Multicultural Literature in Contemporary Italy

Multicultural Literature in Contemporary Italy

Edited by
Marie Orton and
Graziella Parati

Madison • Teaneck
Fairleigh Dickinson University Press

Associated University Presses
2010 Eastpark Boulevard
Cranbury, NJ 08512

The paper used in this publication meets the requirements of the American National Standard for Permanence of Paper for Printed Library Materials Z39.48–1984.

Library of Congress Cataloging-in-Publication Data

Multicultural literature in contemporary Italy / edited by Marie Orton and Graziella Parati.
p. cm.
Includes bibliographical references.
ISBN-13: 978-0-8386-4162-0 (alk. paper)
ISBN-10: 0-8386-4162-8 (alk. paper)
1. Italian literature—21st century. 2. Short stories, Italian. 3. Italian literature—21st century—Translations into English. 4. Multiculturism in literature. I. Orton, Marie, 1965- II. Parati, Graziella.
PQ4257.E5M85 2007
850.8'09355—dc22

2007002507

PRINTED IN THE UNITED STATES OF AMERICA

Contents

Acknowledgments

Multicultural Literature in Contemporary Italy HAD ITS ORIGIN IN discussions with colleagues and with the authors of the stories in this volume. The editors want to thank all the writers who have enthusiastically embraced this project and have been generous with their time and work. We are particularly grateful to those publishers who allowed us to translate and include short stories and excerpts from novels already published in Italian. It is thanks to their generosity that this book exists. In particular we thank: Besa Editore, Cosmo Iannone Editore, Derive/Approdi, Eks&Tra, Fara Editore, Feltrinelli, Fernandel, Il Grappolo, Il Poligrafo and Sinnos.

We are especially appreciative of the colleagues who generously donated their time and expertise to translate the excerpts in this volume: Carmen Di Cinque, Sarah Hill, Jason Laine, Robert Morse, Maria Ponce De Leon, Tristana Rorandelli, Julia Viazminski, James Walker, and John Welsh. Their collaboration has been absolutely essential in bringing this project to fruition.

This project was made possible thanks to the generosity of the Ramon and Marguerite Guthrie Fund at Dartmouth College.

Multicultural Literature in Contemporary Italy

Introduction

Marie Orton and Graziella Parati

IN HER ARTICLE, "FIGLI FORTUNATI DI UNA NUOVA MADRE LINGUA," Valentina Pigmei quotes the Italian-Brazilian author Christiana de Caldas Brito who states, "A migrant leaves three mothers: the biological mother, the mother land, and the mother tongue."[1] Embracing a new culture in order to acquire visibility in a new land and with a new tongue is the difficult undertaking for many migrants who write. De Caldas Brito continues, "It takes time before the pain of leaving one's country transforms itself from a pain as obstacle into a pain as growth. This transformation is a characteristic of life itself and it works for everybody and it affects everybody: every day we have to leave the homeland of our certainties. Every day we need to learn a new language. We are in constant migration."[2] This constant migration that we could call transmigration is directly connected to a translation of languages and cultures, able to create a glocal (the form that a global phenomenon takes locally) space that demands to be investigated.

De Caldas Brito's words are particularly useful in introducing a volume which compiles writings by contemporary migrants in Italy that explore the forms that migrations take in one specific country. She reminds us to keep in mind that migration is not the exclusive experience of a limited number of people. No longer the exception, but more and more the norm, migration (read as change in a multicultural context) affects every individual's daily life. Therefore, discussing migration literature means discussing the recent changes in contemporary Italian culture. Literature becomes the context in which one can examine contemporary Italian multiculturalism and imagine future developments.

This volume is intended as complimentary to *Mediterranean Crossroads: Migration Literature in Italy*, which traced the changes in literature written by migrants in Italy from 1990 to the end of that decade. These texts, which included both short stories and excerpts from novels, concentrated on very specific themes such as exile, displacement, cultural fragmentation, otherness, racism, and other concerns that are characteristic of the writings of a first generation of migrants. Autobiography and autobiographical writing played a major role in these early texts, as often occurs in migrant literature in many different cultures. Collaboration with a "linguistic expert" (native speakers, often writers or journalists) marked a number of these earlier texts. However, it did not take a generation for migrant writers to begin to write without direct, external influences.

Fifteen years after the publication of the first immigrant novels,[3] critics need to examine closely the changes and complexities of subsequent migrant writings. If on the one hand there is some continuity in the choice of themes between early texts and later texts, the level of sophistication has increased and the number of texts published has multiplied.[4] No more just a passing phenomenon, migrant literature in Italy is here to stay, and it closely dialogues with both an Italian cultural tradition and influences contemporary cultural hybridizations.

The question of what qualifies or does not qualify as Italian literature is contested terrain. The category of aesthetics is only one theoretical device through which one can approach literature. Immigrant writings demand a different and complex interdisciplinary approach. Specifically, a cultural studies perspective is useful in talking about multiculturalism and the contribution made by migrants' writings to that indefinable entity that is a national literature. As Leslie Adelson observes, what is at stake in defining that adjective "Italian," is the "need to reconceptualize our understanding of an identifiably [Italian] core of contemporary literature."[5] Although one could argue that postnation cultural issues are fundamental in discussing migration issues, there is the contingent need to articulate a discourse on internal cultural tensions. Literature, therefore, is the ideal forum for examining the anxieties about the present and the future of the Italian identity. The inscription of the other in the Italian context has created general debates on education, employment, and health issues, often confronted through a dichotomy: the right of a majority against that of a minority, the superiority of a native culture vis-à-vis incoming cultures. In an article entitled, "Uno su tre non parla italiano ma qui nessuno è straniero," Roberto Bianchini describes elementary school classes comprised of fifty percent native Italians and fifty percent children of immigrants, transforming traditional schools into international schools.[6] He even reports that in a school where initially children of immigrants were seen as a threat, multilingual children have redesigned the scholastic profile. The phenomenon described by Bianchini could be considered the exception at the beginning of the new millennium, but will soon become the norm in Italy. In fact, the same article estimates that if in 2003-4 there were approximately 300,000 children of immigrants enrolled in the Italian school system, in 2018–19 that number will increase to approximately 700,000.[7] This means that in 2001–2, 2.31 percent of school children were not Italian citizens. In 2002–3, that percentage increased to 2.96 percent. Educated between cultures, these children represent the shifting parameters that define cultural identities.

The identities created in the excerpts from immigrant writers represented in this anthology already perform those cultural changes that demographic statistics attempt to project in the future. We could therefore say that literature imagines today those future transformations that will redefine the multicultural profile of Italy. Often accused of being removed from the tangible problems of life, literature is a space that allows experimentation in the creation of new identities, allows irreverence toward proscriptive roles, and modifies the marginal position occupied by migrants in the social sphere. Literature, in fact, allows a self-constructed visibility, a writing of the self into public existence. Traditional Italianists would downgrade, and therefore marginalize, the texts written by migrants to nonliterary expression of autobiographical or semiautobiographical experiences that have no place in a canonical classification of the narratives that define Italian Literature. This protectionist approach to literary studies epitomizes normative approaches to aesthetics and runs the risk of limiting the ability of literature to interpret the culture in which it interacts. If we consider Benetta Jules-Rosette's statement that "literature reflects society on many different levels,"[8] migrants' uncanonical literary exercises become the key to revealing the connections between contemporary Italian culture and literary expression. Collectively, migrants' writings supply an alternative rhetoric that places migration outside the realm of protectionist discourses that demand regulations and boundaries. Out of line and out of bounds, they are in contempt of literary canons. They also are in contempt of those legal texts that attempt to micromanage their lives and their bodies in Italy. Not being able to vote, to be represented, and to count in politics, migrants write their responses to regulatory legal measures in literary texts.

Unfortunately, most texts by migrant writers are published by minor publishing companies, and are thus confronted with the hurdle of literally becoming visible by occupying a space on bookstore shelves. Not only do migrant writers have to face the literary establishment, but also the complex market forces that dominate the publishing world. Literary competitions and book fairs for minor publishers attempt to draw attention to this flourishing field, but it will take time to achieve that visibility. Some texts are used in schools as tools to educate students about Italy's contemporary multicultural identity, which the students encounter every day. Some of the writers such as Christina de Caldas Brito, Tahar Lamri, and Kossi Komla-Ebri to name a few, frequently meet with students in order to discuss both their own works and the issues concerning migrants in Italy. What is needed is a concerted effort to focus public attention on the valuable contributions that migrant writers are making in Italian literature and culture in general.

The texts collected in this volume directly address this need for public dialogue. Specifically, the goal of this collection is to supply both scholars and students of global migrations with testimonies from the wealth of literary material created by migrants in Italy. These migrants come from a vast number of countries in Africa, Asia, Eastern Europe, South America, and the Middle East. The inclusion of these seventeen authors is not intended to reflect demographic percentages, but is rather a cross section of the current literary production by migrant writers.[9] When dealing with literary production that is so diverse, any pretense of being representative would be shortsighted.

The topics discussed vary widely in each text and the most recognizable difference from the texts included in the previous collecion is the widespread use of humor here, even in talking about painful situations of isolation and racism. Sigmund Freud's foundational text, "Jokes and Their Relation to the Unconscious," defines humor as the force that creates community by distinguishing between those who understand the humor and those who do not.[10] In this case, migrants use humor both to create a community among migrants who have experienced the absurd side of hardship and to portray the life of the migrant in a tone different from the stereotypical representation of the migrant in the press, which often deals with criminal activities and emergencies. In fact, as Mikail Bahktin claims in his classic work on comedy, *Rabelais and His World*, laughter is the weapon of the people in that it liberates them from the oppression of the powerful: "laughter could never become an instrument to oppress and blind the people. It always remained a free weapon in their hands."[11] In these texts, humor certainly functions as an attempt to subvert any essentializing portrayal of what an immigrant is, and what his/her experience entails. At the same time, humor becomes a tool for dealing with the tensions born of the struggle for integration.

Luigi Pirandello defines humor as created by a betrayal of expectations: we laugh if a person falls unexpectedly or behaves uncharacteristically.[12] This definition is particularly useful in talking about texts that represent otherness by relying on humor that addresses a reading audience of native speakers. Otherness is, for natives, a change from the normative structures of the familiar, and instead of presenting such a change as a threat, humor performs difference as nonmenacing and able to create a shared experience.

More recently, Dario Fo has asserted that, "Humor is one of the most powerful tools available to humans in their communicative endeavors. . . . Scorn has always been the weapon of he who has been offended by power and has few alternative resources . . . the grotesque, satire, and irony serve as a concentric mirror; that is, they direct light. They take light and turn it into something that burns. They take words and moments, they . . . concentrate them in images, in ideas until they become a beam of that that burns, that can set fire, that . . . can even destroy barriers. That is exactly its potential."[13]

The texts in this anthology are characterized by their awareness of humor's potential power to subvert. Kossi Komla-Ebri's short story "Home . . . sick"[14] tells the story of two siblings: Fofo, a doctor who has embraced assimilation, married an Italian woman, and tried to forget his African past. His younger sister, the story's first-person narrative voice, comes to Italy to work as her brother's au pair, and makes him confront his choices and relearn his abandoned traditions through a culinary and musical re-education. She feels nostalgia for her Africa, and decides to return. In this narrative, Kossi Komla-Ebri skillfully subverts the Orientalist stereotype of feelings of nostalgia that the colonizers felt for their Africa, a country of privilege for white occupiers. Fofo's sister returns to Africa and experiences nostalgia for her Italian past, which was a very circumscribed and privileged experience of a Western country. In fact, she is nostalgic for those stereotypes of Italian culture, that is, the gourmeted identity of a country that is marketed all over the world: "I take my car, I go downtown and look around the shops, I go to the grocery store and buy some spaghetti, some cans of tomatoes, some meat imported from France, some taleggio, then I go home and cook it all up."

In his short story, "Salvation,"[15] Amor Dekhis creates a protagonist who subverts any preconceived idea of community by developing strategies to avoid any contact with his compatriots searching for support in Italy. Having been in Italy for many years, Dekhis's protagonist searches for an identity in between cultures but he is often stereotyped as a Northern African. People ask him to bring something "typical" to dinner and he has no idea how to cook what is considered "typical" of Algeria. He makes an effort to comply with this friend's requests, because he observes sardonically: "I am aware of the sacrifice that multi-ethnicity requires." Food is the context in which cultural anxieties, tensions, and conflicts are performed, especially when humor is an ingredient.

Cooking and humor define the protagonists' relationships in the excerpt from Igiaba Scego's novel, *Rhoda*.[16] Preparing a dessert becomes the space in which two women, Faduma and Barni, play out their friendship and their differences, their troubles in Italy, and their hope for their future there. The story of the friends' lives takes shape simultaneously as Faduma builds the elaborate tea cake (Barni only eats it; "one made desserts and the other ate them. They had discovered a modus operandi that did not pit one against the other.") Their vexed relationship with Italian culture, the tragedy of Barni's deteriorating health, the trauma of losing her niece Rhoda, all combine with Barni's reflections on how her Somali identity is read in Italy. Pirandellian humor characterizes Barni's reaction to a new friend to whom Faduma wishes to introduce her:

> Barni noticed that her friend was not alone. There was a woman, a *gaal*, with her.

> The presence of that outsider among them disturbed her.
> It meant that she would have to express herself in Italian and that she would not feel at ease. Just a few meters stood between the two of them. In those few meters, she studied the enemy, the foreigner. . . . It was the color of her skin that divided them, that milky white brought [Barni] intestinal discomfort.
> "Oh hi, Barni, this is Sandra."
> "*Barasho wanaagsan,* sister!" replied the girl. . . .

The irony of Barni's describing the Italian as "foreigner" is heightened by the "foreigner's" unexpected ability to speak Barni's language, albeit haltingly. Together the women cook up a new scheme, a commercial venture that aims at cultural inclusion. Humor is used not only to subvert the Italian (mis)conceptions about Somalis but simultaneously (and self-conciously), to subvert the immigrants' similar misconceptions about Italians.

In *Light Beer and Peanuts,*[17] Viola Chandra uses humor to talk about the construction of her protagonist's identity. Valentina, the protagonist, is the daughter of an Italian woman and an Indian man, a lawyer, who has attempted to erase any trace of his otherness. His attempts to erase all signs of her partial otherness lead to a disorder of identity in Valentina. Both her parents are uncomfortable with her inherited otherness: her mother wants her to wear sunscreen so that her skin will not betray her difference, and her father states, "You have got fucking nothing to do with India." On the one hand, Valentina tries to construct a sense of community with migrants coming from different countries, on the other, she turns against her own body by trying to mask any signifier of otherness: she straightens her hair and dresses *all'italiana.* She also falls into the trap of eating disorders, attempting metaphorically to starve her difference by tangibly controlling the space her shrinking body occupies in a culture. Although the situation is tragic, Chandra describes in a comic key the paradoxes that plague her parents' betrayal of identity. She describes her mother's obsession with buying cosmetics that could prevent Valentina from getting a tan, thus making her difference more visible: "In the middle of that chemical arsenal, there were three or four total protection sun-filter creams: a sun-proof screen which was to protect me during my seaside vacation. I would never have become white, but at least I could remain beige. I shared her same desire. Now, I don't really get it: why is it ok to have a black husband but not a black daughter? If you get pregnant with an Indian, do you think that the result can be pink, so it goes well with the bathroom, too?" Unable to swallow identity politics, Valentina "rebels," by using a sun lamp and letting her curly hair grow out, but she still wants to use hair gel because, "You can't say that being natural is always the best thing." The apparent resolution she finds with her own heterogeneity reveals that the different aspects of her identity are still in conflict.

Jadelin Mabiala Gangbo represents a very particular voice among the multicultural narrators in contemporary Italy. His novel, *Verso la notte Bakonga* (*Toward the Bakonga Night*) [1999], focuses on a search for a unique identity that can be constructed without negating otherness. At the same time, the strategies for negotiating identity are bounded by the protagonist's vexed relationship with language. The examination of the interrelationships between language and identity is intensified in Gangbo's second novel, *Rometta and Giulieo* (2001), excerpts from which are included in this volume. Published by Feltrinelli, a major publishing company in Italy, *Rometta and Giulieo* places the author *in fabula* and offers a new model for migration and postethnic narratives. Through the use of mockery, ridicule, and rudeness, breaking linguistic codes, and appropriating elements of traditional Italian literature, *Rometta and Giulieo* emerges as one of the most innovative texts in Italian literature. In addition, Gangbo's novel also plays the role of enacting the relevance of literature at a juncture in time when describing what Italian culture is involves a construction of new paradigms, challenges prescriptive theoretical practices, and defies normative structures.

In obvious reference to Shakespeare's *Romeo and Juliet,* Gangbo reconstructs the famous tale of star-crossed lovers, recasting it as a postmodern story of cultural unbelonging and linguistic complexity. Gangbo frames the issues of multicultural Italy and migrant identity by making his lovers Rometta, an Italian university student, and Giulieo, the son of Chinese immigrant parents. The two meet when Giulieo delivers pizzas to Rometta's apartment. Giulieo epitomizes the liminal space of migrant identity: he never knew his parents, was raised in Italy but has virtually no connection with that country or culture, and is always cast as an outsider. The lovers' story is framed by the story of Jadelin, an African-Italian writer who is hounded by his Italian publisher, Tonino. In a vertiginous interplay of multiple intersecting narratives, Jadelin enters his story and confronts his characters, an intervention that results in Rometta's murder, Giulieo attempting to shoot Jadelin, and Jadelin deleting the story.

That Gangbo's text bases itself in irreverence and defiance vis-à-vis canonical cultural productions is evident in the linguistic manipulations he performs. Gangbo uses different linguistic registers for the two narrative plots and sets of characters in his book. This novel is structured around theatrical frames and scenes: Rometta and Giulieo speak an archaic nineteenth-century Italian borrowed from the Italian translations of Shakespeare's plays. Jadelin employs contemporary colloquial Italian in telling how the novel came about and describing the process of writing it. His modern, native ability to speak the slang of young Italians who are the same age as his characters becomes a problem, however, when Jadelin also becomes a character in Rometta and Giulieo's love story. They do not understand him and accept his justification that his is an archaic form of the language they speak. Gangbo's linguistic manipulation defines the author himself, and Jadelin, the alter-ego narrator, character, and Italian black man, as the internal and, at the same time, external others that challenge any preconceived idea of literature as a multicultural artifact.

Cultural conflicts and cultural stereotypes are scrutinized in a highly comic key in Lily-Amber Laila Wadia's short story "Ravi's Wedding."[18] In this hilarious tale of misplaced expectations and cultural crossovers, the only son, Ravi, goes to Italy to study medicine and instead of coming home to marry the next-door neighbor's daughter, he commits the cardinal sin of bringing home a fiancée from Italy, Maria Cristina. His family goes into crisis attempting to prepare for an Italian daughter-in-law, "We shouldn't embarrass our Ravi by appearing like old stereotypes, all incense and sacred cows. We should present ourselves as a modern family, worthy representatives of the India that is on the cusp of the technological age. We will dress western, we will eat western, we will talk western . . . or at least we will try. Shame on anyone who removes his shoes, eats with his hands, or inadvertently mentions Hinduism or anything like that." They buy a coffee machine they don't understand with grinders and filters in three different sizes, fill their house with imported food, don western clothes, and the mother even buys makeup and gets a makeover. To their shock, Maria Cristina speaks Hindi, doesn't wear a bra, dresses like a gypsy, teaches yoga, and is a vegan. She won't drink coffee because it is forbidden by the Laws of Manu, and she has just finished translating the *Dhyna Bindu Upanishad* into Italian. The trappings of the family's uneasy westernization seem even more foreign to them when they learn that Maria Cristina is an excellent cook of Indian foods and meditates from three to six every morning.

The short story, "The Egyptian Lover,"[19] by Yousef Wakkas, also turns on the play of stereotypes and shifting, confused identities, but in an ironic vein. Wakkas tells the story of Cleopatra, who lands in Genoa sometime in the 1990s full of dreams of going to Cinecittà and making a neorealist film, something like *La Ciociara,* or maybe *La Dolce Vita.* The narrator takes up with her, leaves his wife to go to Egypt as a tourist with Cleopatra, and ends up in prison on racketeering charges. This story plays on stereotypes (the Mafioso stereotype, the foreign woman as prostitute) by exaggerating them to the point of hyperbole. Cleopatra's name suggests the irreality of migrants' exaggerated dreams (to become queen), and simultaneously points to the Italian anxiety that perceives foreigners as untrustworthy invaders.

The empowering force of humor (self-deprecating humor) is particularly evident in the texts in this volume which deal with themes that typify the immigrant experience, such as the impossibility of truly returning to the homeland. Gabriella Ghermandi's short story "The Village Telephone"[20] tells the story of Gennet who returns to Africa and finds herself in the role of a westernized tourist in her own homeland. Disappointed by finding everything in her hometown changed beyond recognition, she rediscovers her home when she leaves the protection of her air-conditioned hotel and stays in a village so small that only one residence has a telephone. By staying in that home, where all private lives become public thanks to the constantly ringing community telephone, Gennet comes to accept the villagers who she initially rejected as dirty and ragged. The short story is thick with beatific but self-critical humor: the author invites the reader to laugh sympathetically at Gennet's Europeanized sensibilities, as well as at the mildly outrageous characters that populate the village, such as Gennet's brassy host, the drunken local priest, and the village witch who shouts romantic advice into the telephone.

The short stories of Carmelo Quijada rely on a darkly comic tone, and the use of irony to examine tensions of integration. "Vendettas"[21] tells the story of an aspiring writer on his way to collect his prize from a contest for migrant writers. He never makes it to the awards ceremony because a pigeon poops on his shirt, so he goes back to the house and begins his vendetta by scattering poisoned popcorn. His battle with the pigeons takes on a more sinister tone as he in turn becomes the victim of violence at the hands of young hoodlums. Again, he plans another vendetta by telling them where he lives and filming their destruction of his apartment. He then turns the video over to the police. The author's second selection, "Back Alleys,"[22] again adopts an ironic comic tone: taking out the trash makes the protagonist envision one day saving a newborn from a dumpster and raising him as his own child, and he also imagines the unpleasant smells that would originate from the dead body of his unfriendly downstairs neighbor.

Though less overtly comic than Gabriella Ghermandi, Fatima Ahmed also deals with the themes of return and becoming a stranger in the homeland. Her short story "Return,"[23] narrated in the first person, tells of the protagonist's return to Phnom Penh, Cambodia, the city of her childhood, after living for twenty years in Europe. Aided by her sixty-year-old guide, Ms. Bopha, the protagonist attempts to "pass" as Cambodian, though her father was Somali and her mother Vietnamese, to avoid the dangers of returning to the military-controlled Khmer section of Cambodia. Like Proust's famous *madeleine*, Fatima's glass of fresh-squeezed sugarcane juice conjures up a host of memories from her childhood, sweet as the juice and bitter as farewell. Her story is filled with the ironies of a woman who is now able, because of her European experience, to return to search for her home in a land where she neither speaks the language nor shares the nationality. The ironies are compounded as her geographic return is contrasted with and paralleled to the return of her childhood memories, though she is unable to navigate either without aid.

Barbara Serdakowski's reflective short story "Elsewhere,"[24] is an interior monologue about the migrant's foreignness in every place. The "elsewhere" of the title has a double meaning: it is both the mirage of the next, better, place the narrator continually contemplates moving to and at the same time, the "other place" is her identity of "origin," which she keeps secret, "my mother tongue, my secret weapon, my hidden identity, my music box with the ballerina inside who is faceless now . . . but that one can still rewind." The narrator's internal monologue is frequently interrupted by questions that are continually put to her by superficial Italian acquaintances: "Where are you from, Madam?" "From somewhere else . . ." "Me, too, I'm from Piedmont, my mother is from Sicily and my father from Molise, I understand you perfectly!" Language functions as a means for disguising and protecting her difference. Because she can speak Italian with virtually no accent, and can speak several other languages, she uses the foreignness of each language to hide her "original" foreignness.

Adrian N. Bravi's text, "Give Me back my Coat,"[25] tells the story of a down-and-out immigrant, who plunges into the depths of despair when his coat is stolen. His Gogolian obsessive search for the stolen item leads him on a wandering path through an indifferent urban landscape. His stream-of-consciousness flows at the same rhythm as his unsuccessful quest. Although his situation is pathetic, the protagonist ruminates on his misfortune, allowing humor to surface. Exaggerations, self-criticism, and irony are the ingredients of Bravi's tragicomic story.

The two excerpts from the novels of Albanian author Ron Kubati, *Leaving with No Return,*[26] and *M*[27] both concentrate mainly on the inability to communicate between cultures. *Leaving with No Return* tells the story of Elton, an Albanian immigrant and student of philosophy in Puglia who ends up acting as translator for the Albanian immigrants arriving by boat to Puglia. The excerpt included here gives the political context for the flight of the Albanians, describing the student protests in Tirana, the subsequent riots, and police crackdown. The novel *M* recasts these same issues, generalizing them by the author's use of an unnamed protagonist in an unnamed place experiencing difficulties in negotiating the problems of personal and professional relationships. In this excerpt, the protagonist lies half-awake in an anonymous hotel room, contemplating the glowing "M" of the metro sign. The constant movement of the metro and the constant shifting of its passengers becomes a metaphor for the protagonist's own placelessness.

The search for identity through a return to the past takes an unexpected and ironic twist in Martha Elvira Patiño's short story "Shipwreck."[28] After days in an open boat, refugees from a war arrive in Italy and hide out in a cave, sending a spy to scout out the local situation. He returns filled with warnings about local corruption, how badly foreigners are treated, and how dissatisfied the local population is due to their overabundance. The group's leader is the narrating voice who tells of their struggles to integrate with the local population, which finally result in violent conflict and are eventually resolved by his marriage to a local woman. It is only at the wedding that the narrator's identity is revealed as Aeneas and the literary allusions embedded in the story become overt. Recasting the *Aeneid* as a refugee's story endows the immigrant experience with epic import, or by the same token, it strips the epic importance from Italy's foundational text. This use of tradition to reveal and re-evaluate cultural expectations of migrants is paralleled in and precipitated by the narrative strategy as the reader's own expectations are brought up short. The reader is brought into the textual humor at the end of the story and surprised by an ending that reveals a new version of a myth of Italy's origins (that all native Italians have to study in school) as well as a re-reading of contemporary migrations. The subdued tone of this narrative gently suggests that the joke is on the reader.

Imed Mahedheb's short story, "Undertow,"[29] tells the tragic tale of a group of Albanians' ill-fated attempt to flee in a rubber raft. The theme of return, so frequent in the literature of migration, here takes on a more sinister interpretation as the guide, Gezim, describes his constant return to his country in strictly financial rather than nostalgic terms: his country's ravaged economy and conflicts that victimize the Kurds have made the black market traffic in people a profitable industry. In this context, the return home is impossible for legal reasons. And in this return to his country, he doesn't lose his home, but his life, and the lives of all the others on the boat. The only survivor, Aleksandra, chooses to drown in sight of land when she realizes that there are no other survivors and that her infant daughter, resting on her chest, has also died. The author describes the suicide as Aleksandra letting herself "be swallowed up by that worldwide sea in which millions of people live, like her, immersed," thus on a narrative level, putting all immigrants in the same ill-fated boat.

As in earlier texts by migrant writers, here, too, the theme of language is pervasive and problematic. Language is a troublesome, often painful topic, and writing in a foreign language represents the loss of the motherland and the mother tongue. Speaking (and writing) in nonnative language reflects all the problems of negating identity that integration requires. The authors included in this volume frequently approach this thorny issue through parody.

Kossi Komla-Ebri parodies the problems of integration in his story of generational miscommunication, "Crossroads Identity."[30] When seventeen-year-old Kuami learns that his family intends to return to Africa permanently, he reacts with all the rage of a rebellious teenager. Kuami's tirade summarizes all the compromises and anxieties of integration, but Komla-Ebri parodies them as they are thrown into relief by the exaggerated rhetoric of a whiny adolescent. Komla-Ebri further parodies the idealization of and stereotypes associated with the homeland in the same exaggerated teenage idiom as Kuami attempts to construct a dialogue with his parents based almost exclusively on an exchange of proverbs: "One who is not invited to the meal cannot complain that the sauce is too hot." "Even the black cow gives white milk." "A tree planted in a river will never become a crocodile." Thus in the story, the anxieties of both migrant and host cultures are drawn in terms of growing pains.

Christina de Caldas Brito's short stories, "The B-Line"[31] and "The Beggar,"[32] deal with idea of language becoming impoverished. "The B-Line" follows a stream-of-consciousness trail of thoughts and memories as the protagonist rides the metro. As people get on and off, the protagonist's words and memories are constantly interrupted by the opening and closing metro doors. The metro car itself becomes a mouth, the passengers are words that cannot communicate: "I have buried all of them. And now I have a graveyard of words inside myself. The words I use at work, on the metro, in encounters on the street, these words are all void of memories. I speak with people, without touching the words inside." The inability to communicate is not determined by lack of words (as in the case of the migrant learning a new language) but rather is limited by human inability to use words. In "The Beggar, " the tattered man waiting outside of a church begging for alms from worshippers does not ask for money, but for words. The beggar is a poet living in poverty because language is impoverished. The author makes clear that the cultural and individual alienation cannot be bridged by formulaic but vacuous language.

Tahar Lamri's short story "The Pilgrimage of the Voice"[33] is a linguistic tour de force, rewriting a foundational myth of Italy in four languages simultaneously: standard Italian, Mantovano, Romagnolo, and Venetian dialects. The myth is told via multiple frames, both narrative and linguistic. The Arab storyteller begins his narration by telling a dream of a family. The family's story gives way to a series of genealogies, which in turn give way to quotations from a Sacred Book. The dream concludes with the storyteller taking refuge in a baobab tree after speaking with the shades of children of all nationalities who recount tales of suffering. "Man is the lord of the word he stores in his belly, but he is slave to the words that he lets out of his mouth. WHAT AM I? I am a heap of words that speaks and always keeps some truth in silence." In this story language itself is the protagonist and the pilgrimage of the voice is the story of linguistic hybridity wherein the modalities of being are revealed as coextensive with languages. Lamri's other two short selections, "You Wicked Wooden Eyes, What Are You Looking At?"[34] and "elevenzerothreetwothousandfour,"[35] employ different linguistic registers. The former, whose title is a clear allusion to Collodi's *Pinocchio,* is narrated through the voice of a child. He discovers difference in school and in the multiple languages that he has to negotiate. The local language, Italian, is for him a language to conquer as the sounds register in his head, but there they remain trapped. "Elevenzerothreetwothousandfour" is inspired by the terrorist attacks in Spain on March 11, 2004. The narrative follows the thoughts of tired commuters on a train that shortly after will be derailed. Lamri includes the voices of teenagers, students, mothers, lovers, and people who cope with the daily dreariness by dreaming of vacations in Italy. A performance artist, Lamri writes short stories that he can also stage. Thematically his narratives explore the ways in which difference is performed in social arenas.

This anthology contains a very small selection of works by migrant writers in contemporary Italy. New texts are being published; new issues arise in their narratives; new writers confront the issues of otherness, difference, marginality, and integration. Inevitably an anthology like this one serves above all as an invitation for scholars of Italian and migration studies to explore the complex shifts occurring in contemporary Italy. This anthology highlights the testimonies that migrants make visible and therefore they add their voices to the political sphere that devotes so much space to debates on who and what migrants are. Comparatively little international attention has heretofore been focused on migrations to Southern Europe. However, Italy's contemporary cultural hybridizations brought about by migrants add to the discussions on global migrations. They demand a future comparison with what is happening in other southern European countries such as Spain or Greece.

Cultures, like languages, are ever-changing entities. Literature serves not only to reflect these changes, but as a possible engine to invoke changes in a specific context. In Italy, where the press and political rhetoric use immigration to displace the many issues that plague its society, literature by migrants allows a different perspective. Literature is a context in which social issues and aesthetic approaches can cross. The title of this collection stresses the concept of an Italy as a location of cultural encounters. The authors represented in this volume reflect on these encounters and describe with humor the changes they have witnessed in Italy and the cultural innovations they forsee.

Marie Orton, Truman State University
Graziella Parati, Dartmouth College

Notes

1. Valentina Pigmei, "Figli fortunati di una nuova madre lingua," *Specchio* (November 27, 2004): 103–4.

2. Ibid.

3. See Pap Khouma and Oreste Pivetta, *Io venditore di elefanti* (Milan: Garzanti, 1990), and Salah Methnani and Mario Fortunato, *Immigrato* (Rome: Theoria, 1990), Saidou Moussa Ba and Alessandro Micheletti, *La promessa di Hamadi* (Novara: De Agostini, 1991), Nassera Chohra, *Volevo diventare bianca,* ed. Alessandra Atti di Sarro (Rome: E/O, 1993).

4. We refer readers to the Web site of the Association Eks & Tra, www.eksetra.net, which currently provides the only database of migration literature in Italy.

5. Leslie A. Adelson, "Migrants' Literature or German Literature? Torkan's *Tufan: Brief an einen islamischen Bruder,*" in *Writing New Identities: Gender, Nation, and Immigration in Contemporary Europe* (Minneapolis: Minnesota University Press, 1997), 218.

6. Roberto Bianchini, "Uno su tre non parla italiano ma qui nessuno è straniero," *la Repubblica* (February 4, 2004): 15.

7. Ibid.

8. Benetta Jules-Rosette, *Black Paris: The African Writers' Landscape* (Urbana: University of Illinois Press, 1998), 148.

9. The selection of texts was also influenced by contingent issues. The vast majority of publishers were most willing to allow translations of these pieces and were happy to see such texts published in English. Practical and legal issues unfortunately limited the number of texts that could be included.

10. Sigmund Freud, "Jokes and their Relation to the Unconscious" (1905) in *The Complete Psychological Works of Sigmund Freud,* vol. 8, trans. James Strachey (London: Hogarth Press, 1960).

11. Antonio Scuderi, *Dario Fo and Popular Performance* (Ottawa: Legas, 1998), 94.

12. Luigi Pirandello, *L'umorismo e altri saggi,* ed. Enrico Ghidetti (Florence: Giunti, 1994).

13. Scuderi, *Dario Fo and Popular Performance,* 90–91.

14. This story appears in the original Italian text entitled "Mal di . . ." in *Destini sospesi di volti in cammino,* eds. Roberta Sangiorgi and Alessandro Ramberti (Santarcangelo di Romagna: Fara, 1998), 125–35. The original titles and publication information for the texts in this anthology will be indicated individually in Italian.

15. "La salvezza," in *Matriciana/Cuscus: Storie di integrazione* (Padova: Il Poligrafo, 2002), 99–113.

16. "Faduma & Barni (aprile 2003)" in *Rhoda* (Rome: Sinnos, 2004), 145–59.

17. *Media chiara e noccioline* (Roma: DeriveApprodi, 2001), 76–88.

18. "Il matrimonio di Ravi," in *Il burattinaio e altre storie extra-italiane* (Isernia: Cosmo Iannone Editore, 2004), 111–26.

19. "L'amante egiziana," in *Fogli sbarrati: Viaggio surreale e reale tra carcerati migranti,* (Rimini: Edizioni Eks&Tra, 2002), 95–100.

20. "Il telefono del quartiere," in *Parole oltre i confini,* ed. Roberta Sangiorgi and Alessandro Ramberti (Santarcangelo di Romagna: Fara Editore, 1999), 73–82.

21. "Vendette," in *Destini sospesi di volti in cammino,* eds., Roberta Sangiorgi and Alessandro Ramberti (Santarcangelo di Romagna: Fara Editore, 1998), 111–17.

22. "Vicoli," in *Destini sospesi di volti in cammino,* eds., Sangiorgi and Ramberti, 117–20.

23. "Il ritorno," in *Anime in viaggio: La nuova mappa dei popoli* (Roma: Adnkronos, 2001), 47–60.

24. " L'altrove," in *Impronte: Scritture dal mondo* (Lecce: Besa, 2003), 135–44.

25. *Restituiscimi il cappotto* (Ravenna: Fernandel, 2004), 9–16.

26. *Va e non torna* (Nardò, LE: Besa, 2000), 170–73, 190–93.

27. *M* (Nardò, LE: Besa, 2002), 7–9, 121–22, 163.

28. "Naufragio," in *Parole oltre i confini,* eds., Sangiorgi and Ramberti, 203–13.

29. "I sommersi," in *Anime in viaggio: La nuova mappa dei popoli* (Roma: Adnkronos, 2001), 11–28.

30. "Identità trasversa," in *Parole di sabbia,* eds., Francesco Argento, Alberto Melandri, and Paolo Trabucco (S. Eustachio di Mercato S. Severino, SA: Il Grappolo, 2002), 89–97.

31. "Linea B," in *Parole di sabbia,* eds., Argento, Melandri, and Trabucco, 28–29.

32. "Il mendicante," in *Parole di sabbia,* eds., Argento, Melandri, and Trabucco, 16–24.

33. "Il pellegrinaggio della voce," in *Parole di sabbia,* 60–68.

34. "Occhiacci di legno," in *I sessanta nomi dell'amore* (Santarcangelo di Romagna, Fara Editore: 2006), 39–40.

35. "Undicizerotreduemilaquattro," in *I sessanta nomi dell'amore,* 109–11.

"Return"

Fatima Ahmed

Translated by Jason Laine

The rice fields extended as far as the eye could see reflecting the clean sky pervaded by light, the tender shoots just peeking out from the veil of water. Farmers working in pairs, feet immersed in the water, beneath the gaze of the palms and the sun high over their heads. Now and again there were naked children leading water buffalo to the fields, the enormous, docile mass subjected to the thin rope held in the fist of the child. We were following a country road made of red earth, transformed into mud by the rain, with huge puddles.

The houses were almost all up on posts, with one or more hammocks hanging from them. When we passed, people were moving their hands to continually rock themselves in the hammock. Dogs and pigs shared food from the same bowl. The farmers called to us, offering lotus flowers: after chatting with them a moment we left to continue our trip.

It was four o'clock in the morning when Ms. Bopha, my sixty-year-old guide, thin as a young girl, took me to the bus station. Hochiminville was still deep in sleep, but some of the people, the merchants, were already up with their wares, ready to head towards a thousand destinations. We got on board a very old, rickety bus. Seats so narrow we were practically sitting on top of each other, air contaminated by the thick cloud from the cigarette smoke. Lots of children, still drowsy, begged us to buy them something:

"Auntie, buy me some sandwiches please."

"Uncle, do you need an orange soda?" And the peddlers would put their wares in the hands of the children, with a sweet and timid glance that did not compensate for their stinginess.

After many hours of traveling through the Vietnamese countryside, the bus arrived at the end of the line. Whoever wanted to continue to the Cambodian border had to rent a car, paying a few thousand lira. After negotiating the price of the trip, Ms. Bopha told me: "Fatima, sit between the driver and me: hold on to him tightly, the roads are full of potholes."

"Yes, ma'am," added the young driver smiling, "here we dance." We essentially danced for kilometers, to the point that when we arrived at the border I felt seasick.

The guide conducted a brief transaction with the soldiers to gain passage through Cambodian soil. The road we took did not have the usual flood of tourists and was used only by locals. We feared the military might object to my travel documents. My only guarantee was Ms. Bopha's word, fairly well-known along that part of the border. They gave me a dubious look. Dressed as I was, I could have passed as a Cambodian headed to see relatives, but, if they asked me any questions, my broken *khmer* would have unmasked me. At home we spoke Vietnamese and at school, French. One of soldiers moved in my direction. I fought against panic and frantically repeated to myself the few phrases I could say fluently. From his suspicious and serious look, the young man seemed to be on the verge of saying something. I caught Ms. Bopha's alarmed look and felt I was lost. The soldier raised his free hand from his automatic rifle, and with a curt movement of his index finger, he motioned me forward.

On foot, we crossed the border and I mentally went and kissed the little sign in Cambodian *Khmer Land.* My eyes filled with tears, I took a fistful of earth and I put it in my pocket, my earth.

A group of Cambodians, with their car, called to us loudly: "Ladies, ladies, going by car?" And there we were, dancing once again over the numerous potholes along the country roads, but it didn't matter, I was finally in Cambodia. We continued towards the town of Neak Loeung to take a ferry.

In Neak Loeung the wait was drawn out under a merciless sun. Life pulsated all around me. Someone offering to change currency, Vietnamese and Cambodians, there were peddlers on foot who followed you with their wares.

The Mékong River was there, majestic, immense, and ready to greet us. Waiting to cross, people were sitting on the ground, tangled up with their bags. It was hot; I was covered in red dust that had risen from dried stretches of the road. Soldiers came and went with their rifles, we felt intimidated by their presence. Not too long ago, these places were theaters of massacres, of unheard of violence exacted by the red *khmer* on an oppressed and defenseless population. How many of the people around me had lived through that nightmare? I scrutinized their faces; there was no longer the innocent serenity of a carefree life, but rather melancholy in the eyes of the elderly, and resignation.

I was looking at a child with her crude crutches who was skipping along with her peers, using only one leg. An elderly woman, seated near me, was following my gaze and smiled at me: "What have you done to that leg, my child?"

"I have had polio since I was a child, grandma."

"Just think," remarked the guide ironically, "a capable French surgeon successfully operated on her so that the poor thing can no longer bend her left leg."

"At least she has two legs. My niece lost one to the mines while she played with her friends."

The elderly woman looked at me again and asked: "Are you Indian?"

"No grandma, my father was Somali and my mother Vietnamese."

"Somali or Indian, for me it's all the same. Where are you going, my child? Where do you live? Excuse my curiosity, I don't often meet foreign travelers who speak Cambodian."

"I was born and lived in Phnom-Penh until I was twenty-one. When the political crisis in Cambodia began in 1970, my father took us to his homeland, Somalia, to save our skins."

"This woman," interjected Ms. Bopha, "despite her leg being the way it is, has done much traveling, she has lived in Somalia, and then in Italy. I don't even know where this Italy is. Just think, she's also married and has three children!"

"May you have a long life, my child. There's hope then for my niece who is missing a leg!"

It didn't seem real to be there among the Cambodians, chatting with them; my eyes were shining with joy. Ms. Bopha resumed the conversation:

"Fatima has lived abroad for twenty years, never able to return to Phnom-Penh for financial reasons, and now she is going to find her childhood city again."

Returning after twenty years! The people near me began to gather around, asking questions, smiling.

"What's Italy like? Is it a bit like France? Is there work? Do the people live well?"

"Look it's the ferry! Grab you bags, call the children!" What a commotion in the crowd. When the boat approached the riverbank and the bridge was lowered, a river of humanity poured onto the embankment, rushing to let the trucks and cars through. A spectacle of a difficult life, the women carrying together their small children and their large rolls of cloth, following their husbands loaded with their own wares. It gave me the impression of an exodus. A river of human bodies pouring over the earth to make room for another wave flowing in the opposite direction. We were all on our feet, crammed in for the trip across. I had lost sight of my little old woman. What a pity! I would have gladly continued the conversation we started on land. I threw some sidelong glances at the people pushing me from all sides, but I didn't catch any signs that they were interested in me. So I gave free rein to my thoughts. It was natural to think about the crocodiles, their unseen and furtive presence was, however, well-known by the inhabitants of the area.

The crocodile in fact was hunted in a unique way by the farmers. Their secret weapon is the *bi*, a type of large squash, the size of a human arm with a somewhat hardened skin. The hunters boil the large vegetable, then attract the crocodiles to their boats and when the foolish reptiles open their jaws, the hunters throw in the still steaming *bi*. The animals swallow the fatal morsel and sink under the surface, but after a few minutes of devastating torment the crocodile reemerges and floats inertly like a log, showing its shiny, yellowish belly.

We had hardly set foot on land when people began grabbing us by the arm.

"Headed to Phnom-Penh? Take my car for a reasonable price."

"Leave them alone! I called them over before you did," protested another driver.

"Phnom-Penh, who's going to Phnom-Penh?" Finally we climbed on board an eight-passenger van. When we left however, there were already more than twenty of us. The man who took care of the passengers went around the sides of the van, then assumed his position clinging onto the roof with both hands. We were so crammed together, we could barely move.

Fortunately we had a cautious driver and we couldn't maintain high speeds. I was watching the landscape go by. Every so often the lush, open countryside of palms gave way to groups of homes suspended on stilts over the swampland. Often before passing through a village I would see on the side of the road a bunch of half-naked children, a forest of hands extended for charity. The regular travelers, knowing this, had some balled-up bills in their hands, ready to toss from the van windows. I looked behind me: a huge cloud of dust rose from the earth, the children diving from the side of the road to try and grab some of the money.

Phnom-Penh wasn't much farther; other cars bursting with people were passing us. There were even some men seated on the roof of a car, while in the open trunk there were other people dozing off, their knees pressed almost to their chins.

Finally, after many hours on that chaotic and stressful trip, we put our feet on the ground once again; we had been folded in half and were numb. There we were at our destination, in front of the Monivong Bridge. On the other side lay Phnom-Penh.

I went over to the sugarcane juice seller and immediately ordered a glass of fresh-squeezed. I fervently took a sip, the first in twenty years. Its taste, its fragrance took me back in time, to that distant day when I left Phnom-Penh. It was a Sunday in May 1970, and it was drizzling. We all woke up very early, overcome by excitement. The house resounded with our calls: "Ishmael, go buy me one of these. Abdoula, where are my shoes?" Dad yelled louder than everyone, wanting everything to be ready as soon as possible. In the kitchen my mother was preparing the last lunch, the pots and lids slipped from her hands and fell with a crash, she was so nervous.

There was knocking at the door, it was our neighbor: "I thought you didn't have time to cook, so I brought you something." She had brought a tray bursting with spring rolls, banana sweets wrapped in palm leaves, and her son had a jug full of sugarcane juice, fresh squeezed. I will never forget that juice, delicious, fragrant and fresh. Another one of her sons came in with a straw basket filled with various candied fruits, from papaya to pineapple, from mango to tamarinds,[1]

[1] The tamarind fruit, also known as tamarind or Indian date, is a thick, dark brown or reddish brown pulp surrounding small seeds inside a hard, brittle bean-shaped pod.

and then the delicious lotus seeds and ginger: "I don't think that you will find these delicacies in Somalia," said our neighbor.

"Do we have space in our bags for these gifts?" asked mom, but our neighbor assured her: "Of course! With eight children, plus two parents, you will have the right to take at least two hundred kilos of baggage." She sighed: "We will miss you very much, we will never see you again," and she started to sob. "We would like to leave too to save our skins, but this is our country." I had the glass of sugarcane juice in my hand, I sent another sip down: it had the bitter taste of farewell!

We said good-bye to our neighbors and began to take our bags downstairs. Dad, who had gone down a half hour earlier, came back in a rush: he had rented a Volkswagen bus with three rows of seats. By chance I glanced up at the balconies and was taken aback. Every balcony was bursting with people! Those closest wished us a good trip, long life, and a good stay in the distant land. I saw the tears in their eyes, tears of pain for their lot: being Cambodian citizens they couldn't leave the country.

At the time Cambodia was desperately trying to remain a neutral country, while its neighbor Vietnam was being torn apart by war. But inevitably the hostile winds swept through and enraged Cambodia's population. The foreign workers quickly fled the country and my family left for Somalia, uprooted forever.

A soft rain began to fall that conferred a rather somber tone on our departure. The Volkswagen started slowly towards the airport, through the window I was watching the landscape go by on the other side. The cocoa leaves, slightly bent by the wind, lined the road, a man and a woman seated on a cart pulled by two oxen, behind them a naked little boy who waved at us. These were the last images that I took with me of my life in Cambodia.

Now I have returned, a glass of sugarcane juice in hand, seeking the past. With my heart in my throat, taking small steps, without a thought for the sounds and the crowd around me, I crossed the Monivong Bridge.

Phnom-Penh, what a magical name! Phnom-Penh, however, had lost some of its beauty. Its marvelous visage, at one time so seductive, today was showing some wrinkles: the war had left its mark. It was my turn to guide Ms. Bopha. I hailed a rickshaw, the omnipresent means of transportation, to show us around the city. We passed by the *Mer-*

cato Nuovo, packed full of people, of colors, of smells. The Wat-Pnom hill was still there in its splendor. But what had become of the fortunetellers who lived there when I was a child? Continuing along its well-cultivated banks, the Tonlésap River seemed to wink at me: "Fatima, welcome, I have been waiting for you." Women were doing laundry while their children were diving headfirst into the water. Life goes on, even if almost every family has suffered one or more tragedies. Lying along the streets, there were many invalids due to mines that pitiless hands had buried virtually everywhere across the Cambodian soil. "Do you want to see the museum of horrors where they display the instruments used by the red *khmer* for torture and the photographs and possessions of the dead?" asked my guide. I shuddered. I felt a chill along my spine even though it was eighty-six degrees in the shade. The fear of the red *khmer* still hung over the city.

"No, the museum of horrors, no, Aunt Bopha, let's go to the neighborhood near the Olympic Stadium, I would like to see our house again."

"Who knows, you may find someone you know," Ms. Bopha was hoping.

There was a little three-floor building on the corner in front of the Olympic market. Our apartment had a long balcony, with heavy, faded wooden shutters. The stairs, somewhat hidden, were the same. I climbed to the second floor: the door was wide open. I silently looked around the foyer: I half expected to see Dad pop out at any moment. "I lived here, many years ago," I said to the woman that had invited me in. I guided myself towards the kitchen, filled by the sweet smells of dishes my mother had prepared. Then I went to the back balcony, where we used to eat sugarcane, all afternoon long, chatting noisily, throwing the husks to the ground. Everyone on both sides of the building in front of ours threw their trash to the ground, and they continued to do the same even now: nothing had changed.

A year earlier it was my brother Abdoula who had been the first to set foot back in Cambodia. He was surrounded by a crowd of children who had accompanied him up the same stairs, as a prodigal son. And he also said, in a low voice: "I lived here, many years ago. In that corner was my dad's bed and over there we read the Koran every night, seated in a circle. In the kitchen my mother was always keeping busy with the cooking, while we kids did nothing but quarrel with the neighbors downstairs."

He went along the entire road with the usual train of children at his heel. At the corner there was a hut, the Wat Moha Montrei, in front of which at one time, we used to have a good time helping with the shows in the square, the *Pàhi.* The Cambodian people love music, poetry, entertainment, and being together to help with a comedy or theater production. Cambodia is celebrated throughout the world for its famous dancers, with costumes made from rich fabrics, adorned with pearls and sometimes even precious gems. The dancers are chosen from among the most beautiful girls and from a young age are subjected to long and elaborate daily exercises. These delicate girls move, barely grazing the earth, accompanied by a melody that wraps you in a surreal atmosphere. At one time the public was not allowed to attend this show, for it was reserved for illustrious guests like the visiting Heads of State or members of the diplomatic corps.

The *Pàhi,* street theater, was also very popular. Toward evening the sound of the tambourine would attract spectators. A circle formed around two actors who would make the crowd collapse in laughter. The children would sneak up to the front row, sit on the ground, and my brothers were naturally part of the crew. Every word from the comedians made them shout with laughter. At times my father appeared after sunset. Pushing through the crowd, ignoring the show, he started looking for his children. In the bright light from his flashlight, he scrutinized each face. My brothers would then quickly form a line and sneak back to the house before him. To a degree my father lived in a world all his own, without mingling much with other people. All he wanted was to have his children constantly under his protection, that is, at home.

Abdoula entered the hut. The old monks, with their saffron-colored robes, moved by the story of his return, invited him for tea. Their faces, lined with wrinkles, marked by time, by the sufferings of war, by deprivation, were brightened by a sweet smile when they told my brother: "You are a Cambodian from beyond the sea."

The sun was high in the sky and I was lost in my thoughts, wrapped in a special solitude along the bank of the Tonlésap River. Ms. Bopha had gone to find a friend and I was walking, walking without any direction. Along the bank of the Tonlésap, I was retracing the same path that I had once taken to go to school by rickshaw. It was exactly there that the waters of the river glided, muddy, around Chruoy-Changvar Island. The Japanese had connected the island to the mainland with a bridge that now, however, lay destroyed by bombs and you had to take the ferry to get across.

One day, during the high-water season, my mom had taken my brothers to visit a friend who lived on the island. Ms. Chanda, from the *Cham* Muslim community, joined us in her skiff. She rowed happily, thoroughly entertained by the joy of watching my little brothers on their first boat trip. The water had covered the island, reaching the height of the floors in the elevated homes. Ms. Chanda brought her boat up to the door and our group walked directly into her house.

You could see the children plunging into the water from their windows: they were swimming and leaping into the river. My brothers watched them with mouths agape. At that time Abdoula was just five years old. He undressed as quickly as possible and counted out loud: "One, two, three." He plunged in and disappeared under the water right in front of my mother who was barely able to sound the alarm: "Help! Abdoula doesn't know how to swim!" Ms. Chanda, without a moment's hesitation, threw herself into the water. Mom cried out, despairing. Other people were diving into the water. Appearing out of nowhere, men came running, interrupting their siesta, or meals. Everyone was searching for my brother.

The river's water was the color of terracotta; it was like searching for a needle in a haystack. And yet . . . "Here he is! I've got him!" Ms. Chanda pulled Abdoula up by his hair, he was semi-conscious.

"Is he alive? Is my son alive?" my mom asked again and again. Then she fainted.

With the help of some friends, my guide took me through the night to a little fishing village a few kilometers from the capital. It was a town inhabited by people who had survived the massacres at Pol Pot. The town was made up of about thirty huts, on the shore of the Mékong, without electricity, without drinkable water. All around was an abundance of banana trees, which created a happy and welcoming atmosphere.

I found myself on the veranda of a little hut. I stretched out on a straw mat, protected by a large mosquito net, beneath the stars. My first night in Cambodia! Impossible to go to sleep! The emotions of the day came upon me: I had the impression I was in a movie, a scene from twenty years earlier materialized before my eyes and made my head spin as if I had drunk some strong wine. Intoxicated by recollections deep in my memory, now resurfacing, I finally fell asleep and slid into the night.

Dawn! My mosquito net was flooded by sunlight; I slipped away and found myself face to face with a python that was observing me from its cage, a meter away. I hadn't seen it the night before; it had been too dark.

"Give Me Back My Coat"

Adrian N. Bravi

Translated by Julia Viazminski

I WOULD HAVE LIKED TO STAY THAT WAY FOREVER, STILL AND ON MY back, on the bed, my hands resting on my stomach, like a dead man who asks nothing more than to stay like that, on his death bead, with a blue flower lying on his chest. That's just how I would have liked to stay that morning. I wasn't able to fall back asleep. I was tossing and turning, closing my eyes, opening them, then returning to my initial position, looking at the ceiling, the spots caused by humidity, the closed window. I was trying to make sense of that supine position that was bringing me memories, stupid ideas, as all ideas are, and I thought that having ideas is really the thing of idiots. Idiots always have grand ideas that have no purpose. But that morning I didn't give a damn about amusing myself with ideas. I wanted only to die and no longer think: "Death is the only thing that can save me from all of my struggles," I told myself. That's how it was. And it would be good for you to know this because the fact that I am here now, alone in this room, with a coldness that is freezing my bones, is all your fault and not anyone else's. Don't play the fool, you know very well what I am mean. And while I was thinking about death, lying on my bed, I realized that it is really not so easy to call it quits in this damn world. It takes courage, inspiration. It is not as if one can wake up at the break of day and decide to die, just like that, as if it were nothing. You need to have talent and clear ideas. In any case, despite the lack of propensity for death that I had always possessed, that morning I would have liked to stay like that, motionless and supine for the rest of my days. I had decided to kill myself. I wanted death to surprise me just as I was, in that stagnant situation with no options. It had to have been around nine or ten in the morning. At that time, I generally would have already worked for a couple of hours. But that morning, you should know, had been a morning of crisis for me: I had been fired a few days earlier, the creditors were knocking at my door, my savings were disappearing and I was beginning to get bored. It wasn't the first time this had happened. Another morning, I had almost decided to throw myself off of the fifth floor. I wrote a letter so that my descendants would reflect on my decision, and I straightened up my house, but unfortunately I didn't even have the guts to set foot on the balcony. I was scared that during the fall some great truth might have revealed itself to me. I don't know, for instance, the real meaning of life, that kind of thing. And then, just as I would have figured that out, inevitable death would come to take me. If I had been sure that after jumping, while I was stepping over the edge, my mind would have turned white like a piece of paper, perhaps I would have done it. But it would have been a bummer if that final revelation had suddenly appeared, just as I hit the first floor or a few meters from smashing into the ground. What would have been the purpose of it all? So it is better to stay ignorant forever. Anyway, as I was telling you, that morning I wanted to commit suicide. I was so fed up, everything angered me and annoyed me beyond words. Seeing people struggle as if they had to make it to who knows whatever age. They want to earn a living? Fine, they are free to do so, but as far as I'm concerned I'd rather be left in peace than deal with those useless responsibilities. I have never understood all that bustling around. Why in the world do they want to involve me in all that anyway? On the contrary, let's be frank, in my case the thought of suicide was born out of not being able to, first of all, kill all those people that I saw on the streets, out of breath, always in a hurry. That was my primary ambition: to rid myself of pretentious people. I wanted to convince myself that, in killing them, I would have done them a favor. However, that failing, I had decided to kill myself without disturbing anyone. In fact, if that morning I had not hit upon the possibility of suicide, that alone would have meant death. Now, the greatest problem became the method, the thorniest phase, full of obstacles and uncertainties. I was tormented, in some ways, since choosing the path to follow poses an agonizing decision. Those who know a thing or two about method maintain that first of all, one must sketch out the plan for the job that is to be undertaken, then measure that against one's own needs, and see what's what. In short, it's a torment that I strongly advise you to avoid! So now, in order to come to some conclusion, I had begun a process of elimination. First of all, I had thought that a bullet to my temple could be the most efficient method. Open the dresser, load the revolver, look at the wall, and pull the trigger without much thought. After having thought about the blood and it squirting about, and that alone having scared the wits out of me, I had decided that at my death there would need to be not even a drop of blood. A pill? Pills have always seemed to me a way to escape reality. Maybe it would have been fine. Pills are usually effective, but they make me anxious, I don't know, it must be because I have never had any anything to do with drugs. Moreover, I was scared of a slow and tormented death. I didn't want to find myself with nightmarish monsters in my head, hallucinations and all those other things that afflict madmen. In order to avoid taking a pill, I would have even thrown myself under the wheels of a car, like the ones that zip down the *nazionale* and make you breathe all the garbage that they spew all over you. But then what if that had not done the job? I'd end up in worse shape than before, a cripple for the rest of my life. And what if I threw myself off a bridge that spans one of the big rivers? There was always the problem of the fall, of what I would have realized in that moment, the truth, the real meaning of life, things that still terrify me. I had thought also of the possibility of setting myself on fire on a balcony. Or I could come up with some excuse, I don't know, something like the rights of door-to-door salesmen or prostitutes, and then go into the town square in front of everyone to make this gesture of protest. But then what the hell do I care about salesmen and prostitutes? So I had opted for a hanging. That would be my death, a romantic death, without any bloodshed or apparatus that I didn't already have on hand. In short, it was a death that was right for me and consecrated me among the souls with distinguished names who rest under the shade of the cedar trees, those people who at one point or another end up becoming great heroes. In fact, from the position I was in, motionless and on my back, on the bed, my hands resting on my stomach, I was looking at the wooden beam that ran from one end of the ceiling to the other, and I was thinking of how I would have ended up: swinging from side to side, half a meter from the floor as if the floor had fallen out from under my feet. In the attic, I recalled, I had put up a rope that wasn't half bad for this type of operation. Nothing was missing. Everything seemed simple and handy, as if someone standing above me were inviting me to kill myself that very day. Before getting up from the position I was in, I began to think about the details. As the first step, I would take the rope from the attic. I would make a slipknot on the end. Then I would have tied the other end to the wooden beam, stood on top of a chair, and slipped the knot over my head; two prayers and a good-bye to my loved ones. Finally, with a simple and decisive little stroke of the foot, I would push aside the chair and good-bye. It seemed the simplest thing that I had ever thought of. So, I had decided to get out of bed and head out to spend the last pennies left in my pocket at the café on the corner where I could say good-bye to everyone, friends and enemies alike. I had decided to toast life and death, hug those scruffy people and say: "Friends, I think that it would be better if I began to call it quits . . . Please forgive me . . . I have ended up in calm desperation . . . I'm getting off. Have a good trip." I thought that I would also say good-bye to you and that maybe I would have given you a slap on the back. I felt such a burning inside that I could no longer stay in bed in that position. I got up. It was freezing outside. I did everything that I normally did in the morning before going out. Afterward, I put on my coat and went out thinking that I would greet my old drinking buddies for the last time. However, I had no intention of revealing my plans. Suicide, by nature, is both pathetic and moving, and I did not want to make a drama out of the whole thing. So as not to raise any suspicion, I could make a date with someone for another drink the next day or who knows when. A freezing wind was blowing from the sea and it made me rub my hands continuously. I buttoned my coat up to my chin and raised the collar. The morning was beginning to show its colors. There were very few people on the streets. "Of course, no one goes out strolling at eleven in the morning," I had thought, "too bad for them." It cheered me up to think that they were all closed inside their offices or warehouses, occupied with their daily tasks. I had taken a short cut and after fifteen minutes had arrived in the square. I felt uplifted like an actor who has just finished his performance and sits in sweet peace to smoke a cigarette behind the scenes. The morning was spreading itself before me like a rug. It seemed so different from other mornings that I felt as if I were seeing everything for the first time, even the tobacconist's disgusting moustache seemed alright to me. I would have given him my hand if he had not been so busy. The wind made me feel good and the idea that on that very day I would kill myself, hanging myself from a wooden beam, filled my heart with joy. I continued to rub my hands and feel happy and carefree. Afterward, I had arrived at the bar to spend the remaining money in my pocket. I had sat next to four or five drinking friends, after having left my coat on a coat rack, as one usually does to avoid being weighed down by clothes. These friends liked to bore themselves around a table. They did it every day. You know that, too. I had asked myself if perhaps they also wanted to kill themselves and were not also there to say good-bye to life. I was almost about to ask which method they had chosen, seeing as for everything one must choose very carefully the best method to carry out the task, but then I had reconsidered. They seemed so sad and worn out, these friends of mine. I had figured out that none of them had any intention of killing himself. A man who is about to die cannot have that face. That can only be the face of a man who is convinced that he'll get by forever, dragging along in this pile of dung without ever managing to pull himself up, I had thought. I had convinced myself that they were seated around the table because they didn't know what to do with their lives, with those doomsday faces. I would have willingly advised them that it would be better for them, and for the whole town, to throw themselves in a ditch than to just sit there doing nothing. They talked about taxes and unemployment, about flexibility and firings. So I took one hundred thousand lire and put them on the table. "What are we drinking?" And since I didn't want to give away the fact that I was happy and that in a few short moments I would kill myself, I added: "Today is the saddest day for me." The waiter brought us a few bottles of red wine. I had noticed that someone was watching me furtively. Talk about ugly, he was standing off to the side, refraining from taking part in all the racket being made by the gathering of scruffy people. I was afraid that someone would ask me something, perhaps about borrowing money, but luckily my mind quickly fell into a fog from the red wine. And between taxes, unemployment, and good company, two or three hours passed. I couldn't stand to be there anymore. At this point I was feeling the confusion of those conversations like a hailstone pounding on the walls of my skull. These ragged people were too talkative. I began to get bored again, to feel really sad, but when I thought about the fact that just a few moments later I would kill myself, I began to cheer up and I felt like toasting to something else. After two or three hours, exactly, you had come in, with the classic face of a cosmetics rep. "What are we toasting, guys?" you had asked. One of the drinking buddies, the one that someone had rightly defined the preeminent belcher, raised his glass and said "To the saddest day." "O.K., to the saddest day," all of the ragged people shouted together. A little later you had looked at your watch saying that you were in a hurry to get to an important appointment with a client: "A big shot, one of those accustomed to spending money," you said. But then, before leaving, damn coward that you are, you had taken my coat from the coat rack and you had gotten into your car. I have never been able to make sense of this act. I had offered you a glass of wine, I had given you my friendship, we had even toasted together to my saddest day. Did you want to see me even more in the dumps? What were you waiting for? Did I have to die in order to satisfy you? I had followed you for a few meters, shouting, "Give me that coat, it's mine, give it back to me, bastard," but you had slammed on the gas and just like that, I had lost sight of your salesrep car. I have not seen you since. I was a wreck. I have always been afraid of small mishaps like this one. I had said good-bye to the ragged people and I had gone home, in pieces, perplexed. I felt beaten. The wind was blowing on me from every direction and it would have taken very little for me to catch a cold. I didn't know what to do with myself. My head was full of taxes and unemployment, but also of complaints and accusations against government, family, and labor unions. "Friends, friends," I said to myself, "don't you see that we are becoming more and more uncivilized?" The cold was intense. Misfortunes never happen alone. I continued to rub my hands, but this gesture now gave me no comfort. On the contrary, I felt really cold without my coat. I was even more distressed than before. I struggled to open the door to the house and then double-bolted it. I felt like the loneliest person in the world, swollen everywhere, without a coat, or anything of value. I couldn't kill myself in that state. It would have been wrong. You have to take stock of reality. I had gone back to bed in the old position, hands resting on my stomach, looking at the ceiling and the humidity spots. I was looking for some explanation for that act. I had even thought that my presence could have been offensive. Then, I decided to wait until you, you miserable person, would decide to give me back my coat. Countless days have gone by, just enough time for a poor soul to freeze to death, and I'm still waiting for you to give it back. If you consider that act some kind of nice gesture, you should know that it's a joke in bad taste. A reasonable person doesn't act like this. Not even a poor fellow without a place to drop dead would take advantage of a friend this way, running off with his coat. Only someone like you, with a dependable job and full pockets, could spurn a friendship to this extreme. Ever since you did this you have been transformed into the embodiment of my distress. I am losing all hope. I wait, rub my hands, read a newspaper, scribble something, and I look around myself. I'm searching for a reason, but then I reconsider and I remind myself that if we were such reasonable creatures, we would resign and accept our destiny. And so I write and then I underline: "Perhaps cows know more than we do how much better it is to be silent when taken to the slaughterhouse." But I am not a cow, and I cannot accept that you took my coat that morning, right when I was about to call it quits with this damn world, once and for all. And free myself from people like you. I am only waiting for you to come and give me back my coat. I ask this and nothing else. I want to put it on one last time. I want to button it up to my chin, lift up the collar, dust the arms off, take a little stroll along the street and then, God willing, hang myself just as I had planned to do that morning, without bothering anyone.

"Light Beer and Peanuts"

Viola Chandra

Translated by Maria Ponce De Leon

My brother hadn't come into the world yet, and my father and I were together in a Bombay hotel, in a modern, ascetic room, and most likely luxurious. In those hotels you can be in Bangkok or in London and not realize the difference. The hotels that have the gift of being identical no matter where they are, almost like international cuisine and Coca-Cola. In the mouth of the native Mexican or on the made-up lips of a fat American, the bubbles go down in the same way and bloat the stomach in the same way. Then the Mexican goes and sells beans at the market and the Yankee goes and gets liposuction at the beautician's.

It was morning and in that hotel room my father was lying on the bed, while I stood next to him looking out of the window. He was asking me if he should leave his French lover for the one from Lombardy. I was not even nine years old and yet I tried to answer him as if I were a wise ninety-year-old or else an astute thirty-year-old manager. Great responsibility for a kid! I think I said something like, "Go where your heart leads," which someone else at forty had already written while drooling the content into a best seller, and I who hadn't even gotten my period yet, was shooting it out in less than ten minutes. What a genius! Or better yet, maybe literature in Italy has a little problem. Afterwards my memories of the two vacations in India get confused. Just a few episodes come to mind and it is so tiring to try and remember. The reason being that at the end of the last trip to India, my father said, "I am never bringing you here again. If you want, you can come back on your own when you are eighteen." That kind of statement for a twelve-year-old was really shitty, but since I was only eight it would have been enough to call the child abuse hotline.

Later, much later, one evening, my father said on the phone, "They really shit on your head, you've got fucking nothing to do with India." Now if you remove from this articulate conversation the words "shit" and "fuck" you are left with only the punctuation, and it is also true that to feel a load of shit plopped on your head like a beret is certainly not beautiful or warm. But it is also true that thanks to his sense of humor, that country for many years has meant nothing more than an unreachable, unreal, and nonexistent place for me. A buried site, or rather, it should be buried underneath shovelfuls of dirt and of course shit, that my father had thrown on it while I risked being left there underneath. Buried alive, as one could say?

A place to be avoided with care, a place to not get to know, to be erased. A place to be excluded because I had been excluded from it. The word of my father had become "law" and I followed it. No appeals. So his "you've got fucking nothing to do with India" was turned over and rehabilitated into my own "India has got fucking nothing to do with me."

"You don't look Italian, are you foreign?" "No . . . that is, my father is Indian." He is foreign, I am not.

From that land I had been exiled, and so I firmly grasped with all my strength on to my travel orders in the new fatherland, Italy, trying to make it completely mine, not just half of it. Despite appearances, I tried to camouflage myself in every way possible from straightening my hair, to avoiding getting tan. It was such a hassle both physical and economical: tons of blow dryers burnt out from excessive use, gallons of total protection sun-screen spread all over my body.

Then later, I forgot the appearances. I went to Morocco, Mexico, and Guatemala, where I immersed myself in the many odors, flavors, lights, flies, countrysides and dark-skinned peoples. Perhaps this all represented for me an acceptable alternative to India, a surrogate, an *éscamotage,* until I returned to India at the age of thirty, with my fiancé, Mattia.

That country with its inhabitants seemed to be a frightening extension of my father, from his judgment to his eyes. A country, together with its inhabitants, which were so hostile as to exclude you and at the same time exhilarate you, while they tease your desires and your enthusiasm.

A country where, when you arrive at the beach all sweaty and all you want to do is spread your towel on the sand, strip down to your bathing suit, and dive into the water, but all of a sudden you realize that "shit," you have just placed your belongings right on a turd, and that while you are swimming you have just swerved away from another one! Oh yes, because the sea represents for those people what toilets are for us. They take a shit just before going into the water or in the water itself. How cute they are: I wonder if they sunbathe in the toilet?

Inhabitants that don't look at you or else never stop looking at you, which causes in you the same effect: erasing your body. Brahmans who don't answer questions and just keep on walking, pretending not to see me. While I ask myself: Did he hear me? Do I exist? Thousands of men hanging out at the bus stop who stare at me obstinately and relentlessly, laughing amongst themselves. They made me yell exasperatedly at someone, at no one, at everyone, into the total vacuum of too much, an unbearable "What do you waaaannnnntttt?" What do you want from me? What's wrong with me? A desperate scream that attracts other glances and more laughter in response. It causes my friend to say to me, "Let's take a rickshaw. I'm begging you, let's get out of here," far away from the crowded buses used by the Indians and enclosed in a protective box on four wheels for tourists. This all made me fall back into that part of me that I didn't want to take on. I didn't want to accept it, but I wanted to be accepted in India. I did exist and I received the semblance of respect only when they were taking my money: in villages, hotels, restaurants or shops designed for foreigners on vacation, for tourists, and for their dollars. But I wanted to be considered one of the people, equal to them. At the same time I would slap them in the face with my diversity: my skimpy tops that didn't cover my shoulders, my jazzy pants that outlined the profile of my ass and my legs, my long curly hair not tied up in a braid, my cigarettes smoked in public places, my bikinis worn on the beach.

I wanted a whole population to accept me and put aside its traditions, its dogmas and its castes. I wanted it to put itself away in order reach out to me: for how I am. I wanted an entire population to accept me: to compensate for the refusal of one single man. He was one of them, the same as them. An entire population was supposed to do that which my father had never done. Instead, the entire population did exactly what my father had always done.

I hated those people in the same way I loved my father. I love those people in the same way that I hate my father. We will never understand each other, at least as long as I expect them and him to adjust to me. They should annihilate themselves for one sole woman who has felt annihilated by one single man. The woman does not admit the responsibility for her acts and she closes her eyes to a millenarian culture, by acting as if that culture didn't exist.

But I did see, I did hear, and I did read.

I saw that dirty little girl, with ripped clothes and tangled hair, who was walking on the road of the large city, begging and leading a mouse on a type of cord leash. I saw the shopkeepers spit at her. I looked away because I felt too similar to her and I was afraid that everyone would notice the similarity.

I saw the women swimming in the sea, dressed in their saris and when they would get out of the water they would try to dry their dressed bodies in the light of the sunset. They probably would get back into their cars still wet, while their men were nice and dry. I kept on looking in the hopes of feeling absolutely different from them and I wanted everyone to notice.

I heard the young husband speak about the baby girl that he and his wife had just had: "Unfortunately it is a girl." Unfortunately? "Unfortunately we are going to have to worry about getting a dowry." The birth of a daughter is above all, the opening up of a debt. That same young mother had been forced the day before she gave birth, to cook the entire morning for a lunch in which she would not have partaken because in the poor and agricultural south, the women don't eat with the men or with foreign women.

I read in Italian newspapers about the wars between the outcasts, amongst the lowest castes, the untouchables that don't touch but do kill those who are considered more untouchable than themselves. Entire villages are exterminated in a war amongst the poor, the last of the last.

I read the statistics gathered in England: the percentage of Anglo-Pakistan women that commit suicide is very high. If they don't respect the rules, such as how a husband is chosen by the family, then they are no longer considered daughters and they lose their parents.

We are orphans of fathers or mothers that are still alive.

One thing which I was never able to get used to was being continuously stared at. Since I had a very typical Indian appearance, I thought that I could have just melted into the crowd and so I dedicated myself to an intense introspection in order to understand the reasons why people stared at me with such insistence. Right when I was beginning to have a clearer perception about my identity, it dawned on me: obviously I was a creature who caused stupor and embarrassment, an enigmatic confusion between the Orient and the Occident. I had some Indian characteristics but my behavior was typically foreign; I was Indian but at the same time I wasn't. I was foreign but not entirely. I had no choice but to learn to live with those curious glances or to mitigate my occidental characteristics: I opted for the first solution because I didn't want to give up being myself.

These words by Sarina Singh, an Australian writer of Indian origin were read to me by Mattia, who had found them while browsing through the Lonely Planet guide to Southern India. We were in Madurai, in a hotel room, that would have been unaffordable for us had we been in Italy, with air conditioning, fan, and marble in the bathroom. I went out into the frenetic, chaotic, busy, noisy, dirty city with my skimpy top and my jazzy pants, combat boots, long curly hair and a lighted cigarette in my mouth.

The challenge continues.

I finally give up when I am in Italy, when the foreigner-outcast is someone else. That person is now the excluded one who is trying to get integrated but is treated with contempt or with compassion. That person is now begging for something that only someone else can give him. Therefore he is dependent on another. He is lacking something: and while I can identify with him I would like to fill his need in order to free him and to allow him to be himself.

Every time that I see an Indian or an African in Italy, I hope that he recognizes me: that he sees in me a member of his family, a daughter, since I am no longer the daughter of my own father.

I try to be adopted by a needy man, someone whose need will allow me to be accepted. By a man whose appearance and history reminds me of my father: a wall without evident cracks in which I never manage to fit, against which I either bounce or crash.

Looking at the most outcast *extracomunitari,* I am moved, I hold back my tears every time that I see one of them, especially if it is an old man, who seems torn away from his land, uprooted, because in him I see my father's suffering and his uprooting. I see the suffering of a boy who has just arrived in Italy, who was once well-off and respected, but now finds himself poor and humiliated by a law professor with his feet up on the desk, quizzing him and in the end who flunks him.

Perhaps because of the color of his skin, a color that in that moment he probably would have wanted to forget, or maybe not even have, so that he could just be a normal student, who is evaluated and appreciated for his intelligence and preparation.

During my last trip with my father to India, I would only eat bananas and grapes and I only drank Coca-Cola. The intense smell that the mango-pineapple-papaya-avocado gave off from the under the beds where they were stored, reminded me of stinky feet. Eating rice and meat with my hands seemed dirty and uncivil . . . everything was just too much and I couldn't bring myself to accept it. I only ate and drank things that were ascetic and familiar. I was only a child; western, too white and too different from Indian children that even then stared at me and laughed. I was too black for some Italians that I had met on the tram on the streets. Too black for them in the same way that the Africans on the street, at the corners, or who washed the car windows, were too black, dirty, smelly, and bothersome for my father. They don't study or work but just live off the money of others.

Since I didn't eat anything except for bananas, grapes, and Coca-Cola, I was a pain in the ass and I would have to return to India on my own. When I finally did go back to India, I wasn't able to really go back all the way. I went around the relatives' houses lacking the courage to visit them because I didn't know if they were still my relatives. I had already experienced the contempt of other Indians and I didn't want to go through that with my relatives, partially because I was afraid that they would be ashamed of me and that they would disown me in the same way that my father had after he took me to visit them.

In Southern India, and even further south in Tamil Nadu, the temple city, there were images of Hindu divinities all throughout the house. The family home had an outdoor shower, screened only by curved wall panels: a cylinder without a roof located next to a well, which was used to collect water in a pail to throw on oneself when one washed.

You had to dry yourself in the sun. I was too ashamed of my curly hair and thought my father was also ashamed of me because of these curls. So, when we went by car to visit a friend of his, up in the mountains, I kept my face out of the window the whole time so that the wind would straighten my hair and then he wouldn't have to be ashamed of me. I could read in his eyes and in his behavior a certain detachment which made me think that he wasn't happy with me. Even today, I read the same things in his eyes. In Italy, when we used to drive to his house, he would look at me, but he didn't like what he saw. "Do you really have to dress like this? You look like a homeless person. Don't you see that the other girls in this town dress well?"

Those jeans and the shapeless sweaters . . . once I got all dressed up and I even had a little shoulder strap purse, just like a little lady that goes and has tea with her friends at 5:00 pm. The only difference was that I would hang out with the daughters of the writer who lived in a dilapidated farmhouse, and were always out on the streets, without curfews or rules, in other words, they were little tramps. If he was not complaining about my grungy clothes then it was about my trampy friends. I always made the worst choices, without even a compliment for my little purse.

One morning in India, I heard that you were looking for your wallet because you had lost it and were worried. We had slept together in the same bed and you were awake and so was I, but you didn't notice. You were speaking with your sisters and I listened to you, without making a move and with my eyes closed. Finally I could make myself useful. I pretended to wake up and I told you: "I had the strangest dream." You were speaking but turned around to listen to me. I was full of emotion as I was thinking: here is the moment. I went on: "I dreamt that a man pointed out a place to me where there was a wallet . . . " There you go, I had magical powers. Therefore you couldn't avoid taking me into consideration. You would have looked at me with interest. I was finally useful for something. You needed me to solve your problems. I was no longer invisible. I was no longer a problem: shit, I solve problems. The only problem was that I was also naïve. So I told you that you would find your wallet under the bed, but it wasn't there. In one moment I went back to being invisible and useless. How could you have been so stupid as to listen to me. . . . you had already checked under the bed. There was only dust and maybe not even that. The rabbit hadn't come out of the hat and I had lost my moment in the sun. I was normal. You could look elsewhere . . . to work, study, hunting . . . thin white women with straight blond hair: attractive.

I used to wear wide-ribbed corduroy shorts or worn-out bell-bottom jeans and big baggy sweaters, and I was always spilling something. If they gave me a cup of coffee I would immediately spill it on myself. People used to think I was a boy even when I was little and my mother took me around, all dressed in pink so that it was clear that I was a girl. "What a beautiful little boy!" "Can't you see the color of her clothes?" I could put my face out of the car window as much as I wanted to straighten my hair, but I would never become blond and white.

White? My mother had even made some feeble attempts. . . . When I came back from a vacation by the sea she looked at me in dismay and surprise and said: "My God! You are so black!" (Ah yeah: the beach, the sea, the sun . . . the melanin! It does happen that some people get a tan . . .) So after a while she came up with a solution: before I left she would go to the drug store, buy anti-wrinkle cream for her face, and firming cream for her body, a jar of cellulite cream and conditioner, a horse-hair glove for bathing, eye cream, dental whitening powder, and some other potions that would be lined up under the bathroom mirror or piled up on the pink vanity in the pink bathroom. . . . Well, in the middle of that chemical arsenal, there were three or four total protection sun filter creams: a sun-proof screen which was to protect me during my seaside vacation. I would never have become white but at least I would remain beige. I shared the same desire. Now, I don't really get it: why is it ok to have a black husband but not a black daughter? If you get pregnant with an Indian do you think that the result can be pink, so it goes well with the bathroom, too?

When my mother wasn't around, my father's girlfriend, the one from Lombardy, would go into action. She didn't have any manias about creams and such, but she did have the one about the hairdresser. In order to make friends with me, she took me to one. Her gift to me was a pageboy hairdo, black but perfectly straight, curled under at the ears and on my forehead. I went home afterwards and looked at myself in the full mirror with utter amazement. She showed her "new Lombard miracle" to my father and said, "She looks nice and tidy." I shared her opinion. So much so, that until I was twenty-six, I continued to straighten my hair. Before going to school, I would have to get up a half hour early in order to work on my hair with the blow dryer and brush.

When I was sixteen, I started using a sunlamp: my first seeds of rebellion. It was only at the end of May of 1995 that I let my hair go curly. The girl with the tight ponytail and the very straight bangs who left for the island of Giglio with her boyfriend in a white VW Golf, from Varese, came back with the same white Golf, and with the same boyfriend, but with her hair down and curly. Even if it was a bit gelled: one frees oneself from dependencies a little at a time. You can't say that being natural is always the best thing.

"The B-Line"

Christiana de Caldas Brito

Translated by Carmen Di Cinque

I HAVE BURIED ALL OF THEM. AND NOW I HAVE A GRAVEYARD OF WORDS inside myself. The words I use at work, on the metro, in encounters on the street, these words are all void of memories. I speak with people, without touching the words inside.

"Eur Palasport, prossima fermata Magliana. Eur Palasport, next stop Magliana."

What shall I do with the words buried inside that I cannot forget; words that sing in the night like cicadas; crazed mango-scented words? All these years I have kept them closed up tight, like little *goiaba* sweets wrapped in corn husks.

"Magliana, prossima fermata Marconi. Magliana, next stop Marconi."

The metro doors open. The cold north wind enters along with the passengers. But the chinook continues to blow on my words.

"Marconi, prossima fermata San Paolo Basilica. Marconi, next stop San Paolo Basilica."

In what region of myself lies hidden that which I think but do not know how to say? My native language is a boat that ferries my thoughts. Carried by the current, my thoughts arrive effortlessly on the other side of the river.

"San Paolo Basilica, prossima fermata Garbatella. San Paolo Basilica, next stop Garbatella."

The words inside assail me like flashes, sudden musical chords, or like something that snaps.

"Garbatella, prossima fermato Piramide. Garbatella, next stop Piramide."

Far from the forest, the lion cannot roar like it used to. The words I left behind were long arms with which I could touch the horizon.

"Piramide, prossima fermata Circo Massimo. Piramide, next stop Circo Massimo."

A woman gets up. I sit down. The metro car is a closed mouth. Fortunately a musician comes in. He speaks with his hands, he does. The sounds of his accordion give a rhythm to the old words that dance in my breast as though in an illuminated room. I smile.

"Circo Massimo, prossima fermata Colosseo. Circo Massimo, next stop Colosseo."

The musician passes around his paper cup and leaves. My lips become closed borders again.

"Colosseo, prossima fermata Cavour. Colosseo, next stop Cavour."

Words are not born in a hurry like the landscapes flashing by through the windows of the metro. It takes a long time to penetrate the fabric of the soul.

"Cavour, prossima fermata Termini. Cavour, next stop Termini."

I have arrived. The automatic door opens. I exit, wordlessly.

"The Beggar"

Christiana de Caldas Brito

Translated by Carmen Di Cinque

He put on his threadbare jacket and headed towards the square, dragging his worn-out shoes as he went. On his shoulder, he carried an empty box.

Begging in this city was becoming more and more difficult by the day. In the congested streets people hurried by without even noticing his presence and, unfortunately, the police did not allow begging on the metro.

The situation improved only on Sundays, in front of the Church of Consolation. The noontime mass, which was sung in Latin and packed, was attended by cultured folk who gave him sustenance.

He covered his corner with old newspaper. He put the box—seemingly tailor-made for him!—against the ribbing of a column, in the space between the door and the bottom step of the marble stairs.

He had no wound to exhibit. His only one, a very old one, was well hidden. But it was on account of that very wound that he had begun begging.

Restless pigeons hovered on the shoulders of saints. One of them nested on the finger of St. Francis. A good choice, thought the beggar, seating himself on the left, under the folds of St. John's robe. The pigeons tended to mess more on the right, probably because there was no shelter provided by the great protrusion of Mary's vestments as on the left.

Very soon the great clock on the bell tower would fire its mechanized sounding of the twelfth hour. During the mass, when they took up the offering, he too would enter the church to leave a little gift. The faithful, well-dressed people, all ladies and gentlemen of cultured aspect, were already approaching. Some foreign maids, dressed in white, accompanied the elderly, their faces emaciated. Two boys with strategically torn jeans eyed two girls whose smiles seemed to emerge from the print of their floral clothing.

"For the love of God!" said the beggar.

The two girls whispered. They threw something inside the box and, still whispering, entered the church.

The beggar's curious fingers began touching that which the girls had dropped in the box, but here were a father, mother, and three children already coming up the stairs. It was better to concentrate on a "for the love of God!" for them. The children's father offered a gift.

"May God bless you!" the beggar thanked him.

He never returned home, after his collection, without first looking at what they had given him. Anxiously, he fingered the girls' gift from inside the box. Only five letters. What could it be? He opened his fingers and saw FAITH on the palm of his hand. What could he do with it? He frequented only the threshold of the church. It would be better to leave this gift in the offering basket for the souls in purgatory. On second thought, perhaps they had no use for FAITH either, but he certainly couldn't leave it outside the church.

With his left hand he pulled out the word that the children's father had dropped into the box: FAMILY. What a nuisance! They thought that he, because he was begging, wanted a wife and children . . . Was it so difficult to understand that solitude was, and would always be, his only companion?

On that sunny morning, a famous judge and his wife emerged from a black limousine to mount the church steps with great pomp.

The beggar pushed the box a little further out, so that it was more easily seen by the judge:

"Please!"

The judge's wife whispered to her husband: "The poor blind man!" "Ah," said the judge, approaching. With a grand gesture he deposited a gift that was so long it barely fit into the box.

The beggar thanked him in the name of God. With his fingers he began to count the letters—sixteen!—and finished counting them in the exact moment that the clock on the bell tower confirmed the beginning of the mass.

Sticking out of the box was ONALLY, which split the air like an arrow in the direction of Mary's vestments.

He pulled the whole word out of the box: UNCONSTITIONALLY. It was undoubtedly a generous gift, but he was neither a politician nor a journalist, Your Honor dear. That wasn't the kind of gift he appreciated. Even if he had divided the word, he wouldn't be able to make use of it. It was true that during popular demonstrations his box would receive many swear words and he would have risen from his bed at dawn to throw them in the garbage, but UNCONSTITUTIONALLY was too big even for the garbage!

It was impossible to carry that word home. It was very cramped where he lived, with words pasted on the wall, words on the table, on his bed and on the floor, inside the closet and in the drawers. There were even words in the bathtub and in the refrigerator. Sometimes, he would go to get himself a beer from the fridge and find in front of himself a cold HERMITAGE or frozen CHAF-FINCH. Other times, when he was taking a bath, his body would sink down between NARCISSUS and MAGNOLIA which floated peacefully on the bathwater.

That beggar who planted himself every Sunday at the entrance to the Church of Consolation was no more and no less than a passionate lover of words. He was a poet! He saw the world through words. He went around the city asking: "For the love of God, words that might open my eyes!" And that is why many believed him to be blind.

He arranged UNCONSTITUTIONALLY better in the box, this time leaving the UNCONSTITION sticking out.

"Give me a word, no matter how small!"

A very thin young man, with long hair, looked at UNCONSTITUTIONAL. He hesitated for a few minutes among the faithful who were still entering the church. He stared at the beggar with a conspiratorial air, threw a word inside the box, and quickly scampered off towards the square. The poet didn't even have to time frame his thanks. He studied the youth's gift with his hands, one word and full of sharp points. At the lightest contact the letters protested and when he was about to pick them up with his hands, the letters pricked his fingers. One of the points was RE. REMEMBRANCE, perhaps? No. That guy was too young to have memories so bitter. . . . He continued to pass his fingers over the word, stopping on an acute angle. He couldn't resist his curiosity. He looked. He had in front of him the REVOLUTION. No, it was no use. He wanted free words, without compromises, without sharp points that wounded, words that let themselves be sweetly caressed, with sounds that could fly, if necessary.

Little by little, the box was filled with other gifts: SOUL (very nineteenth century!), DREAMS (he had had his fill!), RAGE (it was not poetic!), MOON (too explored), MOTHER (what else could you say about her?), HOPE (was it eternal?), DEATH (it would end up in the refrigerator!), SPRING (again?).

Old, second-hand words. He wanted new ones!

"At least one, for the love of God!"

A man with a pock-marked face put a fat packet that sullied the poet's hands into the box. It was a word accompanied by an adjective: ORIGINAL SIN. Did it refer to Adam's sin or to one of the many scars on the giver's skin? The poet was left without knowing.

VIRGINITY, PALLOR, MERCY were deposited politely by three sisters.

How could he continue to be a poet with such gifts? How could he explain, without being tedious, that he wanted to versify the new millennium?

The other alms did not prove to be more satisfying: GLORY, DUSK, FATHERLAND. And so many ROSES (they would end up in the tub), MIRACLES (it would be difficult to make any with this Sunday's offering . . .), PRAYERS (perhaps necessary if he was not to abandon his craft), NOSTALGIA (he had so much of that, for the time when he didn't have to beg for words).

On that sunny Sunday, the poet-beggar understood that he could expect little from the parishioners of the Church of Consolation, only generous in appearance. In the box there were words creased and crumpled like his jacket, words with thunderous sounds, but substantially useless.

He pushed on the church door just at the moment of the offering. He put FAITH, PRAYERS, and MIRACLES, which did not interest him, on a pew. Perhaps they might serve some parishioner well.

Leaving the church he bumped into a couple dressed completely in black. The woman had red eyes. The poet took HOPE from the box and put it into the woman's hand, but the man looked him up and down, shook his head back and forth and sighed. Without saying anything, he took HOPE and put into back into the poet's box.

The poet decided to look for his words somewhere else—what a Sunday!—and hugging his box, descended the church steps.

There were many people sitting on the benches in the square. Some with an expectant air, others with an air of not having anything to expect.

Light and shadow played on the leaves of the almond trees. The thermometer registered twenty-eight degrees. The clock on the bell tower struck two "dongs." Twelve-thirty, thought the poet, and no words. . . .

An old woman was eating dry bread. The poet sat down close to her. Looking up, he saw the sun; a big fried egg. He was frightened by the metaphor that sprang from his empty stomach. The bread that the old woman ate, even though stale, seemed appetizing.

"Do you want some?" the old woman offered him a piece. He accepted. A poet does not live by words alone . . .

When she finished the bread, the old woman took two little meat-filled pastries out of a handkerchief.

They ate the meat pies in silence. He wanted to repay the old woman's generosity with a word, but he remembered the insipid alms of the day. FAITH, MIRACLES, and PRAYERS were left at the church. The ROSES would wilt in the heat. . . . The old woman had no need for RAGE, and as for SOUL, one was already enough. . . . He promised himself that in better times he would dedicate a sonnet to the old woman of the bread. The taste of the first line –"Elderly friend who in the square her bread she did offer"—blended with the flavor of the ground meat.

With his stomach satisfied, the poet noticed that the sun had gone back to being the sun it always was.

"Did you get a lot?" The old woman pointed at his box.

"Nothing of any value."

The old woman rifled through her purse and gave the poet a word that was all folded up.

"May God bless you," the poet thanked her.

"Don't you want to see what it is?"

The poet opened the gift-word: a thick, green FOLIAGE.

"Oh!" exclaimed the poet, "Thank you! Where did you find it?"

The old woman laughed: "It fell on me."

"Do you know that FOLIAGE is much more beautiful than MOON or SPRING?"

"I prefer meat pies," said the old woman.

"Your FOLIAGE has saved my Sunday!"

"Will you take it home?" the old woman asked.

"Certainly!" the poet answered, caressing the word that fluttered between his fingers.

He was so happy that he didn't realize when the old woman of the bread left.

A mulatto woman looked inside the box. "Hey, mister, what are you selling?"

"I'm not selling. I am asking."

"For what?"

"Words."

From afar, the mulatto, incomprehending, kept looking at the strange man.

"Please, one word!" repeated the poet.

"Can it be the name of a person?" asked a little old man leaning on a cane.

"Certainly," answered the poet.

"It was the name of my wife. She died very young. I fell in love with her on account of her very name," explained the old man.

"What was her name," inquired the poet, curious.

"Who?"

"Your wife."

"My wife's name? Ah, it was so long ago . . . I no longer remember."

The poet smiled.

Sowly another beggar approached: "Everything okay?"

"Not everything," said the poet.

"I got three Euros."

"I got FOLIAGE."

"And what will you do with it?"

"I'll put it in the old woman's sonnet."

"Ah," went the other beggar, slipping his hand in his pocket. "I can't give you the Euros but if you want a lira or two . . . "

"LIRA? How wonderful!"

"If it makes you happy," said the other beggar taking out 500 lira coin: "Take it."

"Ah, no thank you!"

"You said that you wanted . . . "

"No, it's of no use to me," said the poet-beggar.

Nor to me, thought the other beggar as he walked away.

Maybe because it was Sunday, maybe because the young woman coming up from the beach was beautiful and shapely, the poet thought her to be a siren on holiday. The young woman stopped, looked at him, changed the direction of her footsteps and returned to the beach.

The poets stayed, imagining what the siren might be hiding under her fluttering wraparound skirt, when—surprise!—there she was in front of him! "It's for you," the siren told him. Carefully, as though her hands were holding sea water, she poured a word into the box. The poet did not know whether to follow the siren or to look in the box. He decided to look in the box: SEA STORM.

The public square was too small to contain his joy: "SEA STORM, SEA STORM, SEA STORM," the poet repeated, "Thank you, siren."

"Aren't you the one who's always at the church entrance?"

"Yes, that's me," confirmed the poet to the almost adolescent mother who was pushing a stroller with a newborn baby.

"I've tidied my son's room . . . "

She left a complete collection of CARESSES in the poet's hand. Some tickled, some seemed to be made of fabric, others still held the wetness of kisses. The poet traced the C of CARESSES with his thumb and forefinger. He would take them all home! You could never have enough of them. He smiled at the teenaged mother who happily went on her way with the stroller.

"My girlfriend fought with me."

"What?" the poet asked, for he had not seen the young man approach with the big suitcase.

"We used to sit on this bench every Sunday," continued the man.

The poet took HOPE out of his box, "Do you want it?"

"If it will help, I will take it," said the young man putting HOPE under his arm, "I always come here, I wait and wait . . . "

"And your girlfriend?"

"She has never come," concluded the boyfriend.

"You only fight with the ones you love," said the poet, thinking about his Sonnet of Peace born after an intense night of fighting with words.

"You only love if you fight," the young man corrected the poet. "I'm leaving this city."

The poet showed the young man his box: "If any of them interests you . . . they are good companions."

"Words? They are the guilty ones! And how they weigh you down!"

He took ABSENCE out of his suitcase: "Take it, please."

The poet fit ABSENCE into his box—and what a strange thing! It took up more space than UNCONSTITUTIONALLY.

"Good-bye," said the young man, "I'm already late."

"Good-bye," said the poet accompanying the man with his eyes as he walked towards the bus stop.

Would leaving the city be sufficient to free oneself from ABSENCE? Would it be enough to give that word to a poet? Knowing the answer, the poet covered ABSENCE with CARESSES.

Dark clouds covered the sun. A first flash of lightening striped the sky with a zigzag followed by a loud thunderclap. Rain, said the poet who was thinking of the young man's farewell, why don't you wash away all the lovers' quarrels once and for all?

Raindrops, like tears, slipped down the poet's face.

"Come under my umbrella," a young woman invited him.

In a gesture of modesty the poet dried the rain from his eyes.

"I quarreled with my boyfriend," said the young woman. "We used to meet here."

"On this bench?" asked the poet.

"On this bench," she confirmed.

"Every Sunday?"

"Every Sunday."

"Why are you just getting here now?" asked the poet.

"I went back home to get my umbrella."

"Cursed umbrella!" muttered the poet.

She took a step backwards, "What?"

"He was here waiting for you!"

"The umbrella?"

"Your boyfriend!" shouted the poet. "Run to the bus stop. You might still find him!"

The young woman rushed off. To protect himself from the rain the poet went under the canopy of a building. He looked at the bench from there. What was worth more to the eyes of destiny, HOPE or an umbrella? The poet rooted for HOPE.

The downpour was over but the words were all soaked. With his box on his shoulders, the poet began heading home. ABSENCE, saturated by the rain, was even heavier than before.

While he walked, he savored in anticipation the pleasure of drying the words. He would take the ones that were useless to him to a friend who had been creating a new dictionary for the past three years. He would have to wring out MERCY for it was drenched. He would light the oven to warm FOLIAGE. He was going to hang it on his front door.

The poet liked choosing a place for every word before making room for his tired body in the bathtub, between NARCISSUS and MAGNOLIA.

In bed, when he placed his head on the pillow—almost always embracing the most beautiful words—his Sunday would seem to end. But it was not so.

The real celebration began after the poet was asleep. The words would become animate; they would leave their drawers, peel themselves off the walls, abandon the cold of the refrigerator or the comfort of the warm sheets, to insinuate themselves, temptresses, into the dark and silence of the night. Only then did they shine. The boldest ones even managed to enter into the poet's dreams.

"Salvation"

Amor Dekhis

Translated by Tristana Rorandelli

I'M NOT SURE WHY A RECURRING ANXIETY SEIZED ME SO RUTHLESSLY. It left me breathless, and this time, I was right in the middle of the chaotic highway traffic. It was right before the beginning of the weekend, and here I was, paralyzed on the seat of my car as it sped along the highway.

In my eagerness to eliminate any unpleasant surprises waiting for me on my answering machine, I decided to stop at a highway service area: it was imperative that I make a call. I refused to even glance at the beautiful hills overlooking a landscape enveloped in a multitude of festive colors. I ran down the irksome succession of stairs and over barriers until I reached the lower level with its bathrooms and telephone booths.

Filled with anxiety and regretting the promise I made to never use a cell phone, I squeezed into the phone booth which seemed to have become deliberately smaller out of spite. I dialed the thirteen numbers in sync with the rapid beat of my heart, but made a mistake on the first numbers which I normally would have dialed without difficulty. Usually attentive to details, I should have taken care of my bladder before attempting the current endeavour. I had to use both hands, one on my pants to keep from wetting myself and the other to hold the receiver. Squeezed between my restless heart and a capricious bladder, I summoned all my remaining strength to make the call.

"We are fine!" my sister-in-law answered.

The phone call was brief but necessary, and pulled me out of my tunnel of anxiety. Once I hung up the phone, anxiety turned into unbridled joy. In the phone booth I jumped up and down, ignoring the line of people in front of the bathroom who were probably staring at me in surprise.

I moaned in relief while emptying my bladder. Then I walked quickly up the stairs, ending up in the usual, unavoidable mini-mart that is located in every highway service area. I was welcomed by the newspaper rack with its overabundance of publications. I thought about finding a possible remedy for the insomnia that tormented me every night; that is, unless I had to accommodate a fellow countryman in trouble and spent the night in complete discomfort sleeping on the floor. My desire to read some magazine columns like *L'Antitaliano, Bestiario* or *Bustina di Minerva* led me to buy a weekly publication that was better than others, the same way one chooses the flu over the plague. With its usual generosity, the cover offered me the small breasts of Marina, the titillating girl from *Big Brother* that was being filmed at Cinecittà.

I was halfway home after spending a month working far up in the mountains. During that time I had remained out of touch and hadn't spoken even once to my distant family.

I was unable to avoid an anxiety attack. The very thought of the warning light blinking on my answering machine terrified me.

In fact, upon my mother's sudden death, I had suffered a trauma or developed some kind of syndrome; whatever the case may be, it was linked to the answering machine. That time, after a similar return home I had received the bad news via the tape on my machine. My obsessive fear that something else might happen back home became an unavoidable burden. Every time I saw the light blinking I put my hand on my chest and could only think of misfortunes, and I would immediately think of my family. Yet I did not want to use a cell phone, even if it might prove useful on some rare occasions. Even my decision to get a phone for my home was the result of a difficult and lengthy process of deliberation, because a regular telephone and answering machine were necessary to communicate in times of need. It served for talking to my family and allowed possible employers to reach me.

Strange gestures, yakking into the air, threats aimed at the houses lining the street, all these odd behaviors by cell phone users have transformed society into a total cell-land, and this has had a completely negative influence upon me. And when you least expect it you find out that people can reach you even when you are trying to hide.

Although I tend to adopt subversive positions regarding cell phones, I openly declared myself a conservative and placed my banner on the side of those who opposed this new object. Stubbornly I swore on my honor that until I became a doctor and needed to save someone, or a fire fighter and needed to put out a fire, or a policeman and needed to prevent a crime, I would radically eliminate the banal expression "cell phone" from my vocabulary.

Before leaving I had read a *surat* from the Koran and addressed an unusual prayer to the phone, begging it to be generous towards me upon my return. At the same time I consoled myself with the thought that I could call on the road, if the public phones worked. But I never called.

While in the mountains I was so swallowed up by my work that I didn't pay any attention to my own feelings. Even if telephone booths weren't in short supply there, when I had the time to walk around, almost all the damn booths I chanced upon seemed to take sides against me: they were always out of order.

After my anxiety subsided and I emptied my bladder, I got back on the highway feeling serene. I turned on the cassette player, filling the car with my favorite music that I always played on my trips. Until I arrived home I followed the wavelike movement of this euphoric rhythm that made the journey inevitably shorter.

When I entered my home there were only two things that needed immediate attention. The pungent smell of stale air reminded me that I had to open the window and air out the room. But the desire to discover what the answering machine had in store for me made me move towards the small table by my bed. I saw the warning light blinking in a flashing dance. I stared at the answering machine, defiantly, like a winner assured of victory. They are probably messages of no importance whatsoever. I pressed the appropriate button to start playing the tape and rushed to the window. I felt I was suffocating and I couldn't stand the waiting darkness of my studio apartment measuring twenty square meters. Because there is only one room and one window, I must live with the combined smell of urine and food. I worked like a slave to change my situation, hounded by the fear of my mother coming to visit me. Now that she had passed on, those promises I had never kept formed a tapestry of guilt. This image summarized my time in Italy and hung in front of the bed, precisely where the kitchenette ends and the bathroom begins.

Beep, the first message started:

"For next Friday we've decided to organize a special dinner, a multiethnic meal," the voice of my Chilean friend Bruno shouted. "There'll be about twenty people, at my place, Haroun, Lisa and Panaiotakis, Bepe and Maria, Buba and Silvana, Honar, Aisha, Abdul, Natasha, Sinisa. . . ." He continued to list off familiar names.

Beep, the second message started. This one was painful. I was filled by an uncontrollable desire to pound the answering machine for being so stupid as to accept such outrageous requests. I wished I could invent a device that would divert unwanted messages and forward them to Prime Minister Berlusconi.[1]

I couldn't tolerate his type of promises any more. I had had enough of those people asserting that Italy needs immigrants, politicians like Fazio, Bianco, and Rosso. Italy needs immigrants otherwise there won't be enough funds to pay for social security, but what did I have to do with it?

If I was sick of this political nonsense, can you imagine how Italians felt? Of course, each of us has personal reasons to feel the way we do. Where could all the immigrants really live? My place or Fazio's?

In fact, for more than fifteen years I had worked like an animal cleaning local restaurants, thus increasing my dignity by paying taxes. And if I thought I was getting somewhere, I was continually reminded of who I am: at police headquarters I was treated as if I had just arrived yesterday every time I went to renew the white-and-blue document that allowed me to be left alone for a few more years. I'm afraid that sooner or later this document will literally cost me a finger.

I was almost overcome by the words being injected into my veins like a poison from the answering machine: "Hello, I'm your cousin Nuori's brother-in-law. *Allah, in his mercy,* has allowed us to become relatives! I got your address and telephone number from your brother. I'm leaving tomorrow for Italy. I only ask you for a small favor, that you meet me at the airport. *And that for the first few days you help me find a job, a home, get my papers, and a residence permit.*" This shameless request opened the book on the dark pages of my stay in this

[1] During his electoral campaign of 2001, Prime Minister Silvio Berlusconi promised to create one million new jobs in Italy and made other unattainable promises.

country. An earlier experience with my cousin Hadi remained engraved in my memory, vexing like an open wound. Until he was deported he had continued to live here without a purpose or papers, and there was no way to protect myself from his aggressive demands.

Sometimes I would ask myself why I hadn't placed a time limit upon my hospitality that would coincide with the length of his visa. Instead I continued to lend him my bed and was quite happy to sleep on a rag at his feet. I lay on the floor in that dump listening to his lullabylike words, filled with complaints which he repeated nightly like a prayer: "I'm going to try my best to stay in Italy. I'll try my best to find a better accommodation, and I'll repay you for your kind hospitality. You know, I have great ideas. Fortune will certainly smile on me. I'll come up with a business plan, and who knows, maybe we'll be extremely rich, maybe we'll own beautiful buildings instead of this hole in the ground."

What was I supposed to say when I heard such foolish things? With a skeptical grimace I just kept quiet. With his big smile, he was full of strength, full of himself, and the will to succeed. But I never saw him growing the wings necessary to take off and fly towards success. Instead, one night he sank like a stone in a sea of penal troubles, and dragged me down with him. Instead of Hadi returning home, the police came to search my place. Hadi had been arrested in a bar fight. And even though he'd had nothing to do with it, once the police arrived, they took one look at him and decided that he looked like the clone of the stereotypical small-time criminal described so frequently in the local section of the newspaper. They didn't hesitate to put him in prison for the night and issue an order for his deportation the following morning.

Even though I never saw him again after that unfortunate event, he made my precarious position even worse. A judge charged me with offering refuge to an illegal immigrant without reporting it. I continued to await a trial that would have who knows what consequences, while back home people kept thinking that the daring Hadi had already reached success in the European paradise. I was besieged with letters and phone calls asking for information regarding Italian life and requests to host other immigrants, until my nervous system was shot and I didn't know which way to turn. I felt the necessity for providential, heaven-sent forces. I decided to go and speak to a special ecclesiastical authority who would give me the appropriate instructions for my salvation. I was almost ready for my trip to Bologna, but then I realized that I should increase my knowledge with more enlightened ideas: maybe I could read about my future described in a book by Giovanni Sartori.[2]

I hadn't the slightest idea how things had turned out for the aspiring immigrant who, according to the message I found on the answering machine, should have arrived during my absence. With no information, I kept staring at my answering machine. I reminisced on those happy days when the Italian telephone company worked unpredictably and I could get in touch with people, including my family, by mail. In the dim light of my apartment I looked around in search of a solution. I felt like someone in need of help and grew faint; I checked to see if I remembered the number of the emergency room in case I decided to pass out. The answering machine continued to play uninterrupted. Once it finished and I had regained some control over my limbs, I called my family for the second time in one afternoon.

This time my brother answered the phone. He was informed enough about the local gossip to reassure me. The aspiring immigrant had been detained at the Rome airport for an indisputable reason: he had little money on him. Although my brother disagreed with those who went in search of the European dream, he was sorry that the young man had failed in his attempt. My brother rather surprised me with an unprecedented patriotic discourse. He lamented the choice among young people, such a precious resource for the future, who left their homeland only to come to a bad end, in most cases. "You know, our young people are proud!" he said, and before hanging up added, "the West only wants them for the humblest jobs, those requiring hard labor. They keep the good jobs for their children, I can understand that, as long as they don't come and deprive us of our resources, and as long as those strange nongovernmental organizations don't come and teach us about human rights in our own country and allow those of the *'les tero'* to prevail. That would cause our nation to collapse."

---

[2] Giovanni Sartori is a prolific writer on social issues. He is Professor Emeritus of the Humanities at Columbia University in New York and Professor Emeritus of Political Science at the University of Florence.

I didn't completely understand what he said. I was only relieved!

Regaining control of myself I continued listening to the remaining messages. Nothing special, a greeting here, another there, except for Bruno's message, which he had left the day before my return. I called him back immediately.

"Each of us will prepare something, but by now all the dishes have been planned, so if you want, you can prepare a dish that is characteristic of your country, but only as a side dish. Something light, an *es*-special salad, an authentic sauce, a *dulce* . . . ," the Chilean proposed.

At first I hadn't the faintest idea of what to prepare. I thought about a couscous, but they had plenty of main dishes. I thought about a *baqlawa* or a *zlabia*, but didn't know how to prepare them, besides they might be too sweet for our friends' taste. I went and inspected the fridge where I discovered only two containers, one with a tomato and the other with a few sweet and hot peppers. Then Bruno's suggestions echoed in my mind, "a *es*special salad," "an authentic sauce." That's it!

Except for garlic, I found the main ingredients for the perfect dish with which I would proudly make my contribution to multiethnicity. But after a month's absence everything was going bad and stank. Yet I imagined a salad made of grilled sweet peppers and tomatoes, and a spicy sauce I call *harissa*. The next morning I cleaned the fridge and went to the market to buy fresh ingredients.

I am aware of the sacrifice that multiethnicity requires, so I threw my heart and soul into the preparation of an original dish that had nothing to do with what could be bought locally. But my *harissa* turned out to be a form of punishment. I was offended.

"What do you eat this sauce with?" Maria asked me that night at the party, "It's hot, isn't it?"

"You can eat it with many dishes, or just with bread."

On the other side of the table my friend Bruno put some of it on the tip of a fork and added the red sauce to his guacamole, the dish he had prepared, even if he clearly wasn't Mexican.

"I guess you don't like the *harissa!*" I said ironically.

He winked at me as if to say that he knew a thing or two.

In observing Bruno's caution, who was used to my cooking, I forgot about poor Maria who was busily eating my little sauce.

Before I could say anything I heard a moan and then some coughing, but it was Maria's shrill shriek that resonated through my bones. Tossing her guacamole and staining the wall red, she collapsed on the floor.

I ran to help. Her husband Bepe stared wide-eyed and choked out in the voice of a dying man: "What did you give her to eat?" He knelt next to her as she kicked her legs and screamed nonstop.

"You'll soon feel better," I said, and offered her a piece of bread. "You'll soon feel better, it's only . . ."

Before I could finish my explanation she kicked me from the ground, her legs half-bare. At first unable to formulate the words, she finally uttered: "Murderer!" Abandoning all reason, for she was previously an open-minded woman, she added: "Assassin! Beware of his food!"

My sauce wasn't like the one in a tube imported from home, especially prepared for European tastes. Being made in the traditional way my *harissa* was like fire as it travelled down the esophagus.

Sadly, because of the nasty looks the group gave me, I realized that this was the end of the party for me. Even though I noticed that Bruno was secretly amused, I left without a word.

I was fighting against the monstrous complex of hostilities that were silently battling in my heart. I realized that I failed even in the smallest of endeavours. Nobody could stand me except to take advantage of me. And I couldn't stand anyone else. I am condemned to isolation.

Within a few weeks the last straw came. The aspiring immigrant hadn't given up and he called me to express his enthusiasm at his own perseverance.

"In my prayers, a new path was revealed to me," he stated so devoutly that even a respected imam would have remained silent. He gave me a short account of his misadventures in Rome.

Only then did I realize who he was: the husband of my cousin Nouri's daughter. Nouri is a cousin a few degrees removed. I thought hard, trying to clarify if he actually was my relative. Anyway, I had no intention of continually turning my bed into a train station for unfortunate adventurers.

So how many relatives did I have by now? My family must have increased dramatically during my absence. Had everyone gone mad down there? They must have started multiplying fast enough to make rabbits jealous, churning out kids in every direction only to leave them to a cruel fate, wandering until they became infected and followed the preaching of Cairo's blind man with his self-styled religious fanaticism. They had come of age, they were ready to run any risk, but they denied their own history, mired the nation in violence, ruined its economy and erased the distinguishing aspects of its culture.

No, no, stay home cousin, at least this unfortunate experience will be a lesson to you that will help you to think more reasonably about the future.

While I listened to him, the antibodies I had acquired against the disease of my relative, Hadi, were awakening in me.

"I'm going to France and then I'll come to stay with you, *inshallah!*" he added.

"Why would you come to see me?" I asked directly.

"*In the name of Allah,*" he repeated the same demands that he had already recorded on my answering machine, "home-job-residence permit."

"I don't believe Italy is right for achieving your dreams! This is only a suggestion, since I don't want to discourage you at all from giving it a try."

"But they say that there is work to be found over there. I'm only asking you to lend me a hand at the beginning."

"I will say only one thing," I replied decisively, "and I apologize for being direct. Do you realize who you are asking for these favors? Someone like me—I barely manage to survive. There's no way you can count on me!"

"Well, I heard that there is always some new law that is passed and then they issue documents to illegal immigrants whose papers are not in order. May God cause this to happen!" he insisted.

It was clear that the rumors of new laws kept spreading since I had arrived in Italy long ago in the 1980s. But now the situation was more difficult. Venomous arguments and iron-clad political policies endangered his dream of immigration. Listening to his persistent requests I sensed his assiduous religious observance and I didn't hesitate to play the bad guy. I saw a combination of two things that wouldn't mix: the fiery dictates of his faith and the drastic policies on immigration, or at least, my personal interpretation of those policies that I had just improvised for this occasion. I had no choice but to take control in self-defence. "If you want to come here you have to convert," I said *tout court.* "Things have changed and amnesties are available only to Christians!"

"What do you mean?"

"You must become a Christian!" I said, feigning a sad, grave tone. "It's a rule that has been introduced only in the past few years. They only want Christians and it's even better if they're Catholics. Is there a priest over there who could baptize you?"

"You haven't become a Christian, have you?" he screamed.

"No, I haven't. By now I'm a veteran here and so I'm exempt from having to follow the new rule, for the time being."

I heard him gasp for air.

"I didn't mean to scare you, but these are the official rumors that are circulating now."

"*There is no other God than Allah and Mohammed is his prophet.* May God protect us from this conspiracy," he uttered a solemn prayer on the other end.

"Maybe you won't have any problems, then, just try to bring a certificate with you from some priest. I know that over there it's dangerous if people find out, but you should be fine if you're careful." In my attempt to shock him, I exaggerated since I felt possessed by the devil by now.

"I wouldn't dream of it! *There is no other God than Allah and Mohammed is his prophet,*" and fiercely he repeated his *sciahada* more fervently before we hung up.

After the phone call I was happy. I'd forcefully rebelled and given him a strong, clear answer that left no room for false hopes since the preservation of my own chaotic existence was at stake.

I realized that I'd adopted a drastic approach; I'd never had such nerve. I realized that people would probably talk behind my back, saying that I was goodness knows what kind of a bastard and how selfish I was, accusations that, in the past, would have made me jump off a bridge to avoid their condemnation. But only in the past!

Now the cord binding me to that world, the world that I had belonged to until yesterday, was broken; but I wasn't going to stop there and simply wait for my unavoidable damnation.

With determination I hurled myself against the small telephone stand, armed with scissors and an iron bar. With one stroke I cut the damn telephone cord. I used my belt to lash the answering machine and the phone to the table, just to make sure they wouldn't try to escape. For the occasion I prepared some "Lipton *Squeezable* tea" according to the instructions on the commercials, but instead of sugar I used "Baygon" insecticide. I rested on the chair in the corner with the air of a *Massu* about to interrogate colonized rebels. I gave them the third degree to force them to confess their guilt, but I got practically nothing out of them since they remained obstinately silent. Once I had finished my cup of tea, I smashed the answering machine and the phone to pieces. Then the tea started to take effect and I was overcome by a sense of wild agitation. I sensed my character was stronger than normal. Given that I had already climbed up a few rungs on the social ladder, I would place my feet amongst the other taxpayers. I started to feel—may God forgive me!—an inexplicable attraction towards those who became angry with the invaders and cursed at them from the church's minaret or on television programs.

I had my head in the clouds while I began making plans to move to Rovato and take refuge in that sacred fifteen meters of space cordoned off around the cathedral. I imagined filling out a form to become part of a group whose name ended with "phobic," then it asked me for the proper term to be placed in front of it. The form told me that once I'd had my fun and the boredom of affluence had plunged me into the depths of despair, I could then begin demonstrating against gays and drug addicts, and then in my free time, I could demolish the mosques brick by brick and replace them with a pigsty. The form then told me, if an act of bravado should cause problems, the Minister Bianco will take care of it, since on several occasions he had already taken the blame for others' actions.[3]

In order to eventually broaden our coalition and fight against retired people and unemployed teenagers—that is, once they have been neutralized as a potential threat—the form encouraged me to buy a cell phone in order to keep an eye on my pigs via satellite.

---

[3] Enzo Bianco is a conservative politician, member of the former Partito Repubblicano. He has been mayor of Catania and a member of the Anti-Mafia Commission. He has also been a minister in the Italian Parliament.

“Rometta and Giulieo”

Jadelin Mabiala Gangbo

Translated by Marie Orton

THE ARTIST’S DAYS, SIRE.

That is what I’m trying to relate for you, the time when I felt I was still an artist, Sire, the time I thought I was a rabbit with the head of a dog, a legless spider devouring an elephant.

My days slipped past like those of a *bastard,* a miserable hybrid who liked to sit crouched in the windowsill.

From there I would think and whistle tunes.

From there I would look up and glimpse things in the sky, then I would drop my eyes and I could see the crashing of the sea, even if there was asphalt down below.

I was the man whose sweat vanished before it touched the ground, whose scent delayed in coming. Therefore I would look at my hands, my Sire, they seemed weak, still childish. I put them in my dry pockets, got down from the windowsill, and went out wandering around the streets.

Still hot, disgusting, hot, Bologna seemed like hell. I needed some water to free myself. Water that ran impetuously down my face. I rubbed the creases in my forehead, crossed the street, and went into a supermarket.

“Are you alone?” I asked Balya.

She was busy with a pot full of mish-mash and legumes over a blue fire that reddened her cheeks. She replied:

“So aren’t you living with us?”

“Yes, of course. It was just a way to ask you where our fellow renters are, if they’ll make it back for dinner, and you will reply, rightly so,

'As if those two villains wouldn't be back in time to enjoy a table that's all ready and inviting. . . .' Well! It's so difficult to understand one another! . . ." and she stuck her head down into the pot.

"Ro'! What dirty gesture comes to mind?"

"Whose mind are you discussing? Mine, now, is lost, noble Balya. It wanders in the dense web of thought. There is not enough space even for me, for those nighttime whims in the beloved company of a good wine. I have a great wish to make a racket in the air of this bratty winter."

"What do you expect? You have to follow your desires . . ."

"If only it were that easy! If my light languishes, extinguished, it would be the duty of some noble soul to rekindle it . . ."

"What enormous absurdity! Rometta, enormous absurdity! Even you yourself could rekindle it."

"And how, pray tell? Maybe with books, or with some crude mechanism that generally vibrates once it makes electrical contact?"

"Ro'! Such filthy ideas?"

"Come on, Balya! There's nothing left for me to do but go and rinse off, now that the filthy ideas have spread my body with honey that I will go and lick away to taste such sweetness . . ."

"Get out! Leave me alone!"

"Notify me about the hour of restoration so I will be able to judge with my palate that happy odor of legumes that is spreading through the room."

"Get out, Rometta! Get out and leave me alone!"

(Exit Rometta.)

Balya dipped the end of her finger delicately into that indefinable soup.

"Just as the luminous eyes of truth hide themselves there, beneath the shadows, the success of this very soup depends on the proper dosage. My instruction is therefore to refine the doses, to add spices but not to excess so that the pepper does not denigrate the laurel and the rosemary does not perish beneath the arrogance of the onion. They must, instead, get married, in order to unite in an embrace from the odor of the hybrid."

Bayla took a taste, cautious and maternal.

"It certainly would not be a subtle, spicy taste that would do damage to this great success."

She opened the cupboard above her head and grabbed a bottle of hot peppers.

"Let's see . . . one? Maybe that's not enough. Three? . . . Mmmmm. . . ." I heard the hot water boiler kick on.

"Four peppers and let's settle the question once and for all!"

The evening light, hidden in an off-white light bulb which hung over the smooth red table adorned with plates.

Balya distributed the soup, her satisfied smile evident in the nod of her head.

"There's still plenty here. If you enjoy it, I'll be back to pour you some more."

"I don't believe that would be opportune," said Tibalda, "to me, this soup, buried an inch deep in oil, resembles the sand that oozes out from under an ocean oil spill, and furthermore, the spicy-hot smell goes malevolently to my head so that it will sting my brain . . . Can we tempt you with a pizza, girls?"

"One with sausage!"

"Basil and mozzarella for me!"

"You, Balya?"

"What's up? You didn't even taste it! What am I saying, you didn't even give it a sniff. . . . Oh, good God! My faith, that you should be muddied by these insults. This is an actual conspiracy that you have organized against me. I already know what kind of ideas you gnaw on in your little, hollow minds. You don't appreciate all the work I go to for you. Mine is a noble attempt to brighten our time together in this house. Oh, my heart! You all want to banish me! You want me to pack every bag that I have and disappear from this house . . ."

"Balya, it's only a pot of soup that didn't turn out."

"It's only my heart that is breaking, noble Rometta, it's only my heart that abandons itself to the most crazy ideas now that it is no longer welcome."

(Exit Balya.)

"I'm opening the window, this winter seems so awful . . ."

"Yes, open it, Paridena, go ahead and open it. It must be the spicy smell of this boiling swill, but the winter this year seems warm to me. Don't you think so, Rometta?"

"Forgive me, valiant friends, but I had stumbled over the questions in my mind. I remembered the days, and their faces appeared before me without remaining . . ."

"Bits of work that you still have to turn in?"

"Are you behind, then, noble Rometta?"

"No, certainly not. It's just that sometimes I fear that I'll be left behind, that I won't reach my truest objective because I'm blinded by the artificiality of what I'm practicing. The days sequester time, and useful are the days only for being counted, one by one. And my fear is precisely this, to sit down one day, having grown old, and assemble all the lost days that I've counted in my life. . . . But just think if there weren't any different days, imagine that after one Monday came another Monday. . . ."

"How would it help your life then, if it were as you say?" asked Tibalda. "What pleasure would you derive, and what satisfaction? As for me, as soon as my studies are over, I will draw my sword to confront every day, whether it is from Mars or from Jupiter. I'll cut down both types with one blow, believe me, Rometta. Better the limited time than the eternity your quiet flesh forces to speak."

The bearer of the pizzas arrived before the world, my Sire. Yellow face and black hair, shiny, slicked back like beings who had been run over. Mixed in an unpleasant odor of strained footsteps with the three white, steaming pizza boxes and the cold beers.

"That will be thirty *scudi*."

"But of course you are mistaken, my young friend with the yellow skin. From our calculations, it comes to twenty-two *scudi* . . ." said Tibalda. "I wouldn't want your intention to be dishonorable, and that from the ancient continent you have come here to rob us."

"For what reason? Oh, you compare me to the mouse that flees with the lowly bit of cheese in its jaws, or to the fox that scavenges among the crumbs of tripe. It's thirty *scudi* and any exception I simply cannot make."

"Who talks of exceptions? It's twenty-two *scudi* given that we ordered three pizzas."

"Plus two beers, Your Clemency."

(Rometta, from inside the bathroom) "Come on Tibalda, leave it alone!"

"No, I absolutely won't leave anything alone, not even the foot odor that came in arm in arm with this guy to disgrace our home . . . The beers, ever since I've lived in Verona, were always offered without charge to those of us who have dedicated ourselves to study in order to render our Country the greatest of all."

"I would happily stay and attend to your chatter, Exquisteness, but time squeezes me like the belt around an overeater, and you really should hurry up or you'll end up chewing on air because your pizzas will be consumed alone. If you would like to consult the price list, please do so."

"Who the hell knows where it ended up, we deposited it in some hole and now it will have to mind its own business just as you'll have to mind yours. . . ."

"Delicate lady, I will show it to you. Here!"

It was there that he'd tricked them, that Chinese, my Sire, with the flyer that he'd busied himself writing according to his pleasure and that he showed from house to house with a mocking smirk.

"Come on, Tibalda, how much do you think two beers are worth. . . ." intervened Paridena.

"Shut up over there, I'm reading: 'only if ordered with a Turkish pizza' . . . Turkish pizza? Did I read that right?"

"Yes, Turkish pizza."

"But . . . I've never read or heard of it . . ."

"Nor had I, ever heard or read any such name of a pizza, yet when I went to ask about a job from Grego, I was curious to taste it. It has a hole in the middle, that looks like a donut, and what little remains of the pizza, that is, just the crust, tastes like urine as much as a public urinal. I would strongly advise you against it, that is, unless you wish to marry yourselves to toothpaste. I extend my regards to the ladies."

(Exit Chinese man, laughing under his moustache.)

"Did you all hear that slanderous, lying, blathering Chinese and I'd say he was highly odiferous?"

❧ ❧ ❧

Before one o'clock, I'd finished reading the story of little Pavel. Not even seventy pages, Sire, the story of a cabbage and foot that begins with a mine exploding.

It took me two hours to rewrite it on the computer, trying to revise the parts that I thought were the most worthwhile. I avoided the mine explosion and left Pavel with his mother. Then, smoking, I found it satisfying to read the finale, I thought it was highly superior to the original.

"Fuck, I could throw it back on the market," I thought. And I continued to praise myself, going to look for a beer.

I never knew if that brief work made any sense, my Sire. It could become a game, the insistent game of folly, the desire to continue living elsewhere, Sire. So, almost bitterly, I closed the file.

And just at the point of concluding my execution, my breathing blocked as if a bottle had been slipped down my throat. On the screen, among many other icons, there was still the one of Rometta and Giulieo. I thought perhaps it was just residual, that I had forgotten to eliminate it completely, but that aside, no other thought could elude the one that loomed up. I decided to buy a little time, just enough to scratch my head, my skin, to roll my eyes around the ample area of the room. I pulled out a cigarette, lit it, and weakly pressed on the mouse.

I was in debt, Sire. It was written on that screen: that I was damned, because music came out of the radio that rested at the head of the bed. Happy music, giddy music, it seemed I could hear it, Sire, from the room where I was staying. Wallpaper carefully affixed to the walls, a minifridge faced in wood panel, graciously stuck in the desk at the foot of the bed. Light material grazed the mattress with an elementary fantasy, and proceeding, one came across the bathroom, small but pleasant, with lacquered white tiles, towels of different sizes folded on top of a plastic stool. Shower cap and bars of soap above the mirror and in the shower, Rometta, bled to death under the jets of boiling hot water.

Silent, I stared at the wall. I stared at the wall, I stared at the wall until the silence bore into my head and the hours flew over my bones. The telephone rang, it rang again and I got up.

I picked up the receiver.

Tonino asked me where I'd been for the last few days.

"Why?"

"Oh, brother, now he's being mysterious, for the love of God!"

"How are you, Tonino?"

"Ah, how do you want me to be, I have a hell of a pain in my back, my car broke down, and then yesterday, damn slut, I met a whore, one of those, Christ, I don't know how two legs can hold up an ass so enormous. You laugh . . . but I'm not kidding, an ass like that requires the hands of an entire platoon to figure out what's going on. God, you'd need three cranes just to lift two cheeks like that. And me, I have all that desire, and I cracked. So I was giving it my best, truly, I really put myself out, I don't want to lose the tiniest angle of an ass like that, fuck! She has an asshole that stinks like naphthalene, and all she says is to stick in my tongue, but holy Heaven. No, don't laugh. Wait. I got inhibited, seriously, I was fucking inhibited in that situation. I was totally disoriented, really upset. What fucker wants to lose an ass like that, I didn't want her to put her panties back on and tell me, "Go fuck yourself, dickhead!" Christ, but you know, those things, for me, really make me sick, holy Heaven, that's stuff for perverts, stick your tongue in her asshole. Ah, shit. But you know, she stank. . . . So, nothing, I told her, 'Listen, it's useless for you to insist on trying to get me to stick my tongue in your asshole, trust me, it's useless, because I'm not going to lick it.' I've never said it, Jade, never said it. So she spits fire and screams, 'Do I stink? Are you trying to insinuate that my ass stinks?' I tell her to calm down and not scream, but she's already lost it and she continues, 'No, but my ass stinks?' So I respond, 'Hey, it's certainly no rose' . . . and so long, ass!! She took off, and ever since yesterday I've been left with this big desire for some ass, damn it."

"What you do to women, Tonino . . ."

"Not what I do, what I'd like to do. Damn it. I could wring her neck, just like a chicken's, the rotten slut. So do you want to tell me where you've been hiding these last few days or do I have to come and pull you out with pliers?"

"I've been at home, Tonino, at home."

"What the hell do you mean, I've done nothing but try to call you."

"I mean it, I've been home. I turned the ringer off the phone, but I was home."

"Bah! You, my boy, you get more mysterious all the time."

"What are you doing now, Tonino?"

"Now, when?"

"I mean now, if you have anything planned. We could go take a walk, I don't know, let's see, if we felt like it we could go and get something to eat, hmm, I don't know, we could see. Let's go out, get a change of air, talk a little bit, how does that sound?"

"Hey, calm down, boy, what's all this hurry? You haven't fallen in love with me, have you?"

"So, will you come by and get me?"

"I have a ton of work, Jadelin, seriously. I'm here waiting for a writer, an idiot, stuff that if they have me publish will put me in competition with the Vatican. Then I have to go to a conference: words from the bench, wordsinyourmouthdiscksinyourmouth, I don't know, all that shit. And goddamn, I have to stay through dinner, and trust me, when I get home I won't do anything but sleep or vomit all night. Maybe we could get together tomorrow if you're still in the mood and you leave the ringer on your phone. How does that sound?"

"Ok, I'll leave the ringer on, and we'll leave it for tomorrow, all right? So I'll see you tomorrow then."

"Be good, you dope!"

I waited for him to hang up before I did, too. Then I dug out my shoes and opened the window.

It's comfortable with your feet on the windowsill, Sire. The soles of the feet absorb something vivid, and as on an afternoon from the roof of my apartment building, I realized that the air was different from the air I breathed in the streets. I couldn't tell if it was more irritating, but I could tell it was different. I looked at my hands, my Sire, they seemed weak, still childish. I put them back into my dry pockets, leaned my shoulder against the window frame, and I still felt like a charlatan, after all, a rabbit with the head of a dog, a legless spider devouring an elephant. I was still the *bastard*, the son of a bitch on a windowsill, who looks up and sees the things in the sky, then looks down and sees the crashing of the sea where there could be asphalt.

It was up to me to decide, Sire, it was up to me to decide what to see.

The sea or the asphalt.

I'd decide on the way down. Understand on impact.

"The Village Telephone"

Gabriella Ghermandi

Translated by Marie Orton

USUALLY IN MY LIFE, GIFTS OR THE THINGS I WISH FOR ALWAYS COME to me when I'm thinking of throwing in the towel, when I give up and let life take its course.

For seventeen years I had dreamed about what returning to my homeland would be like, the places I would visit, the people I would meet, how I would feel, and of course, that indescribable scent of home that would invade me.

Instead, nothing was as I had imagined.

I spent the first fifteen days pursuing my inner journey accompanied by good, old Zeggu.

Zeggu lived in Kechenè, a small district of the poorest inhabitants of Addis Abeba, where the hyenas roamed by night and witches robbed passersby of their energy by day. In Zeggu's village there was only one family who had a telephone, and fortunately for me, it was available to everyone, including Zeggu. Every morning, I woke up early and called that house where a woman with a sleepy voice replied, "Speak."

"Hello. I'm Gennet, a friend of Zeggu. Can you call him for me?"

"Certainly. Wait one moment."

I would hear slow footsteps become lost in the room, a window would open, and then the sleepy voice transformed itself into a scream, "Call Zeggu!"

"Wait one moment," usually went on for twenty minutes, minutes in which fragments of a life reached me across the phone line, laughter, sounds, a radio, children playing. . . .

After that endless wait, Zeggu responded, panting, "I'm coming, I'm coming," which meant waiting another forty-five minutes.

I would see him clamber up the hill that led to my hotel with his aimless step, stopping every now and then to say hello to someone. He was so slow, I would get terribly upset. I would go up to him, sputtering, "Couldn't you walk faster? It wouldn't cost you anything."

He would look at me with his clever eyes, eyes that saw far off. "I only allow you to treat me like this because I feel your pain," and he would hug me.

I made him come with me on my foolish pilgrimage in search of my old life, which I wanted to find preserved intact in some corner of Ethiopia, but which I never found. One day, exhausted, with blisters covering my feet, I sat on the steps of the town square, took off my shoes and stockings, and said to him, "That's enough, I can't take it anymore. I don't want to look for anything, I'm suffering too much as it is."

Zeggu nodded his head with a little satisfied laugh, "It was about time! You see," he took a deep breath, "you need to go with your heart, not with your head."

"What do you mean?"

"Your heart lets life happen, but your head wants to control events instead. Up until now you've been on the wrong path. Let yourself go."

"As if what you propose were that easy!"

"Come to Kechenè tomorrow, everyone knows about you there, you know. There's only one phone but a lot of tongues and a lot of chatter. People are curious, everyone wants to meet you. You'll see, your heart will surely find something there."

I wasn't very convinced, but he had been so nice, and I didn't want to offend him so I agreed.

The next day he came to get me, dressed in his best and all smiles. We wandered for some time in order dig up a taxi. No one wanted to go all the way to Kechenè unless I paid an exorbitant fee.

The only taxi we managed to wrangle a reasonable price from dumped us out at the bottom of the hill that led to his "famous" village.

A little girl in a Turkish dress with a white turban came running up to us holding a tiny cardboard box in her hand. She thrust the box under my nose and with a contagious smile on her face told me, "Chewing gum!" Scattered on the bottom of the box were packages of lemon and cherry chewing gum. I bought one for ten cents.

Completely satisfied, the girl went and sat down on a rock. Her dress hitched up, uncovering her infant genitals. I looked at her with embarrassment, she continued to smile at me. I passed by other girls in the midst of huts, gutters, open sewers. The scent of peppers hanging out to dry in the sun and freshly roasted coffee beans penetrated my nostrils, ancient memories came to my mind, images of women chatting around the pan roasting coffee, images of embraces, the sound of water pouring into the coffee pot, the stone floor of the kitchen foyer in my old house. I instantly felt a knot in my throat.

The road widened, there was a clearing where children were playing soccer, kicking up clouds of dust. Behind them, like a note gone flat, a house appeared with walls of tenuous green and a metal roof. Two purple bougainvilleas covered it and beneath a window, some little girls sat on the ground hugging each other and laughing.

On the other side of the clearing, there was a tiny corner store that also functioned as a bar and two eucalyptus trees with broken-down chairs under them, of course for the bar.

"That's the house with the telephone," said Zeggu, pointing to the house.

We climbed the stairs and crossed the veranda. Zeggu knocked on the door. The sleepy voice shouted, "I'm coming. Wait one moment." I looked at my watch, ten minutes passed and then the door opened. Finally, I could give a face to the voice that had responded to me every morning. A little head appeared in the doorway covered with an elaborately colored scarf, she raised her face and to my great surprise I noticed her lively eyes.

She smiled and throwing the door open wide, she invited us to come in.

The house was lovely, with a hardwood floor and living room done in blue and arranged in a horseshoe around a big fireplace.

Zeggu pointed to the large woman who came trotting up to us.

"That is the lady of the house, Mrs. Ascalech."

We sat down on the sofas. In front of us on a little table sat the famous village telephone.

Slowly all of the woman's daughters arrived, they sat down near me and began asking me about Italy, about my life.

The telephone rang. The sleepy voice went to answer. The familiar ritual that I had heard with my ear glued to the receiver . . . the slow steps, the window opening, and the shout, "Mrs. Abeba is looking for the witch!"

I looked at Zeggu with a questioning air. The lady of the house began to laugh and giving me a slap on the knee said, "Watch."

Like a hurricane, a woman in flyaway clothes and disheveled hair catapulted into the house. I tried to see her face. Her eyes seemed like threatening cracks, they frightened me and I looked away. Without a great deal of ceremony she picked up the receiver.

"What is it this time?" she thundered.

From time to time, the voice on the other end could be heard; it sounded like the voice of a tiny, whining woman.

"That's all the worse for you," the witch replied. "You have to accept it; you're not pretty, you're not rich, you're not even pleasant, and on top of all that, you're getting old. That man is all that I managed to scrape up for you, and if you're not satisfied then find yourself another witch," and she slammed down the phone.

She made a quick round to patrol the room, looked at the owner's daughters, and pointed a threatening finger at each of them . . . "If I suspected that all of you could end up like that one," and she pointed to the phone, "I will give you the evil eye so that you can die in peace . . . NOW."

She came up to me.

"Hi Gennet, welcome home," she gave me a tap on the cheek and left through the courtyard.

"Lazy loafer! Worthless . . . if it weren't for me . . . how would you ever save any souls? You only know how to drown them in the Teggh."

"Who is she screaming at?" I asked Witzerò Ascalech.

"The village priest. He's always drunk."

We ate and the telephone continued to ring.

In the afternoon, we moved to the veranda to drink coffee.

Women arrived, some of them very poor, dressed in colorless, threadbare rags, with runny-nosed infants in their arms, covered in fleas and lice. They sat down with us to drink coffee and eat *hambascia.* A few of them were waiting for telephone calls. The children ran, played, and hugged anyone that came within reach. Anyone that is, except for me, who watched them with an air of slight disgust . . . they were so dirty. The women realized my unease and discreetly directed the children farther away so they didn't disturb me. The telephone rang. A woman jumped up. The sleepy voice went to answer then came to the window and shouted to a boy playing ball, "It's Choni's fiancé from America," and the boy pulled ten cents from his pocket and gave it to another boy who ran to get Choni.

The woman sat down.

A few minutes passed and then a girl appeared, as lovely as a flower, with long, muscular legs and eyes like a wild cat. She sprang up the steps.

"Good evening everyone," she greeted a few children and ran to the telephone.

She started talking with a subdued voice and every so often a little laugh escaped her. She sat with her elbows on the table and her head cradled in her free hand. She took off her shoes and rubbed her calf with the back of her foot, then shook her head, making her braids wave, and started to laugh.

She was a real man-eater, she could knock out any man. After the phone call ended, she came over to the veranda with a dreamy air and tripped in the doorway. Witzerò Ascalech looked at her: "Choni you were more awake when you came in," and they both laughed.

Like a pathway formed by destiny, everything in Kechenè passed by way of that house because of that telephone. Waiting periods, job offers, marriage proposals, love, deaths, the arrival of a veterinary who came to see the cows that had been attacked by hyenas, marble competitions, the births of new babies. Even little accidents, cuts, and bruises.

Even the rest of my vacation ended up with my going back to that house again and again because of the telephone.

Sometimes, the life of the village seemed like a painting, it was almost motionless, only tiny signs, the half-turn of a wheel, gave dimension to the passage of time, to the unwinding of events.

Choni managed to get a visa to go to America and meet her love, the little girl in the Turkish dress sold all of her cherry chewing gum.

The witch began to spend some of her valuable time sitting on the chairs under the eucalyptus trees trying to exorcise the demons of alcohol from the priest's body, and not without a fair share of screams and curses that made the fragile walls of the church tremble along with everything inside it, including the souls of the saints. I found a way to ease my restlessness by lulling myself with those afternoon chat sessions in the company of children and ragged women.

During one of these afternoons, a child stumbled and landed over me, and on my pants wiped half of the egg yolk he carried in his mouth. . . . my stomach turned.

Witzerò Ascalech began to laugh.

"Why won't you hug these children? The love they offer you is sincere, and remains forever inside you, all you need is a little soap and water to remove any dirt," she looked at me to see if she could continue, and sighed, "You know, I've observed you closely. I don't deny that you've relaxed compared to your first days here, but it's hard for you to change your ways, your heart is still closed, and you always have your useless schedules within arm's reach! Look," and she lifted my wrist, "after a month, you're still wearing a watch, you measure time. You're not in Italy, do you understand that? What you're looking for you'll never be able to find, if not here, among your own people, in the pace of your own home. You've lost that in Europe, that slow, easy pace that opens every door. It will make you cry, rejoice, thank your land. Only this way will you find yourself.

That evening, returning home with Zeggu, I stopped on the bridge before my hotel and I threw my beautiful watch into the river.

Inside of me, with this gesture, I accepted and opened those famous doors.

I cried all the following days: I cried in front of my old house with its neglected garden, I cried over the tomb of my father, I cried when the telephone rang and when I saw the witch. I cried and cleansed my heart of the anger over such a long separation. Finally I felt the light in my heart and no longer was burdened by waiting on the telephone, or by busses that never departed, by the long lines to buy sugar, the negotiations with taxis, the hugs of dirty children. My homeland once again felt familiar to me.

The days of my stay came to an end. I had to go back to my other home, Italy, Bologna.

The day before leaving I said good-bye to all of Kechenè. Witzerò Ascalech hugged me.

"You did it, you really came home, my telephone can work miracles, don't you think?" and laughed.

Zeggu went with me to the airport, my faithful old friend.

Just before check-in, Zeggu motioned for me to turn around, and I found myself in front of the witch and the priest. They came up to me, she was pushing him.

"Go ahead, say it!"

"Leave me alone, you ugly old witch!"

He reached out his hand and touched me.

"May God bless you to be happy," and he placed his wooden cross on my forehead.

His eyes were clear.

He turned around abruptly.

"Now it's your turn," he said aside to the witch.

"It's a little of the earth from Kechenè . . . and some other things that I put together. . . .they will protect you."

She handed me a little sack and they went on their way.

I arrived in Italy and the frantic pace immediately attacked me—news programs, the alarm clock, work, dinners, friends, theater, but inside of me was peaceful. In that sacred place I conserved the quiet rhythm of my homeland, even when there was pain. Now I could be anywhere on the planet and I was at home inside myself . . . and anyway, if I ever got lost, I could always call.

"Home . . . sickness"

Kossi Komla-Ebri

Translated by Marie Orton

OUT OF ALL THE YEARS I'VE SPENT IN ITALY, I WOULDN'T KNOW WHICH ones to blame for what's happening to me now. I know very well that I should decide once and for all to cut the umbilical cord that binds me to this bad habit, this sort of sickness.

I can't even remember how it all started, surely with my return to Africa from Italy.

"Italy!" In those days just thinking about it was like touching the sky. For years Fofo (my brother) had been promising that he'd take me to Europe with him. I don't even know how to describe the immensity of my joy when that long-awaited letter arrived. My cousin who lived in the city brought the letter to us, since his mailbox served as the *refugium peccatorum* [sanctuary] for all of the correspondence from our relatives and everyone else in the village.

My father was a little hesitant to let me go.

"A girl traveling to the whites' country all by herself! Don't even think about it!"

My mother took my side.

"She's not going alone, she's going to meet her brother!" As for the "Don't even think about it" repeated by her husband, she nodded to me to leave the room, and that nod made me take heart because I knew, appearances aside, who "wore the pants" in our house.

In fact, the next day my mother took me to the market to buy a suitcase, some second-hand slacks, and my father went to town to get all the necessary documents for the trip.

The night before my departure I saw tender tears mark my mother's face and I had a fleeting sense of guilt, knowing that I was leaving her alone to do all the work in the fields and the house. Papa withdrew into a defensive silence until the last moment, then, when telling me good-bye, he put a talisman of inlaid leather into my hand with a shell and muttered, "Take care of yourself!"

Italy! God, the cold! I never imagined it could be so cutting. My lips chapped, my fingers froze, and my skin took on that gray color of a lizard, though I slathered myself with coconut lotion. The first night was infernal, I spent it in a hotel in Rome where my brother had made a reservation for me: lying in a bed that I would have used for matting in my cottage, I was half-frozen, not knowing that I was supposed to crawl in between the sheets. Fofo explained it to me the next day and laughed at me, when he came to get me at the station in Bergamo.

My brother had sent for me to look after his house and children because he and his wife both worked all day. He, his Italian wife, and their two children lived in Torre Boldone, a little town not far from Bergamo, where he worked as a doctor. They had prepared a room for me in the basement of their house. It was obvious that they were doing well, even though I found that my brother was a little henpecked by his wife, who was the one in charge, just like my mother only more overtly so.

At first it was difficult to communicate with my sister-in-law and niece and nephew because I couldn't understand the language and my brother refused to act as translator. He immediately instructed me to keep my room clean, to wear the "house skates" when I went into the living room, not to take a shower every day because the heating costs were high, not to leave the lights on over the stairs or in the bathroom, not to take three hours to finish the ironing, not to speak our language, and to keep the volume low on the "funeral dirge" of African music. Included in this list of holy commandments there was the prohibition on preparing foods that took too long to cook and especially foods that filled the house for days with the aroma of spices ("that stink").

I felt that I was always agonizing over my faux pas like crunching on the bones during a meal, something that my brother loved to do back home. But who knew why it was that here it seemed to call up some sense of shame for him. I didn't know my brother any more, he let his children call him by his first name as if he were their playmate. He and his wife gave them their way in everything, and they even had to beg those kids to eat meat! They were too spoiled. Myself, for my children (I wanted to have at least six), I would raise them as we do in Africa: teach them obedience and respect. I didn't like how children talked back to their parents.

I smile now thinking about these things, at my shock when I first saw my nephew put on one of his hysterical scenes because a "little skin" had formed over his milk. When I saw my brother get up I was happy, thinking of the well-deserved smack he was going to give the boy, but instead, he simply took a spoon to remove the skin and implore the boy, "Come on, sweetie, just drink a little more!"

I was completely horrified!

I had to take care of those kids, but I could not get them to mind me. One day when I was beside myself, I screamed at them in my language because it was easier for me and they burst out laughing, literally aping my "talk African" with "Abuga bongo bingo!" "And yet," I thought bitterly, "this is the language of their father's fathers!" But I didn't say a word to them.

I didn't know how to act anymore. My sister-in-law made me feel like an intruder, she watched me with an air of suspicion because, out of politeness, I never looked at her in the eyes when I talked to her. One day I heard her tell a friend on the phone that I was sneaky and hypocritical.

My dream of Europe was mutating into a nightmare, too cold, too little time, and then the indifference, the loneliness.

I spent more and more time locked in my room to cradle myself with memories. I quickly used up the sack of cassava flour and peanuts that my mother had slipped into my suitcase. I couldn't adjust to always eating pasta: even though they said there was a difference between tortellini, bucatini, spaghetti, and lasagna, but for me it was all pasta. I wanted to taste *la pate* (white polenta without salt) with a hearty sauce of gombo and chicken with a lot of hot pepper in it, taste it with my hands, take smoking hot handfuls, mince it well, roll it into a ball and press a deep indentation with my thumb in order to easily gather up all the sauce before swallowing it, then lick my fingers deliciously and crunch on a piece of bone.

I smile today at my shame when my body first saw the moon there and I didn't know what absorbent pads were (I'd brought pieces of cloth with me), or the first time I had the adventure of buying stockings, not knowing that they came in different sizes, colors, and prices.

I still see now, as if it were yesterday, the alarmed face of my sister-in-law when she saw me pull my first attempt at doing laundry out of the washing machine—sweaters that were knotted up and white shirts and underwear that had turned pink or were spotted with purple.

I owe my survival to Conception, a Filipino girl who worked as the housekeeper for the family in the house next door to ours and who spoke a little French. We first saw each other from our balconies while I was trying to beat a carpet, then we met doing the shopping at the supermarket. She'd been in Italy for the past five years and her friendship and her advice were like manna in the desert for me.

I quickly learned to cook and keep the house better. I'd work quickly so then I'd have time left over to read or watch TV. I learned very quickly to appreciate the food. I tried to assimilate as much as possible, to completely forget who I was. With time I became more demanding. I wanted my brother to let me go out every so often, I wanted my day off, just like Conception, I wanted the money to send a present to my mother or to buy clothes that I liked and not just take my sister-in-law's hand-me-downs. In the arguments that were born out of this, my brother and I exchanged reciprocal accusations, that I never would have thought I could formulate. He said, "You are ungrateful!" when I told him that I'd found a place working for an elderly woman in Bergamo, because I wanted to be independent. At first, he'd shout, "If we'd wanted to pay for a babysitter or housekeeper, we didn't need to bring you all the way from Africa, you know!" Then when confronted with the firmness of my decision, he played the sentimental card, "So you don't care that you're leaving when we need you, you'd abandon your niece and nephew, you only pretended to care about them! You are completely heartless!"

I alone know what it cost me to leave my brother, resisting the temptation to embrace him, trying to explain to him that I could not come all the way to Europe without at least trying to accomplish something; unlike him, I dreamed of going home someday and creating something of my own, that I didn't want to be a servant my entire life in a foreign country.

So one spring day when the morning air stung my face and nostrils, and nature was rising from her dark lethargy with the sprouting of the plants, and the birds' sweet song of freedom, I made my flight toward independence. I went to live just outside of Bergamo with an elderly lady (Maria) who cleared my residency with the police and got me all of the documents to stay in the country legally. Meanwhile, I enrolled in a sewing course and saved my money in order to buy a sewing machine all my own.

After the first period of anger passed and after a letter from our father, my brother came to visit me unbeknownst to his wife. There at my new house, I found again the Fofo I had always known; we spoke our own language, I cooked our food for him, hot and spicy, which he swallowed greedily . . . with his hands, then he snapped bones with his teeth and sucked out the marrow, making an infernal noise, and I even heard him laugh as we do at home, a belly laugh, and talk, and remember people and events from our village. One day watching him let loose and dance to the rhythm of our traditional music, I laughed at him, "Doctor, if your patients could just see you now!"

And he responded, laughing, "They would say, 'And yet you seemed like one of us!'"

Then he left with a light heart and with the ironic glint in his eye of someone who had fun betraying himself.

My friend Conception came to visit me every other Sunday and together we'd fantasize about all the plans we wanted to accomplish once we'd returned home permanently. My idea was to start a co-op of tailors and make European-style clothes with African fabrics, maybe even to sell to the big distributors in Europe. . . .

I also had the opportunity to meet other co-nationals and so I started greeting the other Africans that I met on the street. Some came to visit me, because I was lucky enough to have my own apartment on the first floor of the house where we could be together and braid hair, listen to music without disturbing anyone, talk out loud. Our meetings were my only chance to show off my flashy *bubu.*

Signora Maria was truly kind. One night while we were embroidering the thousandth doily and as I bent over the lace pillow with tired eyes, she confided in me that we had brought the light and the joy of living back into her house even though initially, seeing us talking and gesticulating from far away, it seemed that we were fighting.

One day Fofo found me at home with some of my girl friends absorbed in dancing to a piece of music from our country. When he arrived, a silence fell out of respect but also full of reproof because many considered him to be a "traitor." Not so much because he'd married a white woman, but because, they said, he'd become like the whites: cold and indifferent toward his people, as if he were ashamed of his origins, and then no one understood why, with all the room that he had in his big house, he never organized an occasional evening to dance at least on the important holidays. He felt uncomfortable and after a little while he ran off with the excuse of needing to see a patient. From then on, he started to call me before stopping by, as they do in Europe. I'm not defending him, but I understood that he had made the choice to stay permanently in Italy and to keep peace in his family, he had to stoop to making personal compromises.

Knowing my sister-in-law, I understood that he couldn't bring "people" home with no warning as we do at home, and invite them to lunch or dinner or even to spend the night. Here everything is different. At home, being used to big families and the fact that we eat just one course, usually with a sauce for a base, then it's easy to heat up a little more, or to stir some *pate* in a pan or crush up some *fufu* to make room for one more guest around the table. Some people blamed my sister-in-law, but I believe that the pace of life here is such that time dilutes feelings, devouring life and people. And if it was fine with him like this, as he confided to me one day, it should be fine with us, because he claimed the right to live his life as a free individual and not as part of a collective as African solidarity required, and besides, he didn't feel obligated to associate with someone simply because that person was black or came from Africa.

"Here in Europe," he pontificated, "everyone must think of himself, end of story. I only feel a duty toward my close relatives and only if they are in need and are deserving."

Clearly, I didn't share his point of view. I only replied, "Fofo, this country, this fog, it's not for me. I miss the sunshine, the holidays in the village, the weather, people's laughter, living together with others."

And still, I went on working, saving, suffocating my homesickness with one single thought and goal: returning home and opening my tailor shop.

Finally, two years ago, with a knot in my throat I embraced Signora Maria, who had been so good to me, knowing that my departure corresponded to her entering a home. Holding back my growing tears with difficulty, I said good-bye to my brother, Conception, and all my friends and I went "home" with my suitcase full of gifts, plates, and silverware, and a dream to fulfill.

After returning to Africa, the first week effervesced and I understood that I could no longer live in the village where there were no lights and no running water, as I had become used to certain conveniences. I could no longer even start a decent conversation with my girl friends from before; by now they had gotten married and some already had two or three children and I felt that they maliciously envied me. My aging parents insisted that they wanted to choose a man for me to marry, but I had already decided on the liberated life of a single person; I didn't want to be any man's servant and even less did I want to give up my plans.

I decided to move to the city, partly to avoid the daily assault by swarms of relatives who came begging, and partly because the heat, the flies, and the mosquitoes had become unbearable to me and I needed to live in an atmosphere that was air conditioned, clean, and calm.

The first year was not very easy, but slowly I managed to build up a steady clientele and one of my clients, Sonia, who had her hair styling salon opposite to my shop, had become my best friend. Sonia is a shapely girl, nice and determined; she returned from Germany where she'd worked "in show business" and came back to invest all of her savings in her salon.

Now things are going better for me.

Honestly, I would have to say, things would go even better for me now if it weren't for this strange sensation of restlessness that every now and again invades me down to my very bones.

Then I take my car, I go downtown and look around the shops, I go to the grocery store and buy some spaghetti, some cans of tomatoes, some meat imported from France, some taleggio cheese, then I go home to cook it all up and invite Sonia to come and have dinner with me. Sometimes we go to have a cocktail at the "Gattobar" and then we rush out to devour a pizza "Da Silvia" and to conclude the evening we go see some nice movie starring Mastroianni and Sofia Loren. Or sometimes we stay at my house and look at all of my photos from when I was "home" in Italy, listening to the songs from the Festival of Sanremo, the music of Baglioni, Ramazzotti, or Zucchero.

Sundays, I cross the whole city to attend mass in the parish with the Combonian missionary priests so that at the end I can talk with them a little in Italian.

Sometimes it's Sonia who invites me to have a beer at the "Baveria," the tavern for the German sailors, whom she astonishes with her perfect German, then we go to her house to eat sausage with saurkraut and mustard and dance Viennese waltzes.

I don't know how to explain this weakness, this mania that I can't seem to get rid of, and which even makes me root for the *Azzurri* when there is an international soccer match. Once after an Italy vs. Germany game, Sonia and I didn't speak to each other for a week.

Ah, Italy! To think that in Italy I wanted so much to go home! Now I feel like a tenant in two countries: sometimes I'm happy for that, sometimes I feel divided, a little unbalanced, as if a part of me remained there, and yet I know that there I would still have suffered from "*mal di* Africa."

Maybe it's just nostalgia, or more simply, "*mal di . . . mal di* Europa."[1]

[1] The term "mal d'Africa" was used by Italians to express nostalgia for a colonial life, or for the exotic life they had in Africa.

"Crossroads Identity"

Kossi Komla-Ebri

Translated by Marie Orton

"Papà, I don't give a damn about your Africa."

Like a rolling river the words burst from Kuami's lips, tumbling frustrated and painful like the frozen waters of a waterfall on the ears of his parents. Kuami didn't know how to keep the words back.

Cautiously, his mother tried raising her hands to stop him, to intervene as always, to mediate between him and his father. Mercilessly, the son made her abort her attempt at reconciliation just as it was born, uniting both parents in his rebellion: "Your Africa means less than nothing to me. And Mamma, spare me your tears!"

He knew how to wound them to the heart, leaving indelible scars, but he couldn't stop himself. His words shot out and hovered in the room, suspended in the air like storm clouds heavy with lightening. He knowingly used a vulgar tone, which was not his way of expressing himself but which he knew would be offensive to them.

"For years you have hassled me with your dreams, your memories, your sacrifices. What do you want from me? I never asked to be born!"

The face of his father, Kodjo, grew even darker. Jaws clenched, his hands gripped the arms of the easy chair. He opened his mouth to say something but then closed it again without emitting so much as a sound.

Unflinchingly, Kuami continued, almost without drawing a breath, with that fixed determination of someone who commits suicide or who is condemned to death: he had nothing left to lose.

"Yes, Papà, I know your story from beginning to end. It's hardly my fault if you had to flee from your country to come here: I know your whole odyssey by heart!"

Odyssey: Kuami distilled an entire life into one word. Having to sell things on the beaches, with legs dragging from thousands of steps sinking into the sand, shoulders and arms overburdened. To survive, every day Kodjo had had to face snarling voices, rolling eyes in intolerant, irritated faces. He had patiently endured interrogation sessions by those who saw in him an occasion to chat and kill time or the chance to ease their loneliness and boredom, turning the merchandise over in their hands forever without buying anything.

In one word his son condensed the course of an existence crowded by nights spent sleeping in cars, a life of illegality, of working illegally in the factory. A subsistence eased by a *sanatoria*[1] after hours of standing in line at the police station, herded like animals behind fences in the sun, rain, and biting cold. Then came the double shifts, the law that allowed families to be reunited, and the cherry on the cake, fingerprinting. . . .

"Yes, I know it all. But what is my fault? You can't blackmail me for my whole life because of this! You made sacrifices so that I could study, and so what? That was your duty as a father. In this society when someone has a child, he takes some responsibilities. In this society, to call yourself a 'father,' it's not enough just to fertilize a female. Here being a father starts in the delivery room, includes diapers and bottles, playing games, and the first day of preschool up through checking homework! So tell me, Papà, when were you here? Were you in the delivery room? No! That was women's work! And I believe that you never once wiped my bottom. And schoolwork? Let's talk a minute about my schoolwork. What help did you ever give me? I know that you didn't know Italian then, and you still don't know it well after living here for twenty years. You never went to parent-teacher conferences! It's true that the teachers speak in a way that even the Italians find incomprehensible and that they set the appointments at times that are impossible to make. But you, with the excuse that they are the teachers, that they know what is right, you always preferred delegating instead of accepting your responsibilities. And as for games, Papà, when did you ever play with me? You were al-

---

[1] *Sanatoria* is a legal term used when the government offers a temporary pardon for a legal infringement. In the context of migration, *sanatoria* refers to amnesties that allow undocumented migrants to acquire documentation and therefore attain legal status.

ways too tired. At the houses of my Italian friends I saw the kind of familiarity that they had with their fathers, and even called them by their first names. What kind of familiarity have we ever had, you and I, Papà? Would you have ever allowed me to call you Kodjo? Sure, you were proud and you swelled up like a peacock every time you took me to play soccer for the city team so that every time I scored, you could hear my teammates cheer for me, "Go Pelé, you're great! Keep it up!"

Little by little as he spoke, the sobs that his mother, Afi, could not repress became more lacerating while she pressed her hands to her chest as if oppressed by his words.

"Yes, Mamma, I know that I'm not allowed to speak to my parents like this, I know that it's against our traditions, that it's something done by those 'little whites,' as you call them. Yes, Mamma, I know how hard you've worked to keep us afloat, a life made of suffocating loneliness for someone who doesn't speak the language, a life of homesickness while you were pregnant with me, waiting at home for hours and days and months without being able to communicate with anyone, waiting for Papà to come home from work. And then hours and hours doing little jobs here and there, even on holidays, babysitting, taking care of old people, being an 'attendant' as they say nowadays. I know all this, but you're not the only ones who have ever done it. You sure didn't do it all just for me, and even if you had, then I still say, you've just done your duty.

"Have you ever wondered what it was like for me to be the only 'colored one' in a class of all whites? Have you ever imagined my painful surprise when the first stupid white child called me 'nigger?' Here I was among them and I never even realized that I was different. It's not like you wake up every morning, look at yourself in the mirror and say, 'Hey! I'm black!' It's others who see you as different. I've always had that feeling of having other peoples' eyes focused on me, and at all costs I had to be better than they were in everything to be respected. And now that I've finally integrated after tremendous work, now that everyone knows me and appreciates me for who I am, you come to me and say that we're going back over there. I'm seventeen now, I'm not baby anymore that you can force things on. In a year I'll be of age. I'll have the right to decide my own life.

"Don't hassle me anymore about Africa: I don't want to go! Why don't you both go? You talk about it so much, you're so homesick for it, why don't you go back home? You always say that you want to go back and that everything was so wonderful back home. You're always wrapped up in this eternal dream of returning and it's always put off. When it's all said and done, I'm probably more likely to go back before you do.

"You know, you have really been a major pain in my butt! I'm sick of having to call any stranger with a dark skin 'Uncle,' of having to wait for all the adults to sit down before I could. I have had it up to here with all the people at those nostalgic parties that you were forever dragging me to where you all danced to that monotonous, repetitive music until you dropped. I know it's a way that you overcome homesickness and reattach your umbilical cord to mother Africa. I understand, but I like soul music, rock, reggae, *rai* and rap."

At this point Kuami, who had been sitting in his chair with his eyes gazing into the emptiness, got up and straightened his gangly body, nurtured by processed, homogenized food, put his hands in his pockets, and began to rock back and forth on his heels. His father watched him with shocked eyes as if he saw a stranger before him. He thought to himself, "No, this can't be my son!"

In the face of their silence, Kuami upped the ante: "I never rebelled when you dragged me back to Africa that summer, after all the vaccines and inoculations just to put up with that sticky heat that glues your shirt to your skin. For your sakes, I put up with the flies, the mosquitoes, the ocean of unknown relatives that invaded us morning and night and demanded that I spoke to them in dialect and ate with my hands. I even pretended to believe all those absurd stories that grandfather told about voodoo. It was the most boring time of my life: if I had known, I would have taken my PlayStation and Game Boy.

"Can't you understand that THIS is my country? My life is here, my friends are here, my future is here: how would I ever become an inventor of video games back home? People can only stay back home long enough for a vacation and that's it, and you could even find it cool. I don't know how to live without lights, TV with lots of channels, clean running water. I wouldn't know how to adapt to life there. Can't you understand? It's like you're asking me to leave a five-star hotel with all its comforts to go and live in a tent at a campsite. Papà, camping can be fun for a while, but in the long run it gets uncomfortable. . . ."

At this point, Kuami rolled over in his bed, covered in sweat. All night long he'd been picturing this confrontation with his parents as an imaginary monologue. Ever since his father had mentioned at dinner that they were planning to return to Africa permanently.

Agitated, he passed his right hand nervously across his face as if to drive out a bad dream. He hadn't been able to sleep. He went into the bathroom to wash his face.

His thoughts swirled and chased each other through his mind. "No, I can't talk to them like that. It would be a disaster. Maybe I could try an approach closer to their culture, their traditions. To discuss it with them, I definitely should have my godfather 'Uncle' Kossi come at daybreak, and inform him the night before to publicly announce a family council. Or maybe tomorrow I'll get up at dawn and knock on their door after I've rinsed my mouth out."

I'd start out like this: "Papà, *dada,* I need to speak with you."

"It's best that we sit in the living room," he would undoubtedly say while my mother would put her hand to her mouth to suffocate her usual, "Oh, God, what's happened now?"

My father would begin, "My son, day has broken."

"Yes, day has broken Papà."

"Did you wake well?" my mother would ask.

"Yes, *dada,* everything is fine."

"Beloved son, we are at peace," my old man would say to give me the chance to speak.

I would say, "Father, I am at peace, too. Please, I beg you *dada* to listen to my words so that they reach your ears and enter your heart. It is true that an elderly man sitting sees farther than a young man who is standing, and that a child does not put his father on his shoulder to help him see the sky. However, it is true that the blacksmith of a village can be the apprentice of another. Here where we live is another world, a different world from the one where you grew up and when one sits in the midst of crouching toads, you can't ask for a chair, you have to adapt yourself."

My parents would undoubtedly look at each other for a long time, feeling proud of me. I would continue, reciting with a convincing voice, "I know of your sacrifices, but that is the way life is: you cannot ask something salty to be sweet. It was written in your *sé,* in your destiny, and you know better than I do that if one is not invited to a meal, he cannot complain that the sauce is too hot. This choice to come here was your choice and I was born here. Now you ask me to return to Africa because you are so homesick. Distance sharpens sadness when memory only conserves the pleasant memories. It is right that this is so, also because the fish that gets away is always a very big fish. But you yourselves have taught me that you cannot beat your drum against another's chest. Each person must make his own choices. Of course, Africa is a part of me. The chicken isn't ashamed of his own cage, but my *sé* is here. I was born here and I've decided to stay here to put down my own roots. And here my voice falls."

After a long silence, my mother would say, "Fo, my husband, have you heard the words of your son?"

"Yes, Afi, I have heard them."

After straightening up from his chair, Papà Kodjo would clasp his hands together as he usually did to gather his thoughts before expounding them:

"Afi, in my turn, I beg you to hear the sound of my voice and to transfer what it expresses so that it can reach the mind of our son Kuami. Tell him that I know that traveling, one finds wisdom and that intelligence is the fruit that is gathered in the garden next door, but nevertheless, even hot water never forgets that it was once cold. A tree cannot grow without roots. It saddens us that our son wants to forget the land of his fathers, and that he speaks the language of his ancestors with reluctance. Certainly, his *sé* brought us here to conceive him in this foreign land. But we know that this is not our home. Even given one hundred years, a tree planted in a river will never become a crocodile. So say our elders, even though I know well that this tree would get wet in the river. Some things we have absorbed in spite of ourselves. It's not that we didn't try to integrate here. That was our desire. But along our road, with only rare exceptions, we found only diffidence or mostly curiosity. Tell our son that his tongue sings the truth when he says, 'One who is not invited to the meal cannot complain that the sauce is too hot.' The trouble was that here we never felt invited and we certainly would not be welcome guests.

"Certainly life here is more glittering than the skin of a serpent: it's like sending a cat to the meat market. I understand that he would prefer to remain here. Of course, he has studied more than we have and he understands the wisdom of books. However, we believe that knowledge is like the baobab tree: no one can embrace it all with two arms. The knowledge of life has an enormous trunk.

"Our family traditions are part of us and he cannot ask us to throw water out of the jar with the excuse that it is going to rain. Tell him that my father, his grandfather, explained to me that the beard cannot teach the eyelashes, and that a father is the destiny of his son. Coming here we sought a better future, more for him than for ourselves. He must remember that not everything here is to be accepted. In this country, we have tried to take that which is good. I understand that he is young and eager, but it happens that youth often cannot manage to see a mouse hiding behind an elephant. Afi, tell our son to reconsider, and tell him. . . ."

Kuami knew that he did not agree with the direction that the conversation was taking. At this point he would have to interrupt firmly:

"Papà, even the black cow gives white milk! Here they say that, 'Things are the same all over.' Even back home things were not perfect, otherwise you never would have come here. Life goes on, and you cannot swallow the saliva that you already spit out. You know very well that 'Two that you will have' is not the same as 'One that you do have.' Anyway, I've already decided."

Surely his mother would raise her right index finger to reprimand him.

"Kuami, your father has not finished speaking yet. You cannot start dancing before hearing the rhythm of the drum."

"But I've already heard my fill of this drum rhythm and I'm sick of it!"

"Listen, my son, if you wish, do not hear my voice, but listen to the heart of a mother, the heart of your mother. I carried you for nine months and nourished you with my own blood. With the help of God, after hours of hard labor, I gave you life. You were not born in your homeland, but were like a wild plant in this forest of cement. In this squalid forest where children grow up on a royal throne, they believe that it's enough to have a seat to become a king. My son, even if today you think you're a giant, you will always remain the fruit of your father's seed. If only for this you owe him respect. You owe him respect my son. Your father is a great man. He has always been an honest man, fair, and a hard worker. No one else in the village could even get close to him when he worked in the fields. The drought destroyed our lands, the harvests were not enough to keep us from starving and we were forced to come here. The *sé* of your father brought him here to bend his back, but believe me, just because a lion has become thin, you cannot confuse him with a cat. Do you understand? Let him finish speaking!"

Then, turning toward her husband she would continue: "Fo, forgive him and finish what you were saying."

After a long silence, he would assuredly pick up where he'd left off.

"Afi, tell our son to think again, and to remember always that if two are running, he can't expect to run in the middle. Life is a continuous choice: who has water in his mouth does not breathe on the fire. Each choice entails suffering and it is not for nothing that we use fire to extract honey. It has been more than two months that I haven't worked because the company closed down. A man who cannot support his family is not a man. Every day I get up and my feet walk tirelessly on the roads and through gates without finding any solution. If we've thought about returning it's because this new law doesn't leave us any choice. You have to go home and wait to be recalled in order to reenter Italy. I know that it's an absurd law because no one would buy a knife hidden in a lining. But this is their country and they make the laws. We have no choice. I say, a thin cow is better than an empty stall. And here my voice falls."

"Father, this law is unjust. By now this country which I consider mine is also yours. A son is at home with his father as well as with his mother. Africa is like my mother and here, I feel like I'm with my father. Why must you force me to choose? You have also contributed to the wealth of this country by the sweat of your brow. Papà, I know well that a hunter's apprentice doesn't show the path to the hunter. You must not think that I'm a foolish child who insists on binding water with a cord, but when one has a headache, one does not try to treat the knee. I believe we must fight to change this evil law. Here I was born and here I want to remain even though I feel I belong to two countries. I want to stay here to study, to live, and so that they can't fool themselves into believing that I will only do the jobs that they don't want. Papà, I beg you, don't give up! At this point, if I have nothing to lose, I'm even ready to stay here illegally . . . anyway, there will eventually be a new law legalizing immigrants, even if they call it by a different name."

As always, his father would soothe Kuami with his tranquil voice, "My son, you must consider well, because a crippled man does not sing a battle song. You must not worry, tomorrow I will get up and will go out again to look for work. The spirits of our ancestors will give us aid, because if you put a burden on your knee, someone will help you to lift it onto your head."

Carefully, his mother would add: "Little one, we live for you, you are our future, our passport with no visa. . . . You will see that we'll find some solution . . . the night is long, but the day comes."

Reassured by that thought, Kuami fell asleep.

"Leaving with No Return"

Ron Kubati

Translated by Sarah Hill

Day and night became the same thing. We were constantly visited by supporters of the Democratic Party and by the so-called moderates. Even the minister of education, whom the government had asked to handle the negotiations, showed up. The room where we had set ourselves up was probably used for staging plays, since we found a big red curtain there. We tore it into red strips to tie around our heads. Now that our "look" was ready, we could go down to the first floor and take some photographs. We were real revolutionaries! Our friends from the Institute of the Arts delighted us with a risqué recording. They had put together a piece dedicated to Hoxha and his widow. Amid gales of laughter, they recalled all sorts of historical figures who had found comfort between the widow's legs before being knocked off, one after the other.

On Wednesday morning things started to get really heated. The crowd surrounding the Students' Building had become noticeably bigger. Control had passed from the moderate supporters of the Democratic Party to those of the free unions. They were great guys. They had big hands and spoke their minds. When three of us fainted and were rushed to hospital, the time for words was over and the crowd decided to make its presence felt. It poured into the grounds of the presidential palace, then, divided into droves, it attacked Tirana's central square, Scanderbeg Square. It was there that the police force was concentrated. With their weapons in their hands, they were protecting the enormous statue of the dictator, Enver Hoxha. Hundreds of thousands of people invaded the square. The crowd had only one goal: kill the dictator. The police started firing into the air. The minster of the interior was observing it all, hidden away somewhere, in constant radio contact with President Alia. Something went wrong between the two of them, since later they would each accuse the other of having given the order to fire on the crowd. Luckily, it wasn't carried out. Now the statue could be desecrated by the crowd, but it was heavy and stable. Specialists were called in to deal with these difficulties. A friend of mine swears he saw Edmond with other, unknown faces, but we never knew anything for sure about their identities. At first they tried with dynamite, but the police managed to deactivate it. When the police gave in, the specialists, who had the equipment for any situation, produced a cable out of nowhere. The cable was slung around Enver Hoxha's neck, but the neck was too massive. It seems an engineer came forward to advise them to pull at an angle of forty-five degrees. Enver Hoxha dug his heels in for a while, then he started to get shaky, toppled, and then fell recklessly, without crushing anyone. Scanderbeg Square yelled as it had never done before. Everyone wanted to see Enver Hoxha from another angle: spread out on the ground.

We students were still shut in. The news was brought to us almost live via the continuous comings and goings of our volunteer correspondents. A few minutes after the fall of Enver Hoxha, the deputy leader of the Democratic Party, Gramoz Pashko, arrived. He climbed onto a chair and told us the news. Then, like all of us, deeply moved, he began shouting: "We got rid of him! We got rid of him! We got rid of that scumbag!"

In Scanderbeg Square, the game was not over yet. The statue had yielded more easily than people had expected. The crowd was not happy. It wanted more. Various possibilities were considered. Two were the most popular: go to the cemetery of national heroes and open and burn Enver Hoxha's tomb, and go to Bllok, the residential area of the Communist politburo. The two places were both on a road on the way to the student zone. For that reason, a third option won out: the crowd came back to us. The statue couldn't be left alone. Perhaps some were afraid that it might raise itself up and get back onto its pedestal. They decided to bring it to us as a gift. The truck they found to do the job wasn't enough. Enver Hoxha was once again tied by the neck and dragged by cables as far as the student zone. Along the way, he lost his head, which broke off from the neck. Somehow, the steel corpse managed to reach us. Some enthusiasts tried to get the head into the building as a trophy, but changed their minds when it occurred to them that it could make us a police target. The statue was disassembled and everyone took a piece. It was said that even the envoys from the little city of Kavaja, the first city to have risen up, had put forward their claim for possession of the head. They would later be killed by the police while returning home with their booty.

We didn't stop the strike. We asked that the news media transmit the news that the government had accepted our request. People came to the windows to meet us and women tried as hard as they could to touch and kiss us. They were crying. They weren't tears of joy, they were truly bitter tears. They had discovered that the monster God was vulnerable, and that their sufferings had been unnecessary. They were crying for a life that had been wasted.

For the first time in its history, the television did its duty and showed the film of the statue falling.

Many other cities had imitated Tirana. The collapse had begun.

Tanks ruled the city. In its desperate last struggle, the wounded regime made use even of the military school cadets, who were pressed into armed demonstrations. It was hard to understand what was happening. We suspected that there was a list of inconvenient people who would be visited during the night. At the same time, an early spring arrived. The air warmed up. The days were beautiful. The university remained closed. In the morning we met up with our friends in the city's main park and there we would play cards on the grass. The girls seemed more attractive than usual. The tanks kept us company a few dozen meters away. Slowly, we even got used to their presence. Each day was like the last, empty and identical.

The news that small boats had left a port in the south, heading west, resonated with our own ideas about how to go about leaving. Everyone started figuring out how best to do it for himself. I contacted a cousin who knew the right people in the various ports of the country. One evening, at his house, we knocked back half a liter of *rakì* to drown his disappointment: he had come back from a fruitless trip to the country's main port. Glasses in hand, we decided to try for the extreme south of the country the next day. The next morning, while I was still engaged in a nocturnal battle with my pillow, sheets, and blankets, he came to get me. "What's going on?" asked my brother. "Nothing. This evening, or at the latest tomorrow, I'll be home, you'll see. I can't ditch him, and in any case I don't think we'll make it." I went out without having breakfast. My cousin didn't even know how we were going to travel. It was as though we had sensed a feeble call that gradually grew stronger. We started walking along a road, which after a few dozen kilometers led to the country's main port. From there, it would be just a few hundred kilometers along the coast and we would arrive at the southern port. The driver of a little bus passing that way recognized my cousin. The little bus took us only as far as the entrance to the most important port city, which was surrounded by the army. My cousin began looking for another means of transport to take us to the southern port. I changed my mind. For me, the presence of the soldiers was the equivalent of a sign saying, "Run away!" For some reason, the soldiers were firing bullets into the air.

On foot, I turned into a road that led along the coast to the port. My cousin started begging me to change my mind, and in the end he followed me. When we were only a kilometer from the port, we saw a huge ship loaded with people setting sail. I wanted to swim to it, but I wouldn't have made it. Without knowing why, I started running.

I run towards the port. I run without stopping. My cousin, older and less fit, follows with difficulty. I can't stop. He can't make it. I drag him by the arm, hoping his heart holds out. Mine is beating as hard as it can. A delivery car stops and gives us a lift as far as the port. They tell us that there's no ship in port. I have no intention of forgetting about it. I would climb onto anything that floats and trust myself to the wind. I know what I want; I just don't know what I'll do.

The port is surrounded by both police and soldiers. I don't know where the entrance to the port is. The soldiers help me. We give them our watches, our money, and any other objects they want. We find dozens of people on the wharf. There's nothing more frustrating than to watch a ship full of people leaving port while you're left on shore. The only thing near us that can float is a former fishing boat with no motor. We jump on and invoke the winds. Our "floater" moves for real, as though our desires were rowing. After a few minutes, we are close to a big ship that has stayed away from the wharf out of caution. The sailors from the ship, which bears a Panamanian flag and is called *Legend,* start making desperate gestures towards us. According to them, we'll almost certainly end up at the bottom of the sea. A guy from our group has forgotten his cigarettes, so he starts asking for some from the *Legend*'s sailors. By a strange coincidence, our craft drifts over to the *Legend*'s prow. It's close enough that our cigarette-requestor climbs up onto the *Legend* to get his cigarettes in person. Encouraged by his example, another guy, who probably doesn't even smoke and just wants to show up the first one, jumps up. That's all it takes. Nobody really knows why he's climbing aboard. Probably everyone thinks that those who went in front of him know what they're doing. Or perhaps it's the ship that makes us climb aboard. My competitive spirit gets going, I overtake a few people, and put myself among the *Legend*'s first five guests. And now what do we do? Everyone is asking the same question. We ask a sailor, or officer, from the ship, who makes himself responsible for our entertainment.

"What should we do?" English reinforced with gestures turns out to be enough for communication.

"Declare the ship occupied. There's nothing else to do." The group surrounding him is at the ready.

"All right. We declare the ship occupied."

It was exciting. We were occupiers. The ship was enormous and occupying it hadn't been that difficult. Essentially, you just had to want things enough. As time passed, another boat came alongside the ship, and the number of occupiers grew. Among them, there was also a number of curious onlookers, who climbed aboard just to say hello. I invested my money and the last swappable objects I had in order to send one of those onlookers to telephone to let the others know. The onlooker was probably charged with making dozens of phone calls, without ever doing it. Nevertheless, a few hours later, there were more known faces and slowly the embracing began. "You too! Hey, so they let you know? Well, look who's here!" At this point the kind of question began to change: "Have you seen my brother? Have you seen my girlfriend? Yes, I really think I did. Look over there, to the left."

The next morning, when everyone is there and there are thousands of us, the ship sets off. The sea pulls it towards who knows where. It's not we who are crossing the sea, but rather the sea that has itself crossed. The dawn is gray, cold and windy. When we had left we hadn't eaten anything for more than twenty-four hours. We no longer understand anything. Our gaze registers everything that happens, but only transmits everything at the end of the adventure, in the form of memories. Everyone is holding onto something in order to face to the waves and the rain that intermingle above us. The city at our backs gets smaller and smaller, but in front of us, we can see nothing.

"M"

Ron Kubati

Translated by Sarah Hill

THE NIGHT HAD TURNED THE JOURNEY INTO A LONG, DARK TUNNEL, at whose end thousands and thousands of lights began to come on, as the train drew closer to the city. I knew nothing about the streets, shops, nightclubs, illuminated houses and who knew what else those lights were brightening. I had no idea about the clothing, the habits, the accent, or the women of that city. A fascinating hesitation stimulated incomplete fantasies that essentially just improved on combinations of pleasant memories, transforming them into improbable predictions. It was a starry night, but as the brightly lit city drew nearer, the sky ceased to count, or rather, the true sky was the halo of promises emitted by a strong field of vital energy. A renewed, child-like innocence opened up the possibility of easier and more generous enchantments to my gaze. The lights over my past seemed effectively to have gone out.

Usually I sleep with the blinds open. It's always the morning light that wakes me up. The first thing I see, when I wake up, is the window. It shows me which room I'm in, and consequently the kind of world waiting for me outside. It tells me where and therefore who I am: if I'm the nice guest who always tells interesting stories, if I'm an annoying son who comes and goes without explanations, if I'm the unwanted drunken friend of the daughter of an apprehensive father, if I'm the taciturn client of a small hotel, if there's someone nearby waiting happily for my reappearance, or if I need to wait until everyone leaves the house before I dare use the bathroom. The window shows me if someone will bring me breakfast in bed, if I have to get up to make coffee, or if I need to go down to get the paper. It tells me if it's Sunday, if I have to run to get a tram, a taxi, a train. That morning I couldn't see the window. The blinds were shut. I didn't even know if it was morning. I remembered only that I had kissed Francesca in my sleep. Her hand caressing my face still gave me a feeling of serenity and well-being. I prolonged the fantasy in the dark, until I decided to explore the bed and its surroundings by touch. Before managing to push a switch, I mentally ran through a series of snapshots from the night before. I waited for the room to reveal itself after switching on the light, with a more disillusioned and circumspect expectation. I looked at the closed window and by now I knew that I was in an anonymous hotel room. I was just passing through. I would have liked to turn out the light, go back to sleep, and wake up somewhere else, another morning. Instead, I went out. It was as though I were waiting for something to spring on me and force me into an irrevocable journey into mechanisms that might somehow transform themselves into who knows what. But the streets were the same as usual: the usual people, the usual faces, the usual rhythms. A strange, disappointing silence created the impression of a large, tired land. At a certain point, however, a large colored "M" invited me down. As soon as I descended, I felt a strange acceleration take over me. The surface energy seemed to be hidden down there below. Everyone was running. They descended marble stairs, escalators, selected their direction, jumped onto trains in movement. Students, workers, thieves, entrepreneurs, gypsies, and refugees all darted towards the trains in a strange, alienating, flattening, and democratic common space. That momentary promiscuity transformed itself into an exuberant, vital magma that spread over surfaces and created cities. I accelerated. I didn't know where to go. I felt above me the current of a vertigo of possibilities that annulled the relevance of my subjective choice. I felt as though I had acquired a credit card which would allow me to live in a multidimensional world that, down there, would not yet reveal its intentions. The buskers were singing. Musicians were playing everywhere. The violin, the harmonica, the cruelty of their delicacy, and the basket to collect 100 lira coins. Art within the cruel and sensitive metro: a gypsy with Hungarian sympathies who wept feelings with his violin, trying to awaken the robot-like travelers holding the change from their just-bought papers. Ads for those waiting: surreal images on the screen from a science fiction film or Massive Attack's latest video. The destinies that brushed against one another, interwove themselves, and were momentarily restrained beneath the suffocating tunnel. The beggars begged. The thieves robbed. The young boys pestered the young girls. The conductors told off those without tickets. Everyone working on realizing a particular project. A multitude of elements assailing me. My perception went crazy. Marvelous confusion improved by the disappointment of disparity. There below it seemed like the workshop of possibilities that channeled themselves in order to realize landscapes, surfaces. Flashes. Everything incredibly full. No empty space, no work for the imagination, no horizon. Just surprise. Roulette. No longer from behind to in front (towards the horizon), but from low to high, from dark to light, immediately, with a leap, with astonishment, from the unconscious to the conscious, from nothing (as the possibility of everything) to the concrete, to the real (by way of drawing lots: only a variant realized) that rose up like the marvel of the magma of everything. The escalators carried you up without giving you any warning of the surface that was waiting for you. Every metro stop like a roulette of landscapes, of variants of reality: now a park, now a street, now the rain, now the night, now a face, now a film camera, now a fire. When you didn't like the landscape drawn by chance, you felt like going back down, hoping that the next drawing of lots would be the most surprising one possible, capable of transforming you from a weight that you drag behind you, into that unknown and supposedly true you to which your inexorable dissatisfaction never tires of laying claim.

❧ ❧ ❧

The feeling of not belonging had never left my chest or my head. Since I was a child, thanks also to the imaginings provoked by the first novels I had read, I had waited hopefully for some event that would reveal something exceptional to me, something that would help me achieve a constant and satisfactory balance with the environment around me. Luckily, children have a license to think the most apparently absurd things. After all, they're children. Society's rules and codes have not yet imposed the outlines of what will be called reality. From the most spoiled to the most unfortunate, sooner or later, already fed up with life and already a little bit left wing, with their sulky expressions, the children stretch out their imaginings pathetically, up to the point of considering the fascinating hypothesis that they were adopted without being told about it. The more your origins are false, the more the present is false. Those directly responsible for your lack of conciliation with the world end up being those omnipotent parents, guilty like all the supposedly powerful, whose imagined removal seems to offer the hypothetical solution to the problem. The claim to another origin, another identity, is the optimistic rejection of a fundamental discomfort. That refusal to accept fully your own parents, your own friends, your own duties, your own language, your own face, your own body, turns into the conservation of that distance that produces a feeling of radical agnosticism. At a certain point, the happy astuteness of this feeling no longer consists of the search for a mythical and inexistent origin and identity, but rather of the projection of satisfying fantasies, whose realization becomes a daily mission. It's as though you were to say: "I don't know where I'm from, but I know where I want to go," or alternatively: "I am not what I was, but what I will be."

The myth of origin, the myth of the past is substituted by the myth of redemption, by the myth of the future, the only one that can offer, with time, a recovery of the past, a reconciliation, an idyllic reevaluation, which is sometimes more pathetic than the initial rejection. As far as I'm concerned, I had never managed to do anything that might earn my own and others' full approval. I had been a talented volleyball player, but my trainer seemed fairly perplexed. I had a sloppy shot and I was pretty much all over the place when I jumped. But I would score a lot of points (who knows how) and so I always ended up as one of the regular team members. Sometimes, however, my shot was truly clean and lethal. "That's it . . . that's how I say to do it," complained the trainer. "He's young . . . he'll go further than anyone . . . I feel it," added the inept, but convinced soothsayer, whispering to someone behind my back. In the pool, too, the lack of a clean style annoyed my coaches. I couldn't manage to follow their advice. During my university studies, it was the same story. Despite my results, my teachers were perplexed, like the editor who, even with the first published copy of my work in his hand, couldn't make up his mind about my linguistic choices. "I like it . . . really. Otherwise I wouldn't have published it. There's something strange, though . . . that I don't understand. But it could work in your favor. Let's hope so," he said, while giving me the addresses of the people to contact about the first presentations.

Next to the train window, behind which there was only the dark of the tunnel, there was a black and white photo of a very old and partially destroyed bus. Near it were several bins that seemed like dumpsters. The image seemed clouded to the point that the physical context could only be intuited. Despite that, something seemed to leak from it, enough to make the image disturbing. I felt strange. The photograph itself might be banal, but seeing it hung in the eternally nocturnal metro train you couldn't help but feel a growing sense of wonder. There was such an evident and clear distance between what you perceived of the environment and the images of the photograph that it enabled you to put parentheses around routine's crushing state of gravitation and its apparently unsurpassable reality. That very old photograph felt more like the future than the past. Not in the sense, however, of a direct representation. It was that feeling of distance, of wonder, that hid a strange hope, which taught me that things can change, despite anything you might expect, that even the most courageous fantasies are possible. If I were a dictator, I would have strictly censored any such image. Without realizing it, I leaned my head against the glass, opening up distant memories in search of a future. And again I thought of Claire.

"The Pilgrimage of the Voice"

Tahar Lamri

Translated by Graziella Parati

I

MAN IS THE LORD OF THE WORD HE STORES IN HIS BELLY, BUT HE IS slave to the words that he lets out of his mouth. What am I? I am a heap of words that speaks and always keeps some truth in silence.

Abdessalam El Sounbati called El Merrakchi, from Marrakech, direct descendant of the last Arab king of Granada, who married four women: Souhaila, Soumaya, Souraya, and Soukaina.

None of them had sons, but Soukaina who gave birth to me. I was the last child after fourteen daughters.

They called me Laayachi because they were afraid I would not see again the season that had witnessed my birth.

My profession and my vocation is to be a storyteller. I have praised Mohammed, Alì's bravery, and Saad Zenati's heroic feats in the square of Jemaa El-Fena and in all the squares of the Orient.

And here I am today to tell you the story of a dream. I have come from the borders of Mauritania to reconnect what history has separated. My story is not different from the stories told by your *filari*, or *fuler* or storytellers from the plains.

The original short story is in in four languages: standard Italian, Mantovano, Romagnolo, and Venetian dialects. In order to maintain the linguistic hybridity of the original text and highlight the difference between standard Italian and the dialects, I translated short sections into Italian, and added the English translation. If the sections in dialect were long I placed the Italian translation in a note.

Zontel al riser, skilled conoisseur of rice paddies and water springs, married Guendalina and they had fourteen children.

Du iè mort ancora putin, tri iè mort in guera e atar iè nega in dal Minciu.

Due sono morti ancora bambini, tre sono morti in guerra e un altro è annegato nel Mincio.

Two died when they were children, three died in war and another drowned in the Mincio river.

Ch'atar set iè diventà grand e ià mis su famiglia.

Ch'atar è diventato grande e ha messo su famiglia.

Ch'atar grew up and had his own family.

Lera: Burla, Orsola, Matilde, Ippolito, Molin, Guerrino e Ulisse cl'era stà in Africa.

Lera: Burla, Orsola, Matilde, Ippolito, Molin, Guerrino e Ulisse che era stato in Africa.

Lera: Burla, Orsola, Matilde, Ippolito, Molin, Guerrino and Ulisse who had been to Africa.

Ippolito knew the language of animals and had the power to heal them with marsh-herbs.

He kept repeating that his powers came directly from Manto, Tiresia's daughter, who had lived isolated, absorbed in silence and in her dreams, in the company of her vocation where the water of the Mincio River ceases to flow. Although Ippolito was illiterate, he knew the *Divine Comedy* by heart. Almost all of it.

Orsola, little Orsola, was the reincarnation of Agnese Visconti. She married a man she did not love and loved a man she died for. It is a story people talk about even today.

Guerino det Cucai, parché l'era bas da statura, l'a mis su na mandria scunfinada e l'a vulì ben sultant ai su gugioi, cal ciamava cun amur, "ime pursei. Ah i pursei! fesi i om pulì cume i pursei," al dzeva.

Guerino detto Cucai perché era basso di statura mise su una mandria sconfinata e amò soltanto i suoi maiali che chiamava affettuosamente, "i miei purc. Ah i purc! Fossero gli uomini puliti come i maiali." Diceva.

Guerino called Cucai because he was short got himself a huge herd and only loved his swine. He called them affectionately, "my lovely pigs. Ah, my pigs! I wish men were as clean as hogs are," he used to say.

Burela l'à mis su n'ustaria in du s'nasava sempar n'udur gaiard da cantina e da brodo. Propia lì, cuma savì, indua ades a ghè l'ustaria di Ranàri. O forse lì davsin, su mia.

Burela ha messo su un'osteria dove si sentiva sempre un odore gagliardo di cantina e di brodo. Proprio lì, come sapete, dove adesso c'è l'osteria di Ranari. O forse lì vicino, non so.

Burela got himself a tavern that always smelled very strongly like a cellar and of broth. Right there, where, as you know, now there is Ranari's tavern. Well, maybe near by, I don't know.

Mulin al sé spusà cun la Giusepa e 'l la piciava na volta al mes e l'dseva: "Sa tagh dè mia ogni tant, li doni li dis ca tagh vo pù ben." Mulin e la Giusepa iè mort la stessa giurnada, ma la Giusepa trent'ani dopo.

Mulin sposò la Giuseppa, che picchiava una volta al mese e diceva: "Se non gliele si dà qualche volta, le donne dicono che è perduta l'affezione." Mulin e la Giuseppa sono morti nello stesso giorno, ma la Giuseppa trent'anni dopo.

Mulin got himself married to Giusepa and beat her once a month. He used to say: "If you don't hit them now and then, women say that your affection is gone." Mulin and Giusepa died the same day. Only Giusepa died thirty years after he did.

Guerin l'à spusà la Pasqualina; da cal matrimoni lì agh sun restà sul mi, cantastorie da stala in stala. Sun chi!

Guerin ha sposato la Pasqualina; di quel matrimonio sono restato solo io, cantastorie di stalla in stalla. Son qui!

Guerin got himself married to Pasqualina; I am the only one left of that marriage: me, a storyteller traveling from stable to stable. Here I am!

Gualfardo, skilled conoisseur of medicinal herbs, married Armellina and they had fourteen children. Two of them died when they were still little angels, the war took three others and two of them were swallowed up by the Ronco river. Seven survived and had themselves a family.

The remaining seven children were: Didnotwantyou, Orsola, Matilde, Ippolito, Carlotta, Guerrino, and Orano, who had been to Africa.

Didnotwantyou fulfilled her father's desire. One day she left the house and never came back.

Orsola, little Orsola when she was a child, was the reincarnation of Agnese Visconti. She married a man she did not love and loved a man she died for.

Matilde married Ribello and they had three sons: Rivo, Lutio, and Nary.

Carlotta married Little October and they had three children: Little Marx, Rosa Luxemburg, and Socialist Idea who married a banker.

Guerrino got himself a huge herd and only loved his swine. He called them affectionately, "My lovely pigs. Ah, my pigs! I wish men were as clean as hogs are," he used to say.

After coming back from Africa, Orano got himself married to Giusepa and hit her once a month. He used to say: "If you don't hit them now and then, women say that your affection is gone." Orano and Giusepa died the same day. Only Giusepa died thirty years after he did.

Ippolito knew the language of animals and the secret language of humans. He had the power to heal both beasts and men with marsh-herbs. His powers came from Gualfardo, his father. Although Ippolito was illiterate, he knew the *Divine Comedy* by heart. Almost all of it.

II

In the Sacred Book, in the chapter titled "Man," one reads:

"How can one buy or sell the firmament or the color of the earth? Remember, we are neither the owners of the freshness of the air nor the owners of the joyful water of the stream. Every pine needle that wavers in the wind, every grain of sand on a beach, every dewdrop in the shade of the woods, the buzz of an insect, are all sacred in memory."

I have come to bring you the words of the sacred book of the Casbah, which is neither a city, nor a village. It is a central area on the outskirts. The Casbah belongs to all of us. Let's say it is a labyrinth. Maybe it is love, but nobody seems to be aware of that. It is a place where there are no women. If women are there, they only live in the apartments. Now in the Casbah there are no narrow streets, but rather streets paved with black tar—streets deprived of any greenery.

Thirty years into the second half of the last century, many of my brothers left behind their large courtyards and came here to your country, looking for fortune. Those men's faces, I have seen them, betray their resignation and at times anger for doing such a stupid thing. But under the early wrinkles on those faces I have also read hope for a world in which there is still room for old stories. Their silent voices say: you too have been deprived of the old courtyards, the old spaces of exchange and storytelling.[1]

In my father's land, my courtyards are no different than the threshing floors of your old farms. They are places of exchange and of feelings. Places filled with laughter and tears. On your threshing floor there is an oak that is like a cathedral, in my courtyard there was a palm tree that was like a mosque. As you can see, they are the same and different. They are like twins, these relatives of ours.

III

It was fate that orchestrated my meeting with Zanubrio. One day, I caught him unawares while he was opening his heart to a blade of grass. He was leaning against a pole at the bus stop and was saying:

> *" U j é una massa d'zent, in Rumagna, ch'i n'supporta i burdel ch'j à la faza negra, o ch'i n'vò ciacaré cun j albanis e ch'i dis che i maruchen j è propi di maruchen.*
>
> *Sta zent la diz che i rumagnul j à da ste in Rumagna, j africhen in Africa e i albanis in albanì, che tota sta zent ch'la ven a que j è bon sòl d'purtè dal malatì, e chi è di lèdar, e quand ch'la va ben, j è di sgrazié.*
>
> *Sta zent la dis ch'a j aven da èsar urgulius d'esàr du rumagnul: a j o capì, mo pu i ciama la su fiola Sue Ellen, i magna int i fast food, d'istè i fa surf, e' sàbat i bala cun la disco dance, i mastìga e' chewing gum, i bev la coca cola, i léz sol i best seller e, stai guérd ben, i s'asarmeia ai Tom, ai Bill o ai Jack di cino americhen.*
>
> *A me invézi u m' piés d'pinsé che in Rumagna uié dal zite pio antighi d'Roma, caglie stedi os averti ae' mond luntan, che da no l'è pas i Fenici, j'Etruschi, i Greci, i Rumen, gli arab, i Tedesch, i Franzis, i Cinis, j'Ebrei e pu 'na massa d'etra zent.*
>
> *Um 'piés d'pinsé che nò a sen i fiul d'tota sta zent.*
>
> *U m'piés d'pinsé che stal fazz novi ch'al zira per la Rumagna i s'porta 'na massa d'stori ch'a n'cnusen, e che i nostar fiul, se no a sem bom, i sarà piò fortuné che no, parchè j arà dal zitè piò antighi cun 'na massa d'stori, d'lezendi, d'rasunament, prema ngn'avema, e ades sè. Me a pens akse. La va ben?"*[2]

---

[1] This sentence differs from the original in Italian. Tahar Lamri asked me to make the changes and in an e-mail message dated February 3, 2005 he indicated the modified wording of the sentence.

---

[2] C'è una massa di gente in Romagna che non sopporta i ragazzini che hanno la faccia nera, o che non vogliono chiacchierare con gli Albanesi e che dice che i

"There are a lot of people in Romagna who can't stand kids with a black face. Or they don't want to talk to Albanians and say that Moroccans are just typical Moroccans. These people say those from Romagna should stay in Romagna, Africans should stay in Africa, and Albanians in Albania. They say that all these people can only bring diseases and that these people are thieves, and when they are lucky, they are wretched. These people say that they are proud of being from Romagna. I got it, but then they call their daughters Sue Ellen, they eat in fast food joints, in the summer they surf, and on Saturday they dance to disco music, they chew gum, drink coke, read best-sellers, and if you pay attention, they also look just like any Tom, Bill, and Jack you see in American movies. Instead I like to think that in Romagna there are cities that are older than Rome. These cities have kept their doors open to far away worlds. Our land has been walked by Phoenicians, Etruscans, Greeks, Romanians, Arabs, Germans, French, Chinese, Jews, and a whole lot of other people. I like to think that we are the children of all these people. I like to think that all these new faces you see around Romagna bring with them a lot of stories that we don't know, and that our children, if we do it right, will be luckier than we were. That's because there will be older cities with a whole bunch of stories, of legends, of arguments, that we didn't have before, and now we do. That's the way I see it. OK?"

Becoming aware of me, Zanubrio smiled; he had four teeth at the most. Then he said to me: "What time are it? What time are it?

Marocchini son proprio marocchini. Questa gente dice che i Romagnoli devono stare in Romagna, gli Africani in Africa e gli Albanesi in Albania, che tutta questa gente che viene qui è capace solo di portare delle malattie, e chi è dei ladri, e quando va bene, dei disgraziati. Questa gente dice che è orgogliosa di essere romagnola: ho capito, ora poi chiamano la figlia Sue Ellen, mangiano nei *fast food*, d'estate fanno il *surf*, e al sabato ballano la *disco dance*, masticano la *chewing gum*, bevono la *Coca-Cola*, leggono i *best seller* e, se ci guardi bene, si assomigliano ai Tom, ai Bill o ai Jack del cinema americano.

A me invece piace pensare che in Romagna ci sono delle città più antiche di Roma, che hanno tenuto le porte aperte al mondo lontano, che da noi sono passati i Fenici, gli Etruschi, i Greci, i Rumeni, gli Arabi, i Tedeschi, i Francesi, i Cinesi, gli Ebrei e poi una massa d'altra gente. Mi piace pensare che noi siamo figli di tutta questa gente. Mi piace pensare che queste facce nuove che girano per la Romagna hanno una massa di storie che noi non conosciamo, e che i nostri figli, se siamo bravi, saranno più fortunati di noi, perché avranno delle città più antiche con una massa di storie, di leggende, di ragionamenti, che prima non avevamo e adesso sì. Io la penso così, va bene?

C'or el? C'or el? C'or el? My name is Zanubrio and I eat glass and iron, *a vut scommetar?* Do you wanna bet? What time are it? *C'or el?* I tell people stories, but nobody listens to me any more. So do you wanna know something? I, I tell stories to things, trees, even to trains, why not? Because not. What time are it, what time are it? *C'or el?*"

"Ten ten," I answered at random.

Then we were silent. When the bus came we got on together. I sat, he didn't. He kept walking up and down the bus asking the time. After a while he came toward me and said: "Are you sleeping? Why did you close your eyes? What time are it?"

"The time before or the time right now?" I answered without opening my eyes.

"Yes, but before is not now and now is not before. Let's say both of them."

I imagined Zanubrio's body in that spot and his mind in another life. Maybe ageless. Who knows, I tell myself, maybe he was born one hundred and fifty years ago.

A dialogue between two foreigners stopped the flow of my imagination:

> *Desso ze tuto un casin con tuta sta jente de fora. I pararia anca brava jente ma soto soto ghe ze qualcosa che spussa.*
>
> *Xe tuto un casin, un continuo buridon, un sgrensamento; i fa un casin de la madona sti marochini, anca quando i camina par la strada in silensio; da quando che i ze rivà me par quasi d'aver na zanza per recia che me fa diventar mato.*
>
> *L'altro zorno in azienda a ghi no trovà uno sconto drio de na fresa, là come un mato indenocià ch'el pregava. E no ghe go dito e no po', qua co se laora se laora. Anca massa che te assemo vegner qua par laorar.*"[3]

Now it's all a hell of a mess with all these people coming from over there. They might look like good people but deep down something

[3] Adesso c'è tutto un casino con tutta questa gente che viene da fuori. Sembrerebbe anche brava gente ma sotto sotto c'è qualcosa che puzza. È tutto un casino, un continuo rumore sordo, una gran confusione; fanno un casino della Madonna questi Marocchini, anche quando camminano per strada in silenzio. Da quando sono arrivati mi pare quasi di avere una zanzara per orecchia che mi fa diventare matto. L'altro giorno in azienda nascosto dietro una fresa, là come un matto inginocchiato che pregava. E no, gli ho detto e no qui si lavora, si lavora. È già tanto che ti lasciamo venir qui per lavorare.

stinks. It's a hell of a mess, it's constantly noisy, and it's confusion. They make a hell of a mess these Moroccans, even when they walk silently on the street. Since they came I feel like I have a mosquito in each ear that is driving me nuts. The other day at the factory I found a man hidden behind a milling machine. Like a nut he was on his knees and was praying. Oh no, I said, oh no, here we work, we work. It's already too much that we let you come here to work.

"Look at me carefully."

Te vardo anca massa maroca. Diria quasi che te vedo dopio e triplo e quadruplo, na montagna de jente che cala come barbari.

Sure I look at you, you Moroccan heap. I would say that I see two of you, three of you, and four of you, a heap of people who come down like barbarians.

Look at me carefully. Am I the cause of your anxiety, of your uneasiness?

Eh si, te vui imbacucarme ti con i to ocioni neri neri, te vui striarme, ma mi non ghe casco mia, non son mia fesso . . .

Yeah right, you want to trick me, with your big deep black eyes you want to bewitch me. But I'm not gonna fall for it. I'm not an idiot . . .

I hear the voices move away. Steps get off at the bus stop.

I opened my eyes and I saw Zanubrio who is sitting in front of me and staring at me. I wondered how long he had been staring. Our eyes met and we burst out laughing. We have been together since that laughter.

In the fall we used to walk in silence, in the fog, listening to the buzzing of electrical cables that seemed to talk exclusively to us. Zanubrio made me take notice of this noise. He taught me to look at colors. His repetitive sentences made me understand what a language could be.

One day, the last day or maybe the first day, Zanubrio became serious and said in a flat voice: "Have you ever thought of where our words go?"

"Into nothingness," I answered without thinking.

Then Zanubrio argued: "What do you mean 'into nothingness?' Have you thought about the radio? *Te mai pinsè alla radio*? How can a radio intercept the voice of somebody who is a thousand miles from us? I know that when I say 'what time are it' somebody could pick up my words. One day, *a so sicur,* I am sure, somebody will answer me. And people also laugh at all the stories I tell to trees and trains but they don't know that one day someone, maybe in 150 years, will just sit down right there and listen to my stories."

Suddenly he became distressed and said: "We have to go to the sea! We have to go to the sea!"

And off we went to the sea. It was spring. We sat on the beach and there we remained without saying a word. Suddenly came a flock of seagulls, and one of them left the flock, circled above us six times, and then flew away. I turned to ask Zanubrio if he had seen the seagull, but there was no trace of him. Then a strong wind picked up. I did not know if it came from the sea or the pine forest. The wind became stronger and stronger. The sea was stormy. The clouds were thickening in the sky. I looked for the road back to the city, but the road had disappeared. I was happy. I started to walk along the beach, southbound.

IV

Maybe after walking for six years, maybe for six days, maybe six minutes, no more than that. I found myself in the Casbah.

South of the Casbah, a man who had at the most five teeth smiled and then told me:

"What time are it? *Sc'hal rahi essa'aa?*"

As I was not answering, the man said: "My name is Slimane, I am a *meddah*, come with me. It's Friday, there will be a lot of people listening to my stories there in the *suk*."

I followed him without saying a word. The *suk* was even farther south. It's a large rectangular square missing a corner. The morning sun was shining and it was dramatic. The air smelled of cinnamon and parsley.

Slimane knew all the languages of Babylon and had read all the books in the library of Alexandria. He did not have a permanent home. So we traveled to all the *suk* in that country.

Every night, before going to sleep, he told me a story. And every night I fell asleep as happy as a lucky child who has somebody to tell him a story.

One night we were in the desert. The nearest *suk* was a thousand miles away. After watching a charming dance of scorpions, Slimane looked at me for a while, then raised his arms and said: "You are halfway through your journey. Travel south and I am sure you'll find the word. I'll see you at the station in Tambacounda."

I was surprised and perplexed and I saw a white camel coming toward us. Once it reached us, it rode six times around us, stopped and leaned down. Slimane got on the camel. A storm suddenly broke out and in the twinkling of an eye, he disappeared from my sight.

I didn't go to sleep, I didn't stand up, but I didn't even want to sit there. So I crawled for a few yards on the sand. Then I let the days go by without counting them.

In my trip south through the desert I walked perhaps, maybe I ran until I was out of breath, maybe I hopped on a camel, maybe I encountered a fennec, the desert fox, that pointed me in the right direction, maybe I did all of these things.

V

The fact is that one day I arrived in Tambacounda.

It is a village as big as a city. It is a crossroads, a meeting place and a place of memory. It is a passage, never a place of escape. It is a place, a site, a location, a spot, a chant, a flank, a land, a region, a *contrada,* a country, a center, a room, a house, a home, a premise, a residence, a corner, a district. Tambacounda is a space, it's a pass. A citation.

I gathered my strength and a cola nut. It helped after a long trip. I stopped for a while in a *tanganà* to eat a *yassa.* Rested and refreshed I headed toward the station. I waited for six hours and six minutes, then I fell asleep. I don't know after how long, a hand on my shoulder woke me up. I turned and saw a man smile at me. He must have had six teeth at the most. He said: "What time are it?" then he adds: "The station clock hasn't worked in seven years."

These words, uttered without a trace of embarrassment, woke me up completely, and I was overwhelmed by an immense joy.

"This is my spot!" I said without hesitation. "Finally a station with a clock that does not work!" I added.

The man answered me calmly: "Friend, you are a foreigner, aren't you?"

I am surprised by the question. The man continued: "My name is Niang, I am the griot of this station. Actually I am the only station griot in the world. I like to make up genealogical trees for the people who travel through. This way I feel closer to the ancestors. If you want to join me, come, but do not ask me any questions. Those who search for facts do not learn."

We left the station. Actually we were already outside because the station had no doors.

Then, as if talking to himself, Niang said: "Once I walked with a friend on streets crowded with people. In the middle of an interesting conversation we were interrupted by a shaft of light. We tried to find each other, but unsuccessfully. And that's how we lost sight of each other for seven years. One day we met again by chance and we started over with our conversation exactly from where we had left it. That explains why the station clock does not work."

Then he pointed at the ground and said: "Look at those wrinkles. Africa is very old and old people are governed by their heart. In Africa when an old man dies, it is as if a whole library burned down, said the great Hampate Ba. The oldest woman in the world is an African. She is three million years old. In Europe those 'red-eared' people call her Lucy, we call her Tikensc in Ethiopia. It means 'the most beautiful.' Maybe she is the mother of the whole of humanity."

Niang talked about Africa for six days and six nights without interruption. On the seventh day Niang grabbed me by the arm and said: "As the word is not in a dream but rather in reality, it is not a fossil, it is the offspring of oblivion and of memory. I am only a traveling griot. I cannot teach you anything else, but I have to walk with you to the south, to the national park."

VI

We started to walk. In Velingara we met two Liberian kids who told us: "There is terrible fighting near our house. We ran away. We walked, and walked and walked some more. We went to Dakar, but there is nothing we can do there. Then we went down to Thiès. Maybe it is better to go to Bamako. If we don't make it there, we'll go to Abidjan."

In Dialakoto we met two *talibé.* The youngest, Bassirou, told us that he gets up at dawn and after praying he picks up his old tomato can and he walks all over the city holding out his can to men of good will. He said that he has learned various chapters of the Koran after three years of *daara.* And if he does not bring enough money to the Marabout at night, the Marabout hits him with a stick. He showed us some marks on his body, "I am luckier than the kid over there," he said, pointing at a child who was walking in our direction. When he reached us, the boy said: "Hello, my name is Iqbal Massih. I am from Pakistan. I am eight and I work eighteen hours a day in a rug factory to pay off a debt that my family made for my sister's marriage. I was murdered one April sixteenth because I said: don't buy children's blood, but I cry less for myself than for that kid over there." He pointed at a child who came from the area around Dienoun Diala, and he said:

"Hi, my name is Mirko. My mother is Serbian, my father is from Bosnia. My grandfather was Croatian, my grandmother from Slovenia. My great-grandfather was from Montenegro, my great-grandmother was from Macedonia. I don't know where I should go. This is my friend." And he pointed to a child who came from Niokolo Koba. "Can he come with us?"

This child said: "I don't have a name. My mother was Tutsi, my father was Hutu. I come from Rowanda." Then many other children came. I cannot remember them all. There were Rom children who had traveled from Rome, Turkish children from Germany, children trapped in the Casbah, children from Cambodia. There was also a naked Vietnamese girl. She appeared in black and white because she came from our memory. So many children, from Medellin and from Cartagena, from Bandung and from Brescia. We formed a long line. Then when we reached Niokolo Koba. At the entrance of the national park of Tambacounda, all the children were transformed: some into zebras, others into elephants, koalas, herons. There were those who even chose to change into the lightest crickets. I continued my journey to Fodekounda. I was neither sad nor happy. I kept looking to find my friends in the trees but I couldn't. Suddenly I heard a baobab calling me. A baobab is a tree that because of its shape looks like a storyteller. In fact when it has no leaves, it appears to have its roots up in the air. I hugged its trunk, his girth was thirty feet around. I climbed up to its branches. I climbed almost to the top and built a nest where I stayed. Every day three men, one with four teeth, another with five, and the third with six used to meet at the bottom of the tree to tell stories every day at seven. There was a fourth man, I don't know who he was. He had seven teeth in his mouth.

I have not come down from my baobab since.

"You Wicked Wooden Eyes, What Are You Looking At?"

Tahar Lamri

Translated by Carmen Di Cinque

THE BLUE DESKS ARE WATCHING ME. THEY THROW ME CERTAIN LOOKS. I only know wooden desks covered with scratched scribbles, from my country, desks that were never plentiful enough to seat all of us. There were fifty of us, we used to have shoving matches, there were so many of us. In this place there are only twelve of us, all lined up in order. Who knows if I'll have a friend to play with someday. There are so few children here. These desks are blue and you cannot scratch anything onto them. They are smooth. Like everything here. Even the teacher's face is smooth. It seems that time leaves no marks on desks or faces. Could that be true? Hmph.

You cannot see the walls of this classroom: there are photos, writings, designs, paper doll cutouts and so much other stuff that it is impossible to know what colors the walls are. There are many windows but little light. You cannot hear the birds singing. Every now and then a train passes and everything shakes.

Yesterday my father said, "Try to be good, we must make many sacrifices here." At first I didn't really understand what he meant, I thought that we had to sacrifice a lot of sheep, like when there was the AIDS Festival, in order to go to school. Then I understood that in a rich country, one cannot live like a poor person. Who knows if I'll have to make "sacrifices," too.

Today the teacher told me, "When you speak to people, look them in the eye," but my grandma always taught me not to look people in the eye: "only animals look each other in the eye," she told me. To help me look people in the eye, Ahmed has been sitting next to me for the past week, Ahmed who is also from my country. When he introduced himself and spoke to me in my language, the sounds of it seemed so strange that I almost didn't understand what he was saying. He said to me in *this* language, "Don't worry, you'll learn Italian very quickly," but when I heard *him* speak *this* language, I began to worry right away, because I know it *in my head* and I understood immediately that he speaks it very badly. Who knows why they don't seat me next to an Italian so that I can learn from him. Well, no matter what, I must learn it quickly because my mamma needs me when she has to do the shopping. I know Italian really well. *In my head.*

"elevenzerothreetwothousandfour"

Tahar Lamri

Translated by Carmen Di Cinque

AND ON THIS CRYSTAL WINTER MORNING A SLASH OF UNWANTED SKY suddenly appeared through the roof of the train. A boom and a newborn's cry rent the silence. And death, death made its way through the sand of sleep, in the rocking of the train that accompanied the commuters to their jobs. It could be any day, this one and one of the third solar month, but . . .

Ana cradled her Colombian nostalgia: just one moment before she was thinking about her hometown, Santa Marta, bathed in tropical rain. She was thinking about Andres, her fifteen-year-old son, left behind in an unstable country where it's considered a luxury to die in one's own bed. She was thinking how inside of two days she would phone him two times. And how every March they would celebrate his birthday in their own special way. She would give him the news that they had been waiting for so long: the documents that would reunite the family were finally ready.

Seated in front of Ana was Ines who, with a smile in her eyes, was reading the message she had printed out this morning before leaving the house: "I have never departed so that I might be able to return. I am here there elsewhere, my embraces or my singular infinite embrace, invented for you alone, belongs to you forever, because it is inside of you, inside of me. My hands have softly plowed your body and by washing your feet I have sheltered you in myself forever. Ancient rites, washing a guest's feet. Surely you have noticed that our bodies find each other naturally and naturally are fused together, one inside the other, in an infinite primordial fluid. But I don't know if you have noticed the scent that hovers around us: earth freshly bathed by the rain. This along with your own scent of green that only I can smell, that I can still smell today on my arm, even this morning after showering, the scent lingering among the constellations of moles that you like so much."

When the boom occurred, before an enraged God appeared, even before that slash of undesired sky, Ines was smiling to herself, her smile alternating with the leaping of her heart. Close to her was seated Angel, who was thinking of doing a little tour of Italy this summer to see *The Birth of Venus* from close up, finally. Angel, while he was thinking, was looking with great tenderness at a nameless mother, sleepy and intent on nursing her baby, almost white, like the dawn that announces a new day. The mother was black, "Angolan," Angel said to himself.

Behind Angel, in that precise moment, between the calm of sleep that was hardly able to leave her eyes, the rocking movement of the train, the derailment and the terrible boom, there sat a young woman, ageless, who daydreamed of sensations and perfumes and embraces and kisses and smiles and whispered words and running water in a faraway hotel room.

In that moment, Anton had opened the door of the day and had entered into this eleventh of March, just like every other day, with a brazen happiness. And Gabriela remembered that she had forgotten to take the meat out of the freezer. And Isabel was seven months pregnant when death mowed them both down, without even asking the sex of her child. She was on her way to have an ultrasound. Yolanda really loved the television show, "One, Two, Three." That was her only fault. And Alberto, absorbed in reading a biography of the painter Cristobal Toral, was aware of nothing. He didn't even hear the boom. Maite was going to negotiate a loan for her newly purchased apartment which she dreamed of furnishing in a new way on a daily basis. And Alvaro "Alvarito," mowed down on the road to high school, would have had his seventeenth birthday at 18:00 hours, soon after that he would have received Limp Bizkit, Linkin Park, and Jarabe de Palo CDs. And Manuel who left behind three children of 8, 4, and 2 years. And Ramon who was in the bathroom this morning and didn't manage to kiss his wife who was already late for work.

And between the boom and us, the news went around the world and thousands of cell phones, crazed with worry, began ringing in the face of God, in the face of fugitive time. In the face of God who watched, without understanding, the trail of red that ran the length of the train, a trail broken like the wings of a defenseless little bird.

"Undertow"

Imed Mehadheb

Translated by James Walker

I worry about the future,
because I plan to spend the rest of my life there.
—Woody Allen

THE SUN SANK TOWARD THE HORIZON AND A BREATH OF SEA BREEZE mixed with the cool scent left by the day's long rainfall. On either side of the muddy paths sat men and women who had met on the road of life and who now watched the Vjosa River, motionless beneath the sky, yet with a still, quiet movement on its surface, as if the river also sat resting, breathing. Something inside them echoed this motion, stirring the depths of their memories, unsettling things there. A man with snow-white hair, who wore alongside the mask of age, that of sorrow, sat with fists on knees, his head bowed forward as if looking down a cliff face. He raised his face to the cool breeze and spoke in Kurdish to a woman who was fussing with a plump, round baby that pawed at her breast with its pink little hand as it sucked away heartily. Nearby, some ragged kids poked at the ground with sticks, while on the riverbank a little loner stood throwing pebbles lazily into the water. Unexpectedly, from a dirt road that penetrated a grove of trees, an inflatable dinghy emerged, towed by a tractor, and everyone—men, women, and children—rose to their feet.

"*Rrini ulu, rrini ulur,* sit back down," yelled a young Albanian man, gesturing to get his point across.

Everyone obeyed. Few of them spoke, and if any of them did have anything to say, it could only have to do with their future, because their future was still theirs and they could paint it whatever colors they wished. And while the women's eyes watched over the children for fear of an accident, with that feral look characteristic of motherhood, the dinghy was put into the water and moored to a piling that stringy mold clung to like greenish tufts of hair.

From the path that wound through the low bushes to the river's edge came a young man, the product of who knows what shadowy corner of human society, who strode the path with an irritating air of superiority and who seemed to think himself God's gift to humanity. Accompanying him was a girl in imitation leopard-print stirrup pants. She showed off her perfect legs with the nonchalance of a Vegas showgirl. Right behind them, a woman walked beside two men, while a horizontal ray of sunshine grazed the face of the baby girl she held in her arms, asleep, with her tiny mouth open as if she were an angel, feeding on the light.

"How is it possible, Imer," asked one of the two men, "that since I've been back in Albania I've barely seen you?"

"Gezim, dear cousin, it's the Turkish government's fault," Imer said, simplifying his response as much as possible. "With the house full of fleeing Kurds, I'm forced to make constant trips."

"Well, then you'll soon be rich!" Gezim exclaimed, clapping him on the back.

"I wish!" Imer answered back, glancing at his cousin with placid, honest eyes. "There are a lot of mouths to feed. We have to look after the families of all the boatmen locked up in Italy, and in order to work in peace everyone's got to have their share, you know." He winked at Gezim, making the gesture of tossing something lightly into the air with one hand.

"Speaking of money," Gezim said, chasing from his mind the flurry of thoughts called up by Imer's gesture, "Arben refused to let us pay for the crossing."

"That's normal. He knows we're cousins," Imer remarked. "Plus I understand you gave a nice present to little Saminet. You can pay next time!"

"Let's hope there is no next time," sighed the woman, rocking her little one who was now awake. "I don't like having to sneak into other people's homes."

"She's worried," her husband Gezim said, excusing her. "She says she has a bad feeling about this."

"Don't worry, Aleksandra! It's going to be fine. You're taking the run with *me* and everyone knows I'm the best skipper in Valona,"

Imer asserted, straightening up his back and shoulders in an oddly proud way.

"This fool," Gezim went on, in an affectionate tone which tempered the insult, "went all the way to Tirana to request a visa from the Italian Embassy!"

"They are never going to give you a visa, Aleksandra!" Imer exclaimed, shaking his head with a knowing smile. "You just have to be patient. Sooner or later Gezim will get his legal status and then he'll be able to request a *ricongiungimento famigliare* for you."[1]

"But we have a baby, Imer," Aleksandra said before an outburst of grief overtook her. After fighting back an emotion known only to those who've experienced it, she went on, her voice lowered, at times broken, but crystal clear: "Remember that my brother, Enver, was swallowed by this sea. . . . One day someone showed up, they talked about a shipwreck. . . . It was a moment, a bolt of lightning, like a window suddenly thrown open on the fate of my dear brother. . . . Then everything closed again. There was no more talk of it, ever."

There was a moment of silence, an outburst of the shadow that Albanians understand all too well, then Gezim spoke to his wife in a voice choked with emotion and tenderness.

"Aleksandra, my love, with you coming to be my boss's maid, everything is going to be easier for us; we'll save some money and, like I promised, if we manage to get our house built before we get legal status over there, we'll come back to Albania anyway: 'more than enough is too much.'"

"Bah!" Imer exclaimed with a sudden shake of his head that expressed all of the contempt he put into that one syllable. "What do you think you'd do in Valona? It's already overflowing with people coming in from the countryside who work for peanuts."

"I know, Imer, I know," said Gezim gloomily, furrowing his brow in thought, then he nodded toward the girl in the stirrup pants and burst out, "Misery offers; society accepts." He sighed and went on: "Before the revolt of '91, a farmer could at least count on seeds, fertilizers, and farm equipment, but today, even the old Russian and Chinese tractors have completely disappeared for lack of spare parts, and our fields have become great clouds of dust and despair."

[1] *Ricongiungimento famigliare* refers to the law that allows documented migrants with a stable job and appropriate housing to request legal entry for their family members.

"There's no working the land like in the days of King Zog," Aleksandra added.

"If it weren't for us 'traffickers,' this country would become a prison full of starving rats—we'd all end up killing each other and *hakmarria* would reign—the law of revenge," asserted Imer bitterly before turning to Aleksandra. "You'll get a little wet—I can't get too close to shore, so as not to get the boat hung up—but I'll get everyone there safe and sound like I always have," he promised, with great emphasis and with innate trust in the strength of his conviction, wholly unaware of the tragedy that awaited them.

When they reached the rubber dinghy, Imer bent over little Valbona and tickled her with one finger, singing to her in the high, affectionate tone one uses with babies. Valbona smiled like the dawn. He kissed her several times on the forehead, then said: "Go ahead and sit down. I have to get the motors ready with my apprentice, who will soon be taking over for me."

He stuck two fingers in his mouth, whistled, then called, "Fatmir, to work," and a sprightly young man of about fourteen who'd been walking up and down the bank with an entrepreneurial air ran toward the dinghy.

While Imer tinkered with the two, 250-horsepower, Yamaha outboard motors, causing the propellers to slosh about while Fatmir watched him with his head cocked like a curious robin, two men came near. The youngest, with a simple, lighthearted appearance that worked to his favor, addressed Imer in an Italian that was not without a healthy Nigerian accent.

"Imer, this Kurdish gentleman, Salah, is saying his people are worried and would like to know when we are leaving."

Imer shut off the motors and addressed the young Nigerian.

"Joshua, explain to Salah that I understand what he's going through because I know they've been traveling for a month and there's still a long way to go to get to Germany." He paused to let Joshua translate into English, then went on. "Tell him that we don't want to put our lives at risk and that we will leave only when we receive the go-ahead," and he pointed to the long antenna of the transceiver one of the men held in his hands.

In the glimmer of the dying day, the silhouette of the hill of Saseno Island, home to the Albanian military base, stood out strong and verdant against the horizon. The crews preparing to hit the seas left the building—renovated by the Italian border patrol, the *Guardia di*

Finanza—and descended the long, snaking path through the thick vegetation to the port. Against broken piers lay the rusted skeletons of four Albanian speedboats, sunken during the revolt of '97, while out in the water two "shark-boats"—Italian *Squalo 5000* patrol boats—were moored. The powerful engines were already rumbling and after a short while the two boats weighed anchor to patrol the stretch of sea between Cape Linguetta and Saseno Island, the corridor used by traffickers headed for Salento.

In the thickening twilight, the radars kept watch over the situation while the two "sharks"—one outside Saseno Island and the other behind the cape—let the water rock them softly as they lay in wait for their prey. On the bridge, some nostalgic figure stood watching the line of the sea on the horizon, marked by a strip of silvery light from the invisible sun which turned the merchant ships into so many shadows. Suddenly the captain of the patrol boat off Saseno gunned the engines and, lights off, veered to starboard, pointing the bow toward Cape Linguetta. He radioed the other customs ship in code that they'd picked up a "moving target." The chase was on. As soon as the patrol ship had cleared the Karaburun Peninsula, the arm that forms the bay of Valona, the infrared binoculars picked up, against the greenish background, the existence of a rubber dinghy, which was quickly intercepted and forced to skirt the base at Oricum, heading back toward Valona.

The skipper of the dinghy sped up, faked a maneuver to cross the shark's bow, then slowed suddenly, letting the huge, floating torpedo—capable of fifty knots—pass him up, then crossed behind her stern. The maneuver worked, but the two patrol boats by now were darting around in tandem, and they flanked the dinghy once more. Again it was forced toward the shore, followed closely by the two captains, dutifully careful to avoid a boarding or any kind of "incident" in Albanian waters.

The renegade dinghy pulled another quick, unexpected maneuver and stopped completely, lighting up the two Italian patrol boats with a spotlight.

"Sons of bitches!" exclaimed the chief tactical officer in charge of the operation. "They tricked us. It was a decoy—a diversion."

He immediately notified the operations center at Durazzo to alert Otranto: the radar was showing more "moving targets" heading for Salento, all out of range by now.

The Albanian policeman on board the Italian cruiser radioed the incident to the only Albanian ship in the area and stood staring at his radio for a good while, snickering with a mixture of enjoyment and admiration that turned his face beet red.

During the last part of the chase, Imer had received the agreed upon signal over the radio. The dinghy, laden with Kurdish refugees, migrants, and a few fortune-seekers, followed along a stretch of the Vjosa River, passed the area of the marsh—at that hour deserted, lonesome, and depressing—then entered the Valona lagoon and started to glide, confronted by the immense night.

The group of people doomed to exile and struggle now faced a great horizontal barrier, a wall of water and darkness, but some of those with vivid imaginations already pictured their future lives in Italy, embellishing them with the smallest details to make their hearts leap with joy, while wealth, happiness, and splendor appeared all around them in their utopian vision. To many others, however—accustomed to finding themselves stripped naked against the lashing winds of misfortune—all of their most cruelly wounded emotions, of shame and of anguish, reawakened in their hearts even more painfully than before. Yet they held on to the solemn silence that they carried with them from their destroyed homes in broken lands.

The rubber dinghy was getting farther and farther from the coast, but Aleksandra's thoughts could not abandon the place so quickly. While little Valbona slept deeply in her mother's tender arms, she turned toward Valona before the flat, dark distance swallowed it up, leaving nothing visible to the eye. On her right she saw a mountain range, sweet and majestic, while to her left, the landscape was softer and a long strip of flat land with two final humps separated the sea from the big lagoon. Valona, bedecked with tiny specks of light, proudly displayed the outline of its large buildings under construction. And while childhood memories crowded Aleksandra's mind, she tried to smile, but her mouth refused, and she saw instead her mother Albana's face raised to the heavens, her trembling hands clasped together, and the anguish in her whole person as she learned that her daughter was about to cross the sea, like her son Enver had.

A tear that had been slowly gathering at the corner of her eyelids, large enough to fall, streaked down her cheek, stopping at her mouth. Aleksandra tasted its bitterness. She closed her eyes so as not to see, or rather, so as to abandon herself to the wave of feelings intermixed with childhood memories and shapeless hopes, like ghosts called up by the sight of Valona—but in the crush of her thoughts, competing with the motion of the dinghy, the sea and her own worries always remained in the foreground. She kept turning, with a continual sobbing in her heart, toward the ever-more distant land, clasping Valbona to her breast, before she fell asleep, though never quite so deeply as to no longer hear the roaring of the motor and the voices, without distinguishing the words.

Awakening from that long, uncomfortable half-sleep, she discovered the dinghy was stopped in the middle of the gloomy expanse. At first she thought she must be delirious, then her thoughts convinced her of the frightening reality while, with wide-opened eyes in the light of the thin sliver of a moon, her gaze took in the gallery of suffering-hardened faces around her.

"Why are we stopped?" she asked Gezim while a strange feeling overtook her that this had happened before, in some vague, indeterminate time, and that she already knew what he was going to say.

"The motor broke down," Gezim answered in a barely audible voice, hoarse with anxiety.

Aleksandra felt something deep inside her give a scream of panic and a shiver passed through her body like a harbinger of doom. In her desperation a thousand different scenarios stewed, each one filled with ill omens. She bent down over Valbona who watched her like a tiny bird full of goodwill, then she tensed her back and face muscles to try to keep the shaking at bay and conquer the feeling of terror that had overcome her. After gaining some slight control over her own anxiety, she asked Gezim: "What about the other motor?"

"It should work—they haven't used it yet. But we can't go on without fixing the broken one. It's too risky to have no backup."

Aleksandra turned toward Imer. She saw him working on the broken motor by the light of a flashlight that Fatmir held and the iron vice that had closed around her heart some minutes before seemed to loosen.

It grew darker and a light, cold wind blew.

Little Valbona took her meal with such a conciliatory air that it almost seemed she was apologizing to the bottle for the liberty she took in sucking on it. Then, to protect her from the cold, her mother put her up against her own chest, inside her buttoned-up coat.

After more than an hour of trying, Imer said in Italian, with a grimace as if he were remembering a tooth being pulled, "This is a bad business." Then he consulted the rest of the group with a look full of desperate energy. He practically exploded: "This Japanese piece of shit won't start and we're closer to Italy than to Valona. Fuck it—if you guys are all right with it, we'll go on with just one outboard, but pray for my return home."

Joshua translated into English for Salah who in turn translated into Kurdish. At first there was a brief silence; the ravages of fate have this peculiar tendency, to tear human nature from our very bowels. Then someone spoke up in the name of the group, with an air of superior wisdom: "Let's go, brother. The Good Lord will surely bless your return journey."

Imer turned the key and pressed the button to start the outboard. He tried a second time . . . then a third. He cursed out loud and lost it, coloring with fear, his body shaken by an imperceptible trembling and setting loose in the dinghy a kind of foreboding haze, a catastrophic vision took hold of everyone's mind, unleashing chasms filled with night.

The skipper went back to work fiddling with the motors and checking the wiring, his eyes showed frequent flashes of impatience in the glimmer of the flashlight.

A long time passed as they waited with heavy hearts.

A Kurdish woman sat hugging herself, rocking back and forth, before she was overcome by an attack of uncontrollable, anguished crying and she started talking to the other women with a crazy, solemn, and tormented air; she remained doubled over, broken by sobs, blinded with tears, wringing her hands and racked by a short, dry cough. Several of the children began to cry, clinging to their mothers. Next to Aleksandra sat the Kurdish man with the snow-white hair and by the shaking of his shoulders she saw that he was crying; a silent, terrible cry. She was struck by his dark and wordless grief and all of these things—realities made up of ghosts; phantasmagoria made up of realities—ended up putting her into an almost inexpressible state. She lost heart again, overcome by wild throbs of near-terror, as if she had just lost something or was about to lose it, forever. She turned to Gezim and said with a voice that was closer to a shriek than to actual words:

"We're all going to die—we're all going to die! I told you—I told you . . ."

"Quiet—be quiet! You're the one who jinxed us," Gezim replied bitterly, shaking his finger at her.

Aleksandra fell silent, clutching her chest with her hand as if to keep the storm within from bursting forth. Only a groan escaped her lips and several times her dark eyes flashed and then went out, like flames smothered in the night. Eventually the time came when she clenched her lips together and swallowed hard, but a pair of tears remained in her eyes and Gezim saw them fall, sliding slowly down either cheek. He gave her a sorrowful hug, then handed her the thermos of tea and said in a voice reduced to a fearful whisper:

"Here, Aleksandra . . . forgive me."

Without looking at Gezim, Aleksandra brought the thermos to her lips, but the tea stuck in her throat, choking her, and dribbled back out of her mouth.

Throughout this interminable time, Fatmir, the apprentice, had only followed the instructions given by Imer, who by now sat with his head in his hands, immersed in his own thoughts. Now the boy stood up suddenly and, with an air of fierce pride, he looked out at the sea like a conqueror. With a disdainful smile playing on his lips he broke the silence and exclaimed: "I'm not afraid of the sea. I'll save you!"

Then the little deviser of schemes, his eyes sparking with cleverness, took the key from the ignition, dismantled it, touched some wires together, and the safety hatch suddenly opened in the bottom of the dinghy, to the sound of the droning motors.

It is easier to imagine than to describe what went through their hearts. The eyes of the crying Kurdish woman suddenly filled with joy, her face still wet with tears. Speaking in Kurdish, she made her way to Fatmir, hugged him, and stroked his hair. These actions were, of course, expressive enough that words were not needed and Fatmir understood her as clearly as if she spoke in Albanian.

Before they could set out again, black clouds gathered, filling the sky, and the wind began to howl across the sea. Imer looked at the dark horizon and said: "They're waiting for us at Santa Cesarea Terme and you absolutely have to land before it gets light. We're running late and the sea has changed, but with God's help, we can make it."

The dinghy, surrounded by darkness, took off again under the force of both motors. Imer stood at the helm next to Gezim, but they said nothing. Perhaps, in some vague part of their minds they were sizing up the threatening horizon against their own tiny lives.

The bodies of the travelers were all huddled together against the cold, searching for warmth, and several had fallen asleep from exhaustion. Their sleep did not last long, however, as the tiny dinghy hurtling itself across the dark expanse struck an obstacle. No one knew what it was, but they all found themselves flung into the water.

The momentum of the boatman's body slamming into the steering wheel knocked Imer senseless. He remained inside the torn fiberglass boat which tilted rapidly, taking on water, as it deflated, until under the weight of its motors it went under, dragging him down with it. Dark concentric circles formed on the surface of the water—a shudder—then nothing.

Gezim ended up underneath the propellers, which snorted like rampaging horses. He tried to defend himself against their furor as he came up, then let himself float on the water's surface, his chest and abdomen unspeakably torn, his intermittent breathing racked by a crackling rattle. Slowly he opened his eyes, which already showed the sullen depths of death, and saw a dark sky spreading over him like an infinite shroud. He let out a wail and only the night witnessed his thrashing convulsions as he disappeared beneath the water.

Meanwhile the waves tossed the children against each other. Their pitiful little bodies were mere specks against the immensity of the waves. They reached out their tiny hands but grasped emptiness, as they called for their mothers in voices choked and torn by the shortness of their last breaths, their eyes wide in expressions that no human tongue could describe. Then, paralyzed by the bottomless cold, their tiny strength quickly exhausted, they submitted and let themselves go. They disappeared into the immensity of that sea as circles disappear on the surface of water, and their bodies settled in that fearful mass grave like so many discarded pawns in a game played by the powerful.

Their mothers, Kurdish women who'd always lived in the mountains, found themselves in the monstrous water of that sea, horribly surrounded by the wind-chopped waves, with only destruction beneath their feet. They disappeared and reappeared, went under and reemerged, hurling desperate cries. They called for their babies, they stretched out their arms in the darkness, but no one heard. And as the rolling abyss dragged them away, it seemed to them that all that water, the entire sea, was hate.

The old, white-haired Kurdish man, outcast of civilization, grabbed onto a child that was drowning, struggled to swim but didn't know how, tried to keep himself up, combating the inexorable, and drank bitterness while the vastness toyed with his agony. Then, with that special clarity and lucidity that reveals the outline of things when they meet with impending darkness, he understood that death was nothing. The frightening thing was not living. Exhausted, he floated to eternity in the gloomy depths that swallowed him down.

Several of the others tried to remain afloat while the self-preservation instinct screamed inside them, blind Self kicking away anyone who tried to grab onto them. Everyone for themselves, they experienced the madness of that sea, swimming around, boundless sleepwalkers in a shipwrecked dream, before slowly drowning in the frozen darkness which claims so many unfortunate people in the dismal march of humanity.

In that disaster of the human intellect grappling with the unnamable, forty-three people perished.

Aleksandra found herself suddenly in the water. At first, everything she could sense was incoherent and chaotic and her heart pounded even in her teeth. Then everything in her set to work—instinct that senses and intelligence that organizes. She quickly brought one arm to her chest and held onto little Valbona who had remained under her mother's buttoned-up coat. Born and raised by the seaside, Aleksandra stretched herself out on the surface of the water, unbuttoned her heavy coat and freed herself from it, holding the crying, shivering Valbona on her chest. She rid herself of all her garments that could weigh her down, then cried out: "Gezim!"

Her husband's name died in the darkness without so much as an echo, and Aleksandra felt this as a calamitous blow. She held her lips locked together frantically for a long time, to control the sobs, then she called out again: "Gezi-i-im! I'm over here! Gezi-i-im, where are you?"

The silence was as deep as before, leaving Aleksandra to stare at the dark with wide-opened eyes, her spirit weighed down by its load of grief.

She allowed the current to take her with it, conserving her energy, Valbona on her chest, clinging to her mother with a child's touching trust which no betrayal can shatter.

The long night was approaching its end. The twilight whitened the crests of the small waves and low wisps of mist streaked along the surface of the water and separated like tufts of smoke when Aleksandra shook her baby and called to her over and over, in vain. She held her eyes fixed on her baby's now sightless ones, wailing an intermittent wail between the clenched teeth of her stiffened mouth—an incoherent, choked moaning, accompanied by a disconsolate shaking of her head—but with no change whatsoever in expression, as if her features had been frozen by suffering. But tears, that first outlet of immense grief, would not come to Aleksandra, immersed as she was in that unending pain and loss, from which nothing else was distinguishable and which shook her every thought, carrying her to the brink of insanity. Then, with hazy eyes, overflowing with astonishment at the violence of her present, she looked around her. The sun was just rising behind her shoulders, casting a weak, wretched light. She saw on the horizon a gigantic cliff, its blue-black silhouette crowned by some low clouds to create a particularly sinister effect, and through an almost physical penetration, that funereal outline added a new sense of gloom to her already ravaged mind. So, by imperceptible degrees, the feeling of grief became a desperate consciousness of everything that had been lost. . . . She wept, torturedly hugging Valbona's tiny, frozen body while a light wind circled around an outcropping of rocks creating a muffled sound, like a low, slow, grief-filled murmur. Then an ineffable smile spread across her bluish lips and a line of sadness creased her cheek. She clasped Valbona to her heart and let herself be swallowed up by that worldwide sea in which millions of people live, like her, immersed.

"Shipwreck"

Martha Elvira Patiño

Translated by Marie Orton

I OPEN MY EYES AND FIND MY FACE REFLECTED IN THE CRYSTAL CLEAR, still water. I slept deeply, but fatigue still impedes any movement, I feel like a dead weight. . . . Observing my face reflected from the bottom of the sea, I am amazed to discover the light shining from my eyes. They are still full of life. I slowly lift my head and the orange horizon streaked with violet welcomes me, it is a marvelous sunset that fills me with joy and brings a grimace that wants to be a smile. There is within us, poor mortals, a spiritual force that goes well beyond pain and will. After fleeing such devastation and then being shipwrecked on the sea for endless days, there is still hope on my face, lined by so many bitter experiences. In these last wandering days on the ocean, I've felt all the fragility with which we humans cross the river of life, and at the same time with a superhuman force we cling to this existence.

We're saved! A sea so calm is a paradox compared to a few hours ago when the furious water swept over our boat and seemed to want to swallow us, aided by a terribly violent wind that battered us from side to side. It was truly a battle to the death to keep our boat afloat without surrendering; I almost went crazy trying to bail out the water that slowly flooded us, bailing was the only thing that worried me and meant surviving. Exhausted, I fell asleep a few hours ago when we had a respite and slowly the tempest subsided. The boat's rocking created a clear sense of tranquillity in me, and the majestic, infinite, horizon then carried away the few worries that I still managed to have.

After the hurricane came the calm, fortunately. Silence. All of my companions are still asleep, I feel next to me the light-weight body of my son Julio who is breathing peacefully. He's exhausted, too. How strong children are, and how often they're able to overcome the trials that the stupidity of adults subject them to. Who knows what destiny is already preparing for them . . . I'd like to offer them a peaceful future, the end of war, but unfortunately mankind is more interested in violence and terror than in reason. It's an endless road, this search for the power to subject each other and for possessions of any kind: land, animals, metal, goods . . . and at any price, even if to obtain it, we end the lives of many defenseless people.

But time passes slowly, and although time tries in every way to dismiss the facts that stayed buried in the past, many of them remain impressed on people, and even if you don't look for them, those facts appear unexpectedly, clear and fresh, and present themselves to your memory with a wealth of details. In fact, it often comes to mind as if it were yesterday, the reason for our flight across the world in search of a place to land. It was a dark night and the birds of evil omen flew overhead when our enemies arrived, silent and hidden, and destroyed our land and sowed terror. My people were unprepared for the attack, and surprised, they fought without any power. It was a long night of desperation: in the chaos, the flames rose over the streets and the houses, everywhere tongues of fire enveloped bodies in agony that were running desperately. My wife was there, in the middle of that inferno, and she was the last person I saw as we escaped from the fire. Behind a cloud of smoke, seeing me turn back to reach her, she screamed at me desperately to run and save our little son. Then her face was lost in the middle of the fire and behind hers, many others; men, women, and children either driven insane by the pain or already having surrendered themselves in the face of death.

We fled as we were, wounded and aching, me, my son, a few friends, and my father. If others managed to survive as we did, then they would be some of the many refugees wandering around the world.

I lost many loved ones on that cursed night and I still carry inside of me recurring dreams where I see a radiant sun appear from which my closest friends come out, and they come up to me, and, wrapped in a halo of golden fire, they comfort me, saying that now they are fine. They all have a peaceful expression, and I feel less guilty. With them is my wife, she's smiling and looking lovingly at our son. Then I wake up, feeling the wound finally ease, a wound made by the emptiness left by so many departed souls and such a tremendous defeat. I'd like to think that was just a bad dream, I'd like to sleep in a soft bed and wake up in my own house, in those spaces where I felt I'd always belonged, and to where I return again in my thoughts.

But today is another day and we finally have arrived in this country, Italy, a name heard so many times, the land of modest, sensitive people who understand our desperation and will receive us with open arms, our new home, where perhaps we will put down roots. But we need to shake off the past bitterness to take on a new life. Above all, a positive spirit is what we need to undertake this new life with our healthy bodies, ready for work. And most importantly, we have a great treasure with us: our identity and the nobility of our hearts.

I hear Leonid whispering something to me. I'd better move closer to him.

"How are you?"

"Ah, I can barely move. But say, did you see what great luck? The storm is over. And what a sunset!"

"Here, lean on me, now you can sit down."

"I feel better than I thought. I slept deeply. Did you see, we're near the shore!"

He's euphoric, and rightly so. In the distance I can just make out palm trees that at first had looked like gulls in flight to me. Leonid moved near my ear again.

"Let's be careful. We must not be seen, help me row toward the cliffs and we'll wait until it's dark to get out."

The night will be favorable for reaching the shore. I already imagine the pleasure of walking in the soft warm sand. It's marvelous to still be alive, the colors of the sunset contrast with the prolonged thick darkness of the torment that has followed us for so many days and seemed endless. The hours pass and the moon lights up the sky with a splendid smile, its light bathes the face of Julio, who is still sleeping undisturbed and tranquil with his face so serene that it seems the face of a god cradled in the arms of slumber. I feel very happy to have him nearby, he's grown so quickly into a serious and curious boy. I, on the other hand, even with my intense life full of emotions, I feel the same as always, as if time had stopped on the day he was born. I see a few white hairs on my head, but inside of me, my heart and spirit are still restless and young.

I breathe in this warm air deeply with its scent of salt that intoxicates me and makes me very happy. Ah, how many people are lost, gone to live in memory and dreams, how many feelings and tears poured out. Fortunately, we still have love.

Many months have passed since we arrived on the Italian coasts, and our welcome was anything but warm and easy. That first night we got off the boat and ate roast fish and drank wine. Then we hid in the caves and as soon as our strength returned, one of the men went to scout out how things were in the surrounding area and in the nearest city. All the rest of us stayed hidden there, cautiously transporting food and clothes. Waiting for news created great irritability among my companions. You couldn't even try to make a joke without someone immediately getting offended; there was tremendous tension in the air, surely we freed ourselves from a continual succession of dangers, the most recent ones during the shipwreck. Being together in a cramped place had become complicated. I, as head of the group, forced myself to keep morale up, but alone at night I wavered. And at certain moments my strength failed me.

One evening when I was more discouraged than ever by the kind of hostility I felt in the air, depressed and afflicted, I fell asleep. That same night I dreamed that I saw my father beaming happily, and even though he now lived in the world of the dead, he urged me to continue my life with energy and he told me not to give up in the face of obstacles, and never stop because I would arrive before long at the destiny written in my book of life. So we started walking in a green expanse, and walking along, I saw some friends who recognized me and waved to me. Then in the middle of a distant wood, an enchanting woman caught my eye. She was dressed in soft, fluttering blue veils and she wandered as if searching for someone. It was Alizāh, my sweet Alizāh. I tried to run up to her, but she magically evaporated and I felt so moved that I abruptly woke up and found my eyes wet with tears. After that night, my will to live magically found new strength.

One day, in the early morning our emissary Antonij finally returned. We immediately surrounded him to hear his news, and everyone was friendly and cordial once again. Our long awaited companion Antonij related many interesting things to us.

"Dear friends, during these long days I've observed how people live in these parts, even though I know that to understand people more deeply, it is necessary to live more closely with them for longer. But I sharpened my senses to observe and perceive the way they live and so I was able to understand many things. Life here will not be as simple as we'd believed. The people, though they are well-off, can't appreciate what they have. Men and women with a home, a job, and who lack for nothing, neither food nor clothing, are always complaining, they would like something more. Many are also very afraid of everything, of the present. They believe that their current state of wealth could disappear, that their job could vanish suddenly, that the arrival of people different from themselves could be damaging to them. And so even though they seem friendly, they're always on their guard. They're worried by the stories of far-off countries like ours, stories of wars, death, atrocities. And from living with all these insecurities and fears, they have become selfish. The people here only accept those foreigners that make things easy, people willing to do the jobs that they refuse to do. On the other hand, there are those foreigners that really are horrifying—criminals who make a fortune trafficking in the poverty of their own people, making those desperate people escaping from their homeland pay a high price for their passage, or reducing the youngest ones in their group to slavery. For their part, the authorities here try to calm the citizens about the arrival of these undesirable people by talking about closing the borders and patrolling the coastline, but it would actually be impossible to do and they'd never really know who to pick up. Besides, they're involved in more lucrative affairs; the powerful groups divide up privileges and have power over how everything is dished out, from ownership of lands to the control of those tiny spaces to set up stalls for selling. Between themselves unwritten rules are in force, rules that don't reflect the actual needs of the people and maintain the status quo, and now, everyone has adapted to this situation in an attempt to scrape a profit from it. Let's just say that a very simple logic rules in this kind of hierarchy: bonds of blood or friendship, that is nepotism. So whoever is without a tradition of relationships of blood is treated as a child of no one, a stranger. And even more so for foreigners. So they, as you can well imagine, are still far from any possible kind of acceptance.

"And walking along the streets of the city, it's obvious how some of them have adapted, dividing up little territories. On the street corners, men who surely came from African countries sell trinkets and woe to any other foreigners who try to enter into competition. One day when I was curiously examining some of the merchandise laying out on the ground, I noticed the suspicious looks of the group: they saw me as a stranger and therefore a potential rival. In the countryside there was a similar situation. People from far-off lands harvest fruit and vegetables, working long hours, most of the time poorly paid. Most of them don't even communicate with the native Italians, they've never learned the local language, and maybe they don't even want to know anything about the people who give them work as if, beyond that wall of words, there still existed a cultural barrier. Fortunately, I also saw something different in the markets: groups of women from various cultures talking to one another, a kind of new universal language, common to all of them, while their children played and had fun together.

"So this is a beautiful and marvelous land, full of natural resources, but I don't know how much the inhabitants deserve it.

"See here friends," Antonij concluded, serious and very melodramatic, "this is what I saw with my own two eyes, but that is much less than what I perceived with my soul."

Then Antonij lay down and our companions brought him something to eat and drink.

I went off by myself to reflect: could I have anticipated a situation like this? Absolutely not, I even thought that our friend exaggerated somewhat. I reached a high cliff by the sea and I sat down to decide what to do. I felt powerless, as soon as possible we had to get out of this hiding place that was suffocating us. Maybe it was necessary to fight, to push ourselves forward violently until we gained some room in this world full of fears and selfishness. But before acting aggressively, I needed to give the people in this place the chance to accept us peacefully. Without losing any time, I immediately started to write a letter to those in power, a letter in which I'd present myself with the honorary title that I had in my country, and I'd ask to meet with them in order to pass on some of that wisdom I'd inherited from my ancestors and I'd also point out some proposals for good political administration. I went on describing the reasons that forced us here. After mentally writing this letter, I stayed on the rocks a little longer. I wanted to enjoy the sun and think about my future plans. I also felt great positive energy guiding me.

I sat there a long time. I watched the foam on the crest of the waves and suddenly I felt the embrace of the warm wind that swept the sand. The sea breeze brought back the thoughts of my beloved Alizãh. Love for that mysterious woman enveloped me like a spell, I was intoxicated by her being, by the enchanting perfume of her bewitching ways: a precious creature with a regal bearing, a magic oasis in the desolation of my sadness and melancholy that culminated in my most sublime desires and gave my body a unique sensuality. She, to my good fortune, always returned this intense feeling that seemed infinite. I would have desired to spend my entire life with her, but my destiny was not to wind eternally through love's labyrinth—other less happy tasks awaited me. And you can't destroy certain commands of desire. Where was her brilliant smile now, her sweet face? My heart beat happily at her memory. At that time, I didn't yet know that, crazed by the pain of my departure, she took her own life.

I am on the hill, I see my radiant son. For him and for all of my friends, this is a great day of celebration. I am about to marry another woman, and thus, in a certain sense, seal the peace between all of these peoples, but how hard we had to struggle to get to this point.

I waited in vain for any reply to my letters. The news that reached me said that the most powerful man of the area was ready to accept us peacefully, but he was thrust aside and silenced by a majority that was doubtful about my origins. At the head of this majority was a strong young man, arrogant, who felt he was the direct inheritor of power. As a response we received an imperious invitation to leave with explicit threats of every kind of hostility against us undesirable types. There was nothing we could do, under duress we had to enter into this contemptible battle that so often men of this earth engage in. Peace, perhaps it is written, must be obtained by violence. People will never understand without having experienced directly what squalor and horror accompany the tales of war. The numerous wars between families, between different ethnic groups and peoples have filled the history of the world with horror, but we mortals are too petty and vulnerable to ever be able to stop this insanity, we began a long battle which fortunately concluded with our victory, though accompanied as victory always is, by the gloomy specter of death.

I hear Leonid, my faithful friend, who calls me: "Aeneas, what is delaying you? Lavinia is waiting for you in the castle and we all want to start celebrating."

I dreamed again of my father, Anchise, who spoke to me from cliffs cloven by a golden river and proudly told me that in this place a great city would one day arise. And it was my duty to restore dignity to this land.

"It is easy to descend into Hell."
—Virgil, *Aeneid*

"Vendettas"

Carmelo Quijada

Translated by Marie Orton

EVERY YEAR IN MY NEIGHBORHOOD, THERE'S A STRANGE PHENOMENON that warns us that it's time for *ferie*:[1] an alarm that was left on blasts us for fifteen to twenty days until the careless proprietor returns home.

It's the middle of the night. We won't be able to fall asleep again due to this incessant, deafening noise. I get up and head to the kitchen intending to iron a shirt. The hallway is stuffed with furnishings and souvenirs from friends and relatives, enough to make you sick. If I get rid of one, I'll have to get rid of them all, otherwise the touchy givers would leave me no peace.

One of the many things that I hate is ironing, especially shirts, so full of pleats, stitching, and buttons. It doesn't often happen that I need to iron one, fortunately, but this time I really can't do without it: I have to go and accept a literary award.

It's been quite a little while now that I keep winning them continually, ever since my father gave me an amulet that he'd prepared for me. It works like this: while I'm writing a story to send in for a contest, I keep the amulet close to the sheets of paper. Once I've finished the story, I make the photocopies, and I put them in a desk drawer together with this extraordinary object.

The large, white envelope that I will use to mail in everything is saturated with positive energy.

Even in the post office, when they receive it, they'll jump back: they'll realize that it's something important, something special.

When it finally arrives in the hands of the jury, they can't do anything but set aside the other stories in the running and "devour" mine, because it's sublime, something never read before. . . . .

[1] The traditional vacation period, usually in the month of August.

The time comes to leave the house, I'm anxious: I need to appear elegant, but not unctuous, a little on the grungy side, but with class.

Hopefully they won't ask me any questions; I wouldn't be able to come up with one sensible sentence (in fact, the amulet only works with stories, to overcome shyness, you need a different one. . . .)

I leave the house out of breath, and I haven't gone ten steps when I feel a silent, light but definite splash. Something hit the collar and the right breast pocket of my immaculate shirt.

At first, I don't want to believe it, then I have to surrender to the truth: it's pigeon crap, greenish, and it hit me dead center.

I hate pigeons, I've always hated pigeons, they are so full of themselves, gray and stinking. . . This time is too much!

I get some popcorn, I lace it with poison, and I let it dry.

I go out to determine the place where they gather, it won't be difficult. When I get to the spot, I only catch a glimpse of one flier, because some bum has caught them in order to roast and eat them. If only there were at least ten of these pigeon-eating bums, this problem would never occur.

In compensation, the rescued pigeon acts like the king of that neglected corner. He scrutinizes me with interest, a sign that he was raised under the protection of many "pigeon ladies."

Afraid of being seen by passersby, I hide in the least visible corner, pour out the contents of my carton, and form a compact pile. The "boss," convinced that I've come to feed him, comes over and gulps down everything in a flash, without leaving the poison time to work (a single grain would be enough to do him in).

He explodes!

Unfortunately, thousands still remain: we're infested by these rats with wings. I manage to plant some poison here and there: without being noticed, I run through all the back alleys, letting one grain fall at a time out of a little hole in the pocket of my jeans. I reload my pocket by the handful and my bag of provisions depletes rapidly. Now it's just a matter of waiting. . . .

The next day I get up early, as always, thanks to the hysterical alarm clock, and I retrace my path of the day before. Deducing that my plan had the desired effect, a demonic expression comes across my face. Before my eyes spreads an expanse of cadavers. They're even uglier when they're dead: eyes wide open, that outline of the purple beak, crazed fleas that scoot in and out from under the feathers searching for an inch of skin that is still warm.

For the "pigeon ladies," who came early in the morning to refill the food bowls, the spectacle is no fun. They are desperate, thinking that they were the ones who brought about the massacre with the leftovers they gather from the garbage of the nearby restaurants.

Now I have to concentrate on the young ones that are crying in their nests; they haven't received their daily dose of food.

I gather up about forty of them and I line up their heads one at a time under my lumberjack boots. I quickly step down hard, smashing everything under my heel.

Fixated as I am on my "urban house cleaning," I don't notice two cars full of tough guys with faces that are hardly reassuring. One of them calls me over. I ignore him to make time to prepare some explanation that justifies my actions. He calls me again: "Hey, excuse me, can you tell me how to get to Molassana?" Relieved, he doesn't give a damn about what I'm doing, I go over to the car. I lean against the door on the driver's side and lower my head so as to see inside the cab. I quickly pull back my arm: that shit who questioned me just put out his lit cigarette against my forearm, while the others begin spitting on me and cursing me. Their words are harsh, full of anger: "You shit of a mulatto, I bet you're fucking our women. . . ." "Italy is ours!" "We don't want it full of slimy blacks . . ."

I defend myself by listing off all of the places that Italians have emigrated to in order to escape poverty and search for a future. I proclaim that in times of need we all must help one another, because we are all citizens of the same world and no one place belongs to anyone . . . In response, I receive a machine-gun fire of insults and spits. I lose patience. I tell them to wait a moment, and I run over to the only tree in the square; I pull it up and I prepare a good, heavy club. I run back to their car and invite them all to come forward. They all come out armed with heavy chains, knives, and even a long sword.

I have to come up with some way to save my skin, I have to utilize that creative power that writers have (otherwise what good is it to be a writer?) The place is deserted, I'm alone here with these guys that are promising to kill me.

It comes to me that there's only one thing to do in these cases: agree with them.

"It's true, it's totally true. I understand," I confess, "because it would bother me, too, if people came to my country to fuck our women and steal our jobs."

For a minute they stand listening to me, shocked. I continue: "You want to take me out? If I have to die, if I have to pay for everything that I've done, just give me time to set a few things in order. This afternoon I'll meet you at my house. Look, here's my address, ok?"

The one who seems to be the leader responds: "Don't think you're gonna get off so easy with us. If we don't find you there tomorrow, there will be a revolution, because nobody makes fools of us."

"I give you my word," I reply, in confusion.

I'm sure they won't come looking for me, but just the same, they shouldn't find me unprepared.

The next afternoon there's a riot on the stairs: a river of guys armed to the teeth heads up toward my apartment. There have to be eighty of them. A big group begins to beat down the door, the others make it up to the roof of the apartment building and begin to lower themselves on ropes through the windows.

I watch the whole thing from my friend's house, armed with video cameras that I got when the consulate where I worked for a few years was demolished and where I'd schemed how to set up that morning.

I took out all of the objects that I needed and the ones that I was attached to. I left all of the souvenirs.

My house looks like a beehive gone crazy. From my position of security, I encourage them to smash everything: "Yes, good, that tacky plate with the lantern from Nadia! That clunky landscape with those overly blue blues and too-white whites from my co-workers, yes, rip it up. . . . Great! That awkward crystal service from Bohemia from my aunt, good! The rotten fixtures, yes, tear them out, ok! Dirty up the peeling walls with your boots. . . . excellent!"

The hoodlums, furious at not having found me, leave the house. I've really done it this time. . . .

When I'm sure that they've all abandoned what is left of my apartment, I start calling: the mayor's office, the prefect, the chief of police, the police commissioner, the office of the district president, the neighbors. I have them all meet me at my house. When they arrive, I assume a downcast air, I even cry. Touched, they reassure me that they can protect me and promise to do everything possible to find me another home far away from this area that has become unsafe for me. And for thirty years, I won't have to pay high rent prices.

Within a week I take ownership of my new house with a view of the sea. It's something from a dream. Without any furnishings, as I explicitly asked. I call my friends and relatives and beg them not to bring me anything to decorate the place, because I would suffer too much if what happened before should happen again.

Two days later, I turn the videocassettes over to the police with the scenes of the afternoon of the revolution. I'll go with the officers on patrol to determine the place where these hoodlums meet. It won't be hard.

"Back Alleys"

Carmelo Quijada

Translated by Marie Orton

EVERY TIME I LEAVE THE HOUSE I ALWAYS HAVE GARBAGE WITH ME that I have to throw out. If I leave without it, I have the feeling that I'm not taking care of my den. But first of all, I take a good look around the dumpster, you don't want to ever, unconsciously, do damage to some newborn that's been abandoned inside.

I'd like to find one, a newborn, in a dumpster.

Maybe he'd automatically become mine, who knows?

I should find out before it happens, so I won't be caught unawares. I also need to find out if I'd have to take it to the police station or to city hall.

It would have to be a boy, though, because then he'd be less shaken up when I tell him where I found him. I'll wait, though, until he's old enough to understand. A girl would take more looking after and she'd be whiny. I'm not up to that.

I'll dress him like his father: jeans, leather jacket, beret, and boots. Fucking cool. I'll also take him around to the groups that I'm part of in the evenings. But I realize that he'll need to socialize with children his own age. And I, as head of the pack, will need to teach him everything about life. I'll take him to the park on Saturdays and Sundays and while he plays, I'll keep a close eye on him. . . . But I'll have to socialize, too, with the other parents: I'll sit on the park bench with them, listen to them ask me what he eats and how he likes it fixed, if he's already had scarlet fever and tonsillitis, etc. I'll have to talk to the other pack leaders, the ones that will have one ear attached to those stupid shitty little radios that leave you stunned . . . maybe I'll have to talk about soccer. What a pain.

But you know, if I happen to come across one of those little beings that scamper around in a dumpster, at least I won't hurt it when I toss my garbage bag in, and I'll just leave him there. And then someone else will find him and. . . . Oh, fuck it.

As I walk around the side streets without any destination, the police stop me, as usual.

"Hey, listen. Where's your I.D.? What are you doing here?"

"I live here."

I straighten up and try to pierce them with a stare, though my stare is often glassy at that time of the morning. I show an attitude of superiority: "I'm the repair man."

"Why are you here at this hour? None of your fucking business," I think to myself. With a challenging tone, I reply, "I always come at this time."

I hear them call: "Headquarters. Alcantara Juvencio with a 'J,' DOB 7/16/63, from Venezuela."

I already know how these delays work so I try to think about my own affairs. I smile as I think of one of my co-workers who said to me once, "Oh God, here come the police! Look down!"

They finished their background check, they hand me back my I.D., and they tell me, "Thank you . . . and have a nice day."

From their tone, I realize that it's 4:30 in the morning and before long I'll have to be at work. It would be more convenient for me not to go home and sleep for nothing, but where can I go?

While I'm trying to come up with a place where I can *amanecer* (wait for the dawn), I hear strange sounds near one of the trash cans. It is the unmistakable sound of feasting from my worst enemies: RATS!

They are enormous, they enter and exit the sewers and they slip into the dumpsters with a crazed frenzy.

Suddenly, an incredible thing happens: two Moroccan boys that were coming from the opposite direction from me, talking between themselves, cross paths with an enormous rat, the hugest I have ever seen, and with total indifference they give it a good kick.

I see the rat sail by in slow motion, directly over my head, I even smell its disgusting stench and I am rooted to that spot for several seconds. The two guys, who by now reach me, say, "Excuse us," and continue chatting, unaware of the shock I've just experienced. The fear makes my bladder start to give signs of incontinence, so I'm forced to head toward home. I speed up. I'm agitated.

Exhausted, I abandon the idea of staying out until morning, I count the thirty steps that remain before I reach my front door. I really want to pee. I already know that I won't be able to make it and that I won't be able to grab the right key on my first attempt. There are six keys in the bunch. . . . I see some water coming from under the front door of the lady who lives below me, and that makes me want to pee even more.

Probably the lady is dead. . . . Yes, in fact, I'm sure of it: she was very sickly. That's why I hadn't heard her complaining for the last several weeks about, "That shit-head who's always making a damned racket overhead all hours of the day and night."

I make it to the john and while I'm unloading, I feel that creeping sensation across my body that you get when you've had to hold it for too long.

As soon as I'm done, I'll call the fire department. . . . No, better not. I'm too tired and I would really like to crawl under the covers. I know if I call them, they'll make a hell of a racket on the stairs with their boots, and then they'll start banging on doors and since no one will open up, they'll try to break down the door. Then the ambulance will come and there will be more noise. I'll call later from work, an hour more or less won't make any difference.

Half-asleep, I think of what stage of decomposition that poor little old lady must be in. I take several deep breaths (but controlled) to try and sense any odor of death. I try to imagine which room the deceased would be in. If it's the bathroom or the kitchen, it's easy enough to wash the tiles, but I'd be sorry if it happened in the living room (because of the carpet).

I need to remember, once the cadaver has been removed, to find out from the relatives of the deceased (I don't wish to seem indelicate), if they intend to rent out the apartment to my friend Piero. That way I'll be able to go and have dinner with him whenever I want to, since I was the one who found him the apartment.

"Faduma & Barni (April, 2003)"

Igiaba Scego

Translated by Julia Viazmisnki

FADUMA HAD PLANNED TO MAKE A DESSERT THAT AFTERNOON. SHE lined up all of the ingredients on the table: flour, sugar, butter, raisins, candied oranges, a bar of dark chocolate (that she was not going to eat under any circumstances; it was for the recipe, not her stomach), pine nuts, ground almonds, a packet of yeast, milk.

Barni Nur looked at her a bit amazed. It didn't seem right to her that all of those things were needed for a dessert.

"All this stuff is for just one dessert?" she asked doubtfully.

Faduma didn't lose composure. She knew her friend's lack of expertise concerning desserts. She mumbled a "yes," out of habit, and continued to mix the ingredients, indifferent to the culinary doubts of her friend.

"But isn't it easier to go buy a dessert ready made at the bakery?" Barni practically exploded, as if she had tapped into an Einstein-esque discovery of the century.

Faduma shook her head.

Barni did the same.

Their two schools of thought were irreconcilable.

A person who called upon bakeries would never keep company with one who made desserts at home.

Despite everything, the two women were friends. One made desserts and the other ate them. They had discovered a modus operandi that did not pit one against the other.

Barni's legs swung loosely from left to right and right to left. The woman was clearly nervous. She chewed her nails frenetically. She could not find peace. Her head did not want to be forced into a corner. It was terribly jealous of her swinging knees. It began to compete with her legs, swinging from one side to another like a crazed pendulum.

Faduma instead continued to mix, as if nothing were happening, almost unaware of the tangible nervousness of her friend.

She, too, was nervous after all.

That's why she was at the stove. Cooking was one of the few things in the world that managed to relax her no matter what.

"What kind of dessert is it?" interrupted Barni, sounding like a retired field marshal.

"A tea cake," responded Faduma with an equally confident tone, but with an added hint of sweetness (even if, truth be told, it didn't take much to have a sweeter voice than Barni Nur).

"Mmmmm, how do I know. All these *gaal* desserts seem the same to me."

"Liar!" smiled Faduma. "When you eat them, I doubt they all seem so alike."

"Well, you'll agree. Eating is a different story. These *gaal* know how to cook. They aren't like us, we only know how to make a couple of dishes . . . and on top of that, they are fried."

"No, our cooking is not so bad, but certainly theirs is healthier . . . anyway, I don't agree with you! Eating is without a doubt a great pleasure, but cooking nears the divine, sister! You combine unformed substances, stir for a bit . . . and voilà, you give them a shape. It makes you feel almost omnipotent."

"What are you saying? You talk like a blasphemer."

"No, on the contrary. It is God himself who gave us food. . ."

"Well, if you put it that way."

They were talking about cooking. Instead, they should have been, and would have liked to, talk about something else. They needed to make an important decision, a crucial one in their lives. And instead, what were they doing? Nothing . . . nothing about nothing. Certainly it appeared that two women sitting in a kitchen bathed in sunlight were just talking about food. But the two women were aware that their conversation was irrelevant. They were only words in the wind that would fly into hyperspace and never return.

Everything had begun that morning. There was a treacherous wind that made one's skin sensitive to the morning sun. It was painful for Barni to walk through that unusual draft, her voice certainly would feel its effect. She had tied a black silk scarf around her neck to prevent that disaster, but she knew in her heart that it wouldn't do much good. She had been out of the house just five minutes when the scarf began to bother her. However, she did not want to take any chances, she preferred to be careful.

All things considered, that scarf was better than an eventual operation on her vocal cords. In fact, to be precise, Barni had already undergone two operations to the said cords. Why? Two nasty nodules. She had noticed them one day when her voice, her powerful voice, had become shaky. At first she had attributed it to a harmless sore throat, but then when her large voice did not return to its field marshal quality, she understood that something had to have happened. She waited almost twenty days before seeing a nose and throat specialist. The doctor she happened upon was a short, bald man with extremely white, crooked teeth. He asked her a lot of questions.

None of them was pertinent to her illness.

Who are you? Where are you from? How long have you been in Italy? What a nice scarf, is it a traditional scarf from your homeland? What language do they speak in Somalia anyway? Have they ever told you that you Somalis are very beautiful people? Yes, much prettier than the other Africans. Are there still Italians there? Don't tell me that there is still a war going on? What do you eat? And that actress, that Zeudy Araya, is she a Somali? No . . . but then who was that beautiful Somali woman? Oh, yes, you are right, the wife of David Bowie, the top model Iman.

Etc. etc. etc. etc. etc. etc. etc. etc. etc. etc. etc. etc. etc. etc. etc. etc. etc. etc.

The doctor had wasted more time chatting than conducting the actual exam. What's more, he had addressed her informally without her permission. These two facts put together really infuriated her. Why did she have to be subjected to the third degree—and worse still, in a tone pretending to show friendship—every time that she moved a step in that country?

And she also hated anyone who told her that Somalis were more beautiful than other Africans. She hated those who said, "Oh, but you all don't have the big nose that the others do." She hated those who wanted to pull her away from mother Africa. She was just like all the others and at the same time different. She really did not like that kind of compliment, for it implied something like, "Oh, you are all monkeys, but you less than the others."

Aisha always told her, "Aunt Barni, you're exaggerating. That guy . . ." in that case it was the doctor, but it could just as easily have been a man or a woman, an educated person or one who had only completed middle school, a businessman or someone in the service industry. "He was just curious. Sure, he was tactless, but just the same he wanted to learn something. Curiosity is a good thing, Aunty. You know that if people are not curious it's dangerous? Do you think that the Nazi skinheads give a damn whether you eat something sweet or savory at breakfast?" Aisha's words were certainly rooted in the truth, but Barni tried to ignore that truth. She was too accustomed to hating to be able to change right then. After all, it wasn't that she needed to change. "Let those racist Northern Leaguers change first," she thought. Why did she have to force herself to understand people who thought that the *negri* had to be treated like slaves, or worse, like butcher's meat?

Barni wasn't willing to understand them, she wanted only to ignore them. It was already hard to walk their streets, breathe their dirty air, and eat their rotten food. It was hard to live like a *gaal* every day. She would have liked to walk the sandy streets of Mogadishu, drink camel's milk, and hear the sweet sound of the sea, her far-away sea. Instead she was forced to live like a *gaal* every day of her wretched life.

She was damn sick of it!

Of course she should have been grateful for the asylum that the country gave her. At least here she was free, very free.

She did not have to run from one end of town to the other fleeing snipers, for example. She had money, a job (though lowly), good friends who were free as she was. She had good reason to be happy or at least at peace. Moreover, not all Italians were racist Naziskins. On the contrary. There were nice people among them, easygoing people, who were intelligent, respectable. But she never saw those respectable ones. She only saw the rotten apples, those that were hateful, who swore and disgraced the land on which they were born . . . those who had forgotten that at one time they had been the targets of other immigration laws.

This category of Italians always had the upper hand in her mind and thus the image she had created of the *gaal* had almost always been negative. What's more, Barni knew in her heart of hearts that she needed someone whom she could blame for the poverty in her homeland. She had found in the *gaal* the perfect scapegoats. When everything went wrong in her country (that is, always), well, she would get angry with the *gaal* around her. They weren't guilty of anything (or better, they were not individually at fault, their past and present governments on the other hand were a bit to blame), but she considered them guilty just the same. She was unfair and she knew it! Anyway, didn't they do the same thing? The politicians never fixed the problems of the unemployed youths, of pensions, or the economy. And instead of explaining, "Be patient, my country, the economy isn't doing well, we must tighten our belts for a bit, make some changes and sacrifices," they said: "It's their fault, the immigrants. They take away your jobs and pensions and weaken the economy." And they pitted one against the other so that they could remain untouched in their corruption and general eat, drink, and be merry attitude. Yes, the whole world was like that after all. Italy of the year 2000 was not so different from corrupt Somalia of the dictator Said Barre or Germany after the Weimar Republic. The scapegoats were important for masking global crisis.

Anyway, the doctor, after a thousand words, diagnosed her with nodules. She was operated on two months later and she didn't much like it, especially the shots. But what was that Italian proverb? Troubles always come in threes? This is why Barni preferred to wrap herself up like a sort of salami. She didn't want to run into that notorious "three." She didn't want to undergo another operation, and the additional resulting shots.

Aisha sometimes found her aunt ridiculous and Rhoda, too—when she was still with them—laughed about Barni's way of bundling up excessively. Faduma was the only one who never laughed about it. She understood her friend all too well. She knew that Barni had a terrible fear of needles and shots. Faduma didn't want to attack someone who in her own way was already suffering.

Every operation consisted of different shots, between the anesthesia and various treatments. Naturally this was Barni Nur's worst nightmare.

She had tried everything to overcome this phobia: *sure* of the Koran recited weekly, *baqshiis* to spiteful *ginn*, overflowing cups of fragrant chamomile tea (a bit nauseating), yoga exercises copied from some magazines she had read distractedly in some waiting room.

But everything had been wasted, useless, meaningless!

Upon seeing a needle, her reaction was always the same: a faint worthy of a silent film diva, followed by a huge sense of embarrassment. Barni could not stand this sissy behavior, so—in order to avoid feeling even more ashamed—she preferred looking like a ridiculous salami and dressing up that way. There was nothing in the world she hated more than acting like a damsel in distress! Barni had always known in her heart: she would have liked to have been born male.

To Barni, men were fortunate. Of course, they were a little dense, but they were definitely lucky. They always made out better than women in any corner of the globe. They were not forced, as she and her sisters were, to wear their sexuality like an evil yoke. They were free. Women instead were just objects to be covered with a ton of burkas or to be unveiled with a thousand excuses. Whether they were nude or covered made no difference after all, either way, nude or covered, women were never free. Barni would have liked to be a man because she thought she would finally be free. "Yet how disgusting it would be to wake up with an erect penis every morning." That's what made her a bit sick, so in the end she decided she was grateful that destiny had brought her into this world as a woman. Perhaps she was not free, but she was most definitely superior (since she was a woman).

So, that morning, wrapped up like a sausage, Barni had headed out for the visit that Faduma Aden had arranged with her. Her long-time friend had been very mysterious about what they would do that afternoon. Faduma was usually candor incarnate. She was not a woman capable of trickery and secrecy. She was a great woman that Faduma! She had even forgiven Barni for her betrayal. Barni hadn't trusted her friend enough to tell her about Rhoda and after the initial pain, Faduma had understood, forgiven, and almost forgotten. It wasn't really a question of trust. The truth was that she, Barni Nur, was ashamed of the state of her grandniece. For the first time in her life Barni had envied her friend. Faduma had grown children who were upright and religious. What did Barni have in comparison? A heathen slut. She had envied Faduma with all her being. And in so doing she had risked losing her friend. Barni never imagined that keeping the secret about Rhoda from her friend would have been such a blow to Faduma . . . she had made a big mistake. Barni hadn't understood, until that moment, that Faduma considered Rhoda a child of her own equal to her other children. Rhoda was not a touchstone for Faduma. Rhoda was a piece of her.

However, Barni's friend was not the type to hold hatred in her heart, thank God. She vented and screamed like a mad woman, but then she always put the pieces back together.

And she had put them back together once again for Barni Nur.

"Who knows what she has up her sleeve," the woman asked herself in relation to that blind date. On the phone the night before, her friend had been too evasive.

Yes, she had definitely been too evasive.

Barni had tried to set a trap for her, but there was little she could do. Faduma's lips were not only closed, but absolutely sealed.

"Let's meet in piazza Capacelatro at nine. Don't be late," was all she said.

Barni was more than on time. She was a half hour early. The anxiety caused by that broken secret had kept Barni from sleeping. She usually spent her free day with her head buried in her white pillows, but that day after morning prayers she had not been able to fall back asleep. She made herself a strong coffee and left the house. She knew she would have been early, but that didn't matter. It was better to be out of the house walking than in the house racking her brains. Walking was at least good for keeping her from worrying. Sure, her neighborhood was not the best place to take a walk (she was well aware of that!), but that slightly grim, squalid atmosphere characteristic of her neighborhood didn't bother her that much. Her employers naturally were horrified when they heard the name of her neighborhood: "You really live in Primavalle, my dear? Poor thing!"

Usually the name Primavalle was a holy terror for the ladies of Parioli or Prati. In the seventies and eighties it was that part of the city known for trafficking, heroine, and muggings in broad daylight. In the seventies and eighties, one didn't live in Primavalle, but simply tried to survive. Then things slowly began to change, strangely for the better. Perhaps it was the city itself that was changing for the better. The fact was that day after day the district became less dark, less threatening. Coffee shops, stores, markets, social clubs, two movie houses, and even a library cropped up. This changed the face of the neighborhood. Families decided that Primavalle was not such a bad place to raise children after all. And just like that, the neighborhood filled with people. Sure, it still was not absolutely safe to go out at certain hours of the night, but where else (in Rome, Italy, or the rest of the world) was it safe to go out at all hours of the night? There were certainly many problems yet to be fixed, but the neighborhood was making giant steps towards normalization. Even the extention of the metro as far as Battistini had helped the area to free itself from a past filled with daily crimes. Above all, Barni liked (as did her niece Aisha) seeing many colored faces in the neighborhood. There were Filipinos, Poles, Egyptians, Romanians, Peruvians, Ethiopians, Argentineans, Indians, and many others she didn't have the strength to mention. She did not feel then so far from home when she walked the streets of her neighborhood. She did not feel that cold sensation in her gut that used to eat away at her when she cleaned the chic toilets of chic *gaal*. Even the Italians seemed nicer to her in Primavalle. She had friends in Primavalle. There was the man at the Hallmark store where she bought notebooks for Aisha, the grocer at the corner who gave her herbs every day, the newspaper vendor who updated her on the latest global events. And there were many more still: the blond girl in the café, the bearded optician, her neighbor who was always laughing, the enthusiastic fan of the Roma soccer team in his eighties who had his daily sweet honey croissant. Those characters added something to her day. She spoke to them slowly in Italian, but never making errors. After all, she had attended school in Italy or, as they said where she was from, she was an "Italian type." She had studied Dante, Ariosto, and Leopardi. And she had even enjoyed it! Now, as an adult, she realized she should not have liked it. One must study one's own history first and then others' history. When she was little, she knew all about Garibaldi, Mazzini, Cavour, King Victor Emanuel II. But she knew absolutely nothing about her own national heroes. She did not know a thing about the Darawish, Saydka, or Ahmed Gurey.

This ignorance about her own roots had ruined Italy for Barni. The lack of historical understanding was the seed that had sprouted into civil war in her country.

She excelled at her studies of Italian, always receiving an eight out of ten on her compositions. She was also a whiz at conversation. She knew twelve-letter words and she made fancy statements worthy of any show-off in town. So what happened to her? Where had her fancy Italian gone?

She had simply repudiated it.

In hearing people say: "You blacks don't know Italian!" Barni had ended up believing it. She abandoned Dante, Ariosto, and Leopardi and in their place she adopted scandalously ungrammatical verbs.

Her language became confused and approximate. And she ended up becoming that stereotype of an immigrant woman that society (or better, the media) wanted to see in her. Barni gave herself up out of laziness, without fighting, without believing in it for real.

Seeing her friend roused Barni from her thoughts. Faduma was of course on time, as always, upright as a pillar in front of the bus stop. Barni was surprised in realizing once again that her friend looked like a Miss Universe. How was it that a woman as sensual as Faduma had decided against remarrying? For Barni this was one of the unsolved mysteries of history, a bit like the murder of JFK or the building of the pyramids.

If she had not been a woman, Barni would have married Faduma herself. She was not only beautiful, but she was also loaded with personality.

Barni noticed that her friend was not alone. There was a woman, a *gaal*, with her.

The presence of that outsider between the two them disturbed her.

It meant she would have to express herself in Italian and that she would not have felt at ease. Just a few meters stood between the two of them. In those few meters, she studied the enemy, the foreigner. She had a small, round face. Actually, her whole body was small and round. She was young. She was roughly the same age as Rhoda . . . the same age as Rhoda if she were still alive. Her hair was long, very black, and held together in one thick braid. Her hands were small and she had extremely long nails painted black. She was not a classic beauty. But she had something capable of attracting men and women. Barni found her interesting. But this didn't change her opinion: the presence of that outsider bothered her. It was the color of her skin that divided them, that milky white brought her intestinal discomfort.

"Oh, hi Barni, this is Sandra."

"Pleased to meet you," Barni said in a dry tone.

"*Barasho wanaagsan,* sister!" replied the girl in labored, but correct Somali.

Barni could not believe her ears. She put out her hand and shook Sandra's firmly. She wanted to check whether that girl was real.

"Where did you learn Somali?" asked Barni in Italian.

"Oh, you are flattering me. Unfortunately I don't really know your language . . . I know many words, phrases here and there . . . but I couldn't hold a long conversation."

"But where did you learn?"

"You don't remember me?

Barni searched her memory. She didn't remember ever seeing that round face before, but she didn't have a good memory. Moreover, to her white people (especially those with round faces) all seemed alike to her. Barni thought for a bit, but no memory came to the surface. The girl didn't say anything. She waited patiently to reveal her identity to the woman she had met long ago.

"I'm Sandra. I was Rhoda's seatmate in high school."

Now the memory emerged slowly from the abyss into which it had fallen. The name and the figure alone didn't explain anything. The connection was missing. Rhoda was that missing link. With this said, everything became clearer.

"And to what do I owe the pleasure of this return?"

"Well, first of all my condolences."

"Thank you."

"I know it's painful, it was for me as well. I loved that crazy girl, though I don't think she ever understood that."

Barni felt connected to Sandra. She had also sensed that Rhoda rarely felt loved in spite of her efforts.

"I know," was all Barni managed to whisper.

"And also, I don't think that Faduma has mentioned to you . . ."

Barni looked at Faduma confused. Then she shook her head.

The girl grinned.

"I'm happy! At least that way I will have the chance to pitch the business idea to you."

"Business?"

"Yes, Mrs. Nur, b-u-s-i-n-e-s-s!"

"And what in the world would that be?"

"To open an ethnic store in Primavalle. We will sell the things that your countrymen sell on the streets. I have a vacant shop in Pietro Maffi Street. My grandfather left it to me. We would put in some money, you know now there are funds for entrepreneurial women . . . Faduma also has some savings and her children will help her . . . and you all, you . . . right, so you all will contribute your experience. It will be perfect, Mrs. Nur . . . Faduma and I have been talking about it for ages. Naturally . . . we will call the store Rhoda."

The girl came up for air with a smile. Then she waited for Barni's reaction.

Barni was speechless.

The girl fell back to her sales pitch. "You don't have to decide right away. We'll go now to see the place and then you can tell me."

And that was what had happened that afternoon. Barni had . . . they had caught a glimpse of a dream.

Faduma Aden, as usual, had been right to make that dessert. They needed energy to make a decision about the business.

“Elsewhere”

Barbara Serdakowski

Translated by Tristana Rorandelli

TODAY YOU TELL ME ABOUT OTHER PLACES, ABOUT PERFECT PLACES with their fresh air, about everything one can find there, all that one would be able to do, but only there . . . Here, as we already know, certain things are impossible, everything has already been explored, we are aware of faults, of restrictions. It is true, better places do exist, and fresher air, elsewhere there is infinity, we know this, and the “desire to leave” immediately returns.

“You know, life is great in Spain, and in Barcelona there’s only art . . . ,” you tell me.

Is it possible that such thoughts never fade away? That they are always right there, under the skin, in one’s capillaries, in the epidermis? I’ve been living here for many, many years, but one word is enough and the suitcases and boxes are almost ready to go. I’m already thinking about schools, the first month’s rent, expenses; four thousand euros will be enough to get started, as for the rest we know how to manage, nothing can stop us, by now we are experts.

To leave once again for another place is no longer a departure into the unknown, it is a destination like all other destinations, it is only a matter of moving, you just need gasoline. Why is it that every time I remain in “this place” for a while, I inevitably have the impulse to go somewhere else?

Days are fragile, they break easily. Am I a female citizen of the world? Yet to belong *to the world* mostly means not to belong to anyone. To be plankton in the collective plankton, filtered by the teeth of an unaware sea mammal. Yes, the world is small indeed, but in any case, it is too vast to allow us to inhabit it in its entirety.

“After all we already speak the language, the children will learn fast. There they have a great school system and they are even better organized than here. What about bureaucracy? Well, it does exist, but it's not worse than here, you know! There is the sea as well."

"They say that rents are lower. . . ."

I bit my tongue. I was already thinking about leaving. Imagining that I was looking at apartments and choosing one with a balcony, with a garden and large windows. One thing was certain, there the bread wasn't tasteless, here on the contrary I have never gotten used to it. Who knows, once there, I might even miss the bread. How many things had I missed because of my departures, unexpected things, objects that I didn't love, façades that I was indifferent to, shapes that I had never before noticed.

"Look, Amsterdam is also very lively . . . ," you say.

I rule it out because of the language. Strange, a few years ago I wouldn't have imposed this kind of restriction upon myself. Years damage you and are as slippery as an eel.

"No, forget it, the climate is too unpleasant," you say.

I let out a sigh of relief. I'm getting old and can only manage one place at a time. The possibilities are decreasing. I feel a bit of frustration, but maybe it's better like this: for instance, I almost never think about Africa anymore.

If *my* mixed language were to become a sound, it would be a sound of many branches. Like an oak with the leaves of a maple, of a eucalyptus, of a myrtle, and many evergreen pine needles. In different languages one's thoughts don't always follow the same trunk. You make your point by utilizing different images. You can't always jump from one image to the next without risking the loss of the listener's attention. I speak, they look at me with curiosity, I seem incoherent, I stumble because of a word that I can't come up with, in my mind I translate an image they won't understand, I haven't said anything, they are no longer listening . . .

In the background Youssou N'Dour is playing, the words are round, comforting: but what did he actually say? I relax and listen to the sweet sounds; are his words also sweet?

"I think more clearly when I don't understand . . ."

The sounds of your words and the way you discard their meaning trouble me. For you meaning is optional, a little like *L'après-midi d'un faune* heard on the radio by someone who doesn't speak French. Do I write meanings or sounds? One day people will read my work and say: "I like the musicality of this writer. I wonder," they will ask, "I wonder, what did you actually say?" There is something that I lost along the way, something that escapes me, "when sound and meaning will no longer be inseparable, what will I become?" My mind can't help me, I let it go.

My coffee is salty. I don't like to speak my *first* language. People look at me with curiosity. They try to guess its origin and interpret the sounds. My language is whispered, it sounds like a waterfall, I seem to be talking like a bird but I was actually angry. I say one word, they laugh because it sounds like one of theirs. They will never let me speak.

"What you're saying sounds so cute! Talk, talk, say something else!"

"What do you want me to say?"

"It doesn't matter (they can't understand, anyway). I like to hear you speak."

This is not my home. Others are aware of it as well. They know the difference. For me there is no way out of it, even if I were in my own country I would still be in "their homeland." Two years, or three, five maybe, but no more than that. Yes, if you have been away from home for more than five years, you will never again be one of the locals. If you have been away for too long, you might as well remain in the place you have moved to, becoming forever infected. However, you can always leave the place where you landed, there isn't any minimum stay that allows you to become one of the locals. You will always be asked: "Where are you from?" And thus the syndrome of the "other place" is born because you can always go elsewhere, for the others nothing changes. To New York, maybe, to London or Berlin. Perhaps there nobody will ask you anything, except for spare change. There nobody talks about origins, could it be because of the climate?

"Honey, what do you think, should we go to Barcelona?"

Sure, you decide, you pick a place. After all, the only thing that matters is our life together, what we do, not how others perceive us. These are empty words, umbrellalike words for rainy days. The truth is that we live through our memories. This *inner* life is strange, when everyone else lives a life *on the outside*. Our world, our home, our fatherland are inside of us, their network is outside, surrounding them. How does one live with the absence of the other place?

"An *espresso*? *Macchiato*?"

How nice, this girl already knows my habits! And why do I feel this happy? She says hello to me, she recognizes me, as do the newspaper vendor and the person at the health food store. The newspaper vendor always talks to me about France. He heard me speak French. I explained to him that I have nothing to do with France, but he insists that I do. I have only been there twice, I can hardly remember the stairs of the Eiffel Tower, *le bateau mouche sur la Seine*, I had the flu, I was feeling very sick. But for him I am French. He is right, poor thing, if I am not French why on earth do I speak French to my daughter? Why? No, seriously, why? How should I know? I don't feel like thinking about everything, that's just how it all turned out, that's just how it is.

The café isn't empty, I am not alone, but what is curious however is that Youssou N'Dour's own words mixed with French are playing on the radio. I understand a little bit, I feel the rest. It is not bad to enjoy the language of others without understanding, I think in blatant contradictions. Inside I feel like I am dying.

"Please, one more," I tell the girl.

She gives me a strange look but understands, and the cream-filled croissant is brought to me on a red napkin, a strange choice of background color for a drawing of a young man holding Medusa's head: Perseus Café!

"*Merci,*" she looks at me and smiles, she thinks I am joking, she says: *"La vie est belle,"* who knows why, maybe it's the only thing that she can think of in French.

"*Gracias y hasta luego.*"

After paying I thanked her in Spanish. She no longer smiles, she thinks I'm making fun of her. I'm not teasing her, I'm searching for myself.

But how about my *mother* tongue, my secret weapon, my hidden identity, my music box with a ballerina inside, who is faceless by now, but with the music from *Doctor Zhivago* that one can still rewind? That's another story. I can take it out of its box unexpectedly, I could really surprise people, just a few words uttered one after the next and I would bowl them over. By now they have heard me speak too many languages, but only those that are similar to theirs. They have even studied some of these languages in school but not that one, that one belongs to me. When I hear people speak those words on the street I don't approach them. My children recognize them, they press my hand, they pull me by the sleeve and nod: yes, yes, they have recognized the language, it is indeed that magically secret language of mom's, that nobody in the family understands but that can be heard sometimes at home, on the phone. We hold our breath and walk past them with furtive glances and in silence.

"*Tak wlasnie wczoraj . . .*"

". . ."

"*No nie, bron boze, to tylko trzeba zalatwic zanim . . .*"

"*Tak . . . Tak . . . chyba tak . . .*"

". . ."

"*Wczoraj to dostalam, tym razem doszlo dosc szybko.*"

I am not desperate. By now at the police headquarters they look at me with downcast eyes. I stand out from the other people with their haggard faces, the result of sleepless nights. Those that still carry their other place on their faces, those who could still go back and pretend that nothing ever happened. I carry my other place in my womb, like a baby who will never be born, yet who will neither grow nor die.

"I'm Polish! Nobody knows that . . . they all think that I'm American, or Swedish, except for the newspaper guy. . ." *Shuut.* Please, don't tell anyone. I can't stand that glance that seems to say: "Really? So you're from Eastern Europe . . . !?" Those girls are great at taking care of the elderly, cleaning homes and then they do that other thing . . . I am a different Polish woman, one cleansed in no man's land before arriving here, I no longer bandage my wounds. I wear black stockings in October, even when it is eighty degrees outside.

"Honey," you touch my face softly, "maybe we made a mistake by coming here; but no, come on, we really made a good decision!"

"I don't know, maybe we really did make a mistake," I confess, but I immediately regret having said that.

It is strange how ideas lose their meaning when expressed out loud. If I were to leave tomorrow, nobody would be surprised. Foreigners are nomads, everyone knows that. Besides, one foreigner is as good as another. They aren't pillars on which one can lean, they belong to another place, they are evanescent. Even those who are well established, doctors, scientists, might not be here tomorrow. The fact is they aren't reliable, but, on the other hand, they are better paid. They bring knowledge from elsewhere, a foreign name in the medical field inspires one with greater confidence, even more so if it is English or German, because it indicates "a true specialist." As long as the name doesn't sound South American, or even worse, Pakistani, since they only help their own people and they speak directly in Spanish, Portuguese, etc. Language is important for questions regarding one's health.

"Where are you from, Madam?"

"From elsewhere . . ."

"Me too, I'm from Piedmont, my mother is from Sicily and my father from Molise, I understand you perfectly!"

"I was born in my country, but, you know, I didn't grow up there, I went elsewhere, and then after a few years, I moved somewhere else, but not for very long, then my father. . . ."

ENOUGH! Only one move is allowed. You can be born in a place and then go to one other, preferably "here." This provides a point of reference. But not in my story. From the very start I lose my listeners. They look at me with astonished eyes, a worried expression, and keep glancing nervously at their watches. An unpleasant feeling of general uneasiness arises. I'm merely one example. Isolated cases don't matter. Only groups really matter. The Albanians living in Italy, the Senegalese, and the Korean communities. They can even study and maintain their traditions, experience their culture which is welcomed here. But not me. I cannot be linked to anyone else, cannot be tied to any group. Thus I am I. But I always stand alone.

I am about to go home, I have already drunk my coffee, I think that maybe in Barcelona . . . I already feel tired from the trip. I can ask for empty boxes at the pharmacy, to save money.

Along the way there are always the same streets edged by centuries-old stones and those plants whose name nobody recalls. You know, the bushes with very green leaves that are always full of flowers, even in the middle of highways, even close to the sea, even in dry Sardinia. There is the same man who owns the refreshment booth. And there are always the same sandwiches with prosciutto, mozzarella, tomato, and arugula which are no longer sold to respectable families, but to the dirty hands of shipwrecked people. The clientele has really changed in the last few years. But I see him, with his ever-graying skin, still selling those sandwiches. With an expression of disgust on his face he pockets the money and returns home. I am a foreigner like they are but they look at me the same way they look at him, the sandwich guy. The sandwich man prefers me, I am not like him, but I am not like those people either. By now I am a family cat, at least I am vaccinated, whereas they are still stray cats. They would give me a piece of steak, while they would only give them some fat. The fillet won't fall from the table.

As a matter of fact we are a bit like pets, they love us very much, but if they had to choose who to throw off the roof . . . but some of them love us, very, very much. And if they never had to choose you wouldn't even notice the difference. The hierarchy of the last to arrive. In the restaurants aren't they always the ones who clean the toilets? All right, clean the toilets! (Even those with a college degree).

"Hello!"

He looks at me with a smile, he finds it hard to recognize me, he finally does, it has been a long time since I was last there, he realizes that I won't buy anything, he loses interest and becomes a little irritated. He is very busy, I should understand that one only says hello to the regular costumers. I haven't gone there in a year. Foreigners are like that, easily changing their habits. A local wouldn't have changed his regular coffee bar, but I did.

My Italian is good, sometimes they can't tell the difference.

"How did you learn to speak so well?"

"I'm pretty good with languages . . . ," is my witty response.

"How strange, I talk to you and it doesn't seem like I'm talking with . . . with . . . I mean, it's the same as speaking to one of us . . . It's very strange indeed, and actually if I don't think about it . . . it's impressive! But how do you manage to do it, how long have you lived here?"

"In Canada they called us allophones."

"Extraordinary!"

"In theory it means 'one who speaks a different language.' In reality, they are probably referring to the two main languages: meaning those whose mother tongue is neither French nor English."

"It's incredible, I can't believe it, I can't even detect an accent, nothing, really nothing. . . . Look, I know a lot of people, I even have girl friends who are foreigners, I mean people who've been living here for years, you know, they all have an accent. This is unbelievable!"

"I have to get off, this is my stop, I'll see you at the gym . . . or maybe not, I might be moving to Barcelona, anyway bye!"

"Barcelona?" I hear her mumbling.

I don't want to leave. I don't feel like it anymore. I'm happy. Resigned? Could I have lost my *elsewhere*? Maybe for every *elsewhere* there will always be yet another *elsewhere,* so I might as well keep the *elsewhere* that I already have. These are the thoughts of the locals: I was born *here,* everything is *here,* my *here* is as good as another *here.* Will I stay?

"I don't feel like leaving," you say.

We look at each other, relieved, we feel safe. But everyone knows that foreigners are unpredictable, maybe next time it won't be Barcelona.

"Ravi's Wedding"

Lily-Amber Laila Wadia

Translated by John Welsh

"MAMMA! MAMMA! COME QUICK! RAVI'S ON THE PHONE!" I PUSH open the parlor door and run down the narrow hallway to the kitchen out back—the one separated from the rest of the house by a little terrace and a screen door in order to keep the women and the cockroaches out of the men's sight. I get wrapped up in a hot cloud that smells of peanut oil, green chili peppers, freshly ground coriander, chopped vegetables, and chickpea flour. I pause for an instant to catch my breath and put my hands on my hips. "Mamma, run! Ravi's on the phone from Italy!"

"My God, he couldn't have picked a worse time," says Mom, drying her wet forehead with the inside of her arm. "Will you fry the rest of the *bhaji* for me? Make some of the ones with onions and potatoes." Her hands are covered in chickpea flour. She searches desperately for a dishcloth, but she can't find anything within reach. She runs into the parlor and answers the phone—the one that sits in the corner on a glass shelf supported by two elephants made of ebony.

I haven't seen my brother for over a year, so I'm pretty anxious to hear the news. I grab a *bhaji* from the fryer and gulp it down so fast I burn the roof of my mouth. Even though I know Mom hates it when you don't listen to her orders, I can't resist the temptation to follow her into the parlor. It's way too hot to stay in the kitchen, even with the ceiling fan set to maximum speed. I don't know how my mom managed to cook in this sweltering heat without fainting. Even though we have a permanent cook on salary, she insists on making the *bhaji* with her own two hands every time that Aunt Preeti and Uncle Hemnant come to visit—even if it means dying over the stove. She says it's a subtle way to let her sister-in-law know that when you have guests—even family—it's not enough to serve lukewarm tea and open a bag of *Petit* cookies.

Mom plops down on the green velvet sofa and carefully lifts the phone off of the glass shelf with two fingers, trying her best not to get it dirty.

"Ravi *beta,* how are you, my son?"

Dad is reading his daily newspaper in a rocking chair near the window. His pant legs are rolled up to his knees and his feet are soaking in a little basin filled with cold water and salt. He suffers from poor circulation, and this time of year his feet puff up like two giant mangos. Dad lowers his glasses from the paper and eavesdrops, trying to piece together a mosaic from the bits of dialogue he manages to overhear.

Mom sees me, covers the phone with her hand, and tells me to go get her a wet towel. I reluctantly obey, dragging my feet on the floor so that my rubber slippers squeak.

My dad gives me a reproachful look. Dad almost never communicates with words, unlike my mom who never stops talking—not even when she's alone! Dad's eyebrows are so expressive they could tell the entire history of the Indian independence movement better than any documentary. He developed this extraordinary ability during thirty years of marriage, partly out of sheer laziness and partly out of necessity, since it's so difficult to interrupt my mom.

I haven't heard from my brother in two weeks and I'm dying to talk to him. I'm one hundred percent sure that my mom is going to forget to pass me the phone so I have to hang around waving my arms in the air to remind her.

"It's too expensive. Don't you know how much these international calls cost? You shouldn't fritter away your brother's money in useless chatter, understand? Just say: 'Hihowareyou? Imissyoucomebacksoon.' How much can a twelve-year-old girl possibly have to say anyway?"

I grab a towel, wet the corner and run back to my mom in the parlor. As I'm handing it to her, I notice that she is trying to hide a tear by pretending to scratch an eyelash. I'm shocked! It's not that I've never seen my mom cry—she's the queen of melodrama, but most of the time she cries and screams in stereo, usually for the benefit of our neighbors. I've never seen her try to hide her tears like this.

"Here, take it." I hold out the towel, but she doesn't see or hear me. I pry open her fingers and stick in the wet corner of the towel. I have to literally push her fingers closed again to make sure that she will hold on to it.

"Will you take it already? What's the matter? Is your hand paralyzed or something?" I ask, annoyed.

"Shh," says my dad, getting up from the white and blue striped chair and leading me away underneath his arm. "Don't disturb her. It seems like a touchy subject. Who knows what the devil your brother is saying to worry her so much."

Dad and I find a spot at the edge of the parlor. We're still within earshot, but we stay hidden from sight.

We hear Mom change herself into a blackbird. "But *beta, beta,* my little boy, my son. What am I going to tell Aunt Samira? What will I tell her? What will I tell her? You tell me, you tell me what I'm going to say to her."

"What does Aunt Samira have to do with anything?" I ask my dad. He responds with the raise of an eyebrow.

We had been neighbors with Aunt Samira for years, until her husband had to move to Hyderabad for work. She isn't really related to us, she's just my mom's best friend, but in India the terms "aunt" and "uncle" are used for older people as a sign of respect.

"But what the devil is happening?" I ask. Mom uses the corner of her white sari to dry the tears that now flood from the banks of her high cheekbones like water bursting from the river Ganges during a monsoon. The white towel I brought her lies on the ground completely ignored.

"Shh! Will you be quiet! How can I understand what's happening if you don't stop talking!" Dad bursts out.

I stare at him with my mouth wide open. He frowns and tilts his head to hear what Mom is saying.

"Certainly, *beta,* yes certainly *beta* . . . yes my son, I am happy for you. . . . No, no I'm not just saying that . . . It's just that you caught me off guard . . . you never said anything about this before. . . . Yes, yes, it's okay, *beta* . . . Dad?"

Hearing himself called, Dad runs to the phone but Mom abruptly pushes him away. She glances down, covers her mouth with her free hand, and finally realizes what she has done: her beautiful white sari is completely covered in chickpea flour.

"Mina? Yes, yes, Mina's fine," Mom continues, rolling her eyes and showing me the pitiful state of the sari.

I gallop to the telephone and try to jerk it out of her hands. "Can I talk to Ravi for one minute? Come on! Let me talk, I'm begging you!"

My mother's fingers grip the phone like a pair of tongs, but she finally eases up and I wrestle the phone away.

"Your sister insists on saying hello," she says to my brother. She looks at me severely and says, "Hurry up, your brother doesn't have a fortune."

"Bhayyia!" I scream in excitement. My mother counts the seconds out loud as they pass.

"Little sister! How are you?" My brother's voice is like shelter from the storm.

"I'm fine, how are you? Is it snowing in Italy?"

"How silly! It's July! It's hotter here than it is in India."

"Really? I'm learning to play piano you know. I've already had three lessons. And I cut my hair too. Now it just comes down to my shoulders."

"Mina, your brother doesn't work day and night at the University of Florence to waste all his money listening to your foolishness," Mom pipes in.

"Okay, Ravi. . . . Yeah, that's Mom going on about how I'm making you spend so much money. We'll talk to each other soon. Yeah, yeah, come back soon. I love you, too."

Mom smiles and nods, "Tell him that his mother loves him very much."

But it's too late, and the phone just starts to crackle. I put the receiver down very carefully, as if I were laying a baby in a cradle. I turn quickly to my mother.

"You get to spend hours and hours talking to him and I don't even get time to say a real good-bye!" I shout.

"Shh, shh, Mina, there's no need to shout, we're not deaf," my father intervenes. "Well, what did our little biomedical researcher say? Is there any hope of renewing his scholarship?"

"Rama, Rama!" Mom invokes the heavens as she runs from the room. *"Rama, Rama!* First I have to go to the bathroom."

Father and I exchange worried glances. What could have happened? Did he lose his job? Does it have to do with that Moratti education reform bill that he was talking about before? Mom never takes the name of the god *Rama* in vain. It's obviously a sign that she is extremely agitated.

"What is it, Mom? What did he say?" I flutter around my mother like a Biafra mosquito.

"Nothing," she sighs, folding the sari that she has attempted to clean.

"What do you mean, nothing?" asks Dad's right eyebrow.

"He said that he's getting married."

I take a step back to support myself against the wall. Dad's eyebrows sink. No one has the courage to speak. Finally Dad starts to cough to break the silence.

"I guess the first person I have to tell is Samira," Mom sighs.

My father's eyebrows consult each other about their next course of action. When they finally decide he asks, "But who is he marrying?"

Mother looks at him as though he had asked for the square root of 13,456 times 234.

It's my turn to rephrase the question. "But is he marrying Radhika?"

Two shiny droplets stick in the corners of Mom's eyes as she stares at me.

"No," she says after an interminable silence. "No, he's marrying Maria Cristina."

"And who's she?" I ask confused.

Dad tries to digest the name, but it seems to stick in his stomach like the peppers he ate at dinner. My mother is contemplating her little toe. Dad stares at her until he divines the thoughts of his wife.

It's not easy for a mother to hear that her son is getting married. Being told on the telephone from thousands of miles away only makes it worse. It should be a moment of great joy, but in that moment a mother begins to fear deep down that she may lose the special place she has always had in her son's heart. From then on, the boy drifts outside of the gravitational pull of the mother planet and rotates around another woman. In fact, from the very moment a male child is born, a mother begins to worry about the type of woman who will marry her baby boy.

My mother never had those fears. She was sure she knew the kind of woman her son would marry: a girl who would be gracious, intelligent, and very kind to her in-laws. She would have illuminated our lives like a starry sky. She would have given us at least three beautiful grandchildren. This girl had already been found and chosen, and her name was Radhika. She was the twenty-five-year-old daughter of Aunt Samira, my mother's best friend. Even though Ravi was five years older than she was, the two of them grew up together: they had played together, they had gone to school together, they had even vacationed together. They knew each other very well and they got along splendidly. A mother couldn't hope for anything better. Radhika was a wonderful, good-looking Indian girl: two deer like eyes and a thick, shiny ponytail that reached all the way down to the bottom of her back. She was an excellent classical dancer and she had fluid and harmonious gestures. She knew our family and our traditions, she was religious, respectful, an excellent sitar player and singer, and she was even an excellent cook.

Mother tries to shake herself out of a trance.

"Maybe I will tell my brother and my sister-in-law first when they get here. Even better, it must be them now. Did you finish frying the *bhaji,* Mina?" Mother starts toward the door.

Without responding, I run to the kitchen—otherwise I know that all the frustration my mother is trying to restrain will erupt on me like an avalanche of incandescent lava. But I don't want to be too far away from their conversation at such an important moment, so I tell the cook to put the rest of the vegetables in the batter, brown them in oil, and call me when he had finished cooking them. I hide myself outside the door of the parlor to eavesdrop.

Uncle Hemnant, my mother's little brother, is about fifty years old. He is bald and well put together. He has always been a fatalist. He takes life as it comes, and people with a philosophy like that can't help but be rewarded by fate—it seems as though nothing ever goes wrong for him. Aunt Preeti, on the other hand, being the kind of person who offers you cookies from a box when you visit her, has enough energy to make a thousand pessimistic speculations.

"Come on, come on, you're all crying for nothing. You'll see that in two weeks he will change his mind and this Maria Cristina will be a Maera Chimera: nothing but a far-off memory. After all, I myself encouraged him to have fun in Europe. At least there the girls don't have so many scruples as ours. It's good for a man to have a little experience," says Uncle Hemnant.

"Will you clean your ears? Your sister said that he gets married in two weeks," remarks his wife. "And the girl is even five years older than he is."

The uncle suddenly turns serious.

"What need is there to marry her? Why buy the cow when you get the milk for free? It's not like he got her pregnant, right?"

My mother looks at him with terror in her eyes.

"Well done, Hemnant. That's exactly what she needed," scolds the left eyebrow of my father. He moves toward his wife and massages her rigid back and her beautiful round arms, trying to reanimate her.

"Well, what does it matter? These are modern times, nowadays these things even happen around here. Plus if she's not very far along, no one will notice anything. A couple extra layers of sari and you can hide a watermelon! How nice, to have a little granddaughter that looks like Gina Lollobrigida." Uncle Hemnant thought he would remedy his faux pas by lightening the mood, but he only managed to intensify the dense cloud of tension that hung in the room.

His wife told him that it would be better for him to go into the kitchen and eat something to keep his mouth shut.

"Who do you think the granddaughter would look like?" I can't help but ask Uncle Hemnant. He ignores my question and goes toward the kitchen skipping and singing: *"I'm getting married in the morning . . . ding dong the bells are going to chime. . . .* Do you know that song, Mina?"

"Yes uncle. It's from *My Fair Lady,* I saw it on videotape."

"Good, good. Are you happy you're going to have an Italian sister-in-law? You'll have to learn to make pizza instead of these *bhaji.* Mmm . . . but these vegetable fritters your mom makes are really outstanding. I'm going to try one of the spinach ones." He shovels one hot *bhaji* after another in his mouth. "Who knows what a tasty little cupcake your brother has gone off to find, huh? What do you think she's like, this Maria Cristina?"

"Is Britney Spears Italian, Uncle Hemnant?" I ask.

"No, dear. She is a doll, but I think she's American. Let's see, I think you're too young to remember Sophia Loren. In terms of famous Italian women today, let's see, who is there. . . ."

My father had joined us in the kitchen and he finishes my uncle's phrase: "There's Sonia Gandhi."

"Lord save us!" Uncle Hemnant puts his hands on his throat and pretends to suffocate. "I hope Ravi hasn't gone all the way to Italy to find someone like that! Otherwise all the lessons I gave him were in vain. That would be like going to England to be Margaret Thatcher's sweetheart! A proper Italian woman should have two bewitching eyes, supple lips, big breasts and a backside so beautiful and firm that you could set a pitcher of tea on it." Uncle Hemnant pantomimes his ideal of the Italian woman and I start to laugh out loud because it's really funny to see him walk around shaking his protruding backside.

"That's the only thing in that head of yours, Hemnant. Here we are talking about the future of my son and all you can do is joke," scolds my father.

Uncle Hemnant continues unperturbed. "I hope her mother is a nice little dumpling and brings at least a half dozen nymphomaniac friends and cousins. You know, other than your father who seems to have taken a vow of abstinence, we have a great need for affection in India!" Uncle Hemnant laughs in my father's disgusted face while he polishes off another six *bhaji.*

Aunt Preeti is the one in charge of the feverish preparations to receive our future relative, even though she herself only knows how to tell her servants how to open boxes of cookies. Mom goes around like an automaton, chiming *Rama Rama, Rama Rama* and other prayers under her breath and looking around as though everything—all this racket in the kitchen and the reorganization of the furniture to fit two beds in my brother's old room—was just some kind of movie. She doesn't even notice that her refrigerator, for the first time in its twenty years of life, has become carnivorous. Aunt Preeti had sent Jeevan on vacation, and in his place she had hired another cook that wasn't afraid to touch sausages and lamb shanks. He also knew how to make English crème and Russian salad. She even forced my mother to buy a new set of dishes with crystal glasses, repaint the guest bathroom, and fill the bar with bottles of imported whiskey.

Mom has no idea what to with all the little cans and bags she finds scattered in the kitchen, but Aunt Preeti patiently shows her the merits of Knorr's mushroom cream, frozen asparagus, and boxed ravioli with Bolognese sauce.

"You won't be able to give her spiced potatoes with onions and chapati for breakfast," she says when Mom complains that she doesn't know how to use the mix to make these American fritters, these "pancakes."

"It's written on the bag how you make them. You just add a bit of water, cook them in a nonstick pan and pour on a little melted butter and maple syrup."

Aunt Preeti is not usually a person who accepts compromises, but she has to allow my mother to substitute honey for the maple syrup. Even though he looked in all the imported food stores, Dad was unable to find this last ingredient.

Aunt Preeti then convinces my mother to blacken the long gray hair that she wears in a bun at the nape of her neck and to wax the little hairs on her chin. She even persuades her to try a layer of makeup. My mother gets the first manicure of her life at the beauty salon.

"It's a good thing you're with me now, Mina, or else you wouldn't even recognize me," says Mom with a trembling voice, but she acknowledges the clear improvement of her appearance. My mother is by no means ugly, it's just that she let herself go over the years and doesn't place much importance on her physical appearance. She also loves fried Indian sweets to death.

Aunt Preeti also takes advantage of the visit to the beauty salon, but she is much more ambitious than my mother. Not satisfied with her chic new look—jet-black hair cut in the latest style and her eyebrows plucked to perfection—she decides to get a new peach-colored suit in a boutique that assured her it was an exact replica of the latest Giorgio Armani spring-summer collection.

"You'll make a great first impression with our daughter-in-law," says Dad, admiring the first evening dress and jacket Aunt Preeti has ever worn in her life. It fits her very well because she is so tall and slender.

I notice a look of jealousy silently make its way over the crosswalk of my mother's face, but she doesn't say anything. She picks out the sari she will wear to the airport to pick up her future daughter-in-law. It is made of silk, emerald green with a red border. She twirls the twelve golden bracelets she will give to her daughter-in-law at their first meeting. She would have liked to bring everything that was necessary for an Indian-style welcome: rose garlands, dried coconuts to ward off the evil eye, bright red paste to make the dot on the forehead as a sign of blessing, and rice to scatter about her head to bring good luck and abundance . . . but all these things had been tacitly forbidden, first by Aunt Preeti and then by all the others who had been contaminated by my aunt's "modern" form of thought.

"We shouldn't embarrass our Ravi by appearing like old stereotypes, all incense and sacred cows. We should present ourselves as a modern family, worthy representatives of the India that is on the cusp of the technological age. We will dress western, we will eat western, we will talk western . . . or at least we will try. Shame on anyone who removes his shoes, eats with his hands, or inadvertently mentions Hinduism or anything like that."

At this point, perhaps I should say a word in defense of my family. We are part of a substantial middle class in today's India: those who have voluntarily embraced Japanese technology and are never quite sated with American film and television, but who still feel out of place in a t-shirt and jeans and generally prefer the traditional flavors of their childhood to the bottled, freeze-dried fare that crowds the supermarkets.

Nevertheless, on the way to the airport I sit next to two perfect strangers trained by the lash of Aunt Preeti's tongue. They are my parents, suffocated with the fear of meeting their future daughter-in-law for the first time.

The plane is two hours late and my dad is melting inside the dark gray suit he had purchased for the occasion. He misses his comfortable cotton tunic and he asks my mom with an imploring look if he can take off his silk tie—at least until they announce the landing of the Alitalia jet.

Mom is a Botticelli-like splendor in her emerald green sari with brick red lining. She twirls and twirls the little golden bracelets and unconsciously scrapes all of the red blush off of her cheeks. She throws a compassionate glance toward her husband.

I catch sight of my brother coming through the glass door and I start to jump up and down in my pink chiffon dress with its matching shoes and stockings. "Here he is! Here he is! But I don't see Maria Cristina."

My mother follows my hand and hangs her head. "Me neither," she admits. "What if she didn't come? What if it's all over?" I hear a note of relief in her voice. The last two weeks had not been easy for her. The most arduous trial had been telling the news of the upcoming wedding to her best friend Samira, whose daughter Radhika was destined to marry my brother. Even though we haven't heard from her since, Aunt Samira apparently took the news well and Radhika had been sent on vacation to visit a relative in America in order to spare her the embarrassment of having to show her face at the wedding.

Ravi opens the glass door forcefully and throws himself into my mother's arms. She squeezes him tightly but leans her head over his robust shoulders to catch a glimpse of his fiancée. Even my father's eyebrows give a negative response: there is no trace of the Italian girl.

A few steps behind my brother, there is a girl with dark brown, dusty hair in dreadlocks. She has a pierced nose and another piercing in her chin. It must be another one of those souls looking for salvation from some fashionable guru. She's dressed in loose cotton pajamas with purple and black stripes and an unbuttoned black shirt. It's easy to see that she's not wearing a bra. On her feet she wears natural leather sandals and dangles a hair-skin bag in the wind.

After asking about the health of all of his relatives and giving a brief account of the trip, Ravi turns in search of his future wife like a man in the park looking for a lost dog.

"Ah, here you are," he says to the girl dressed as a gypsy. "Allow me to introduce you to my family."

"Namaste," says the girl, reaching her hands out and leaning her head forward.

My mother's jaw turns so stiff that the whole welcome speech she has prepared exits in a single syllable: "Ugh," she grunts.

My father's eyes stall on the girl's turgid nipples as they struggle against the transparent material of her blouse.

Since I am the only one not left speechless, I introduce myself and I ask the gypsy girl why she still has pajamas on in the middle of the day. My mother would never let me out without brushing my hair or let me wear wrinkled clothes in public.

My parents glare at me, but Maria Cristina starts to laugh. She laughs like a little bell in the wind and her gray-green eyes caress me as she speaks, "But I'm dressed as an Indian, my dear. Can't you tell?"

I notice my mother's face relax a bit. She is pleased to not be the first one to commit such a faux pas. After all, a twelve-year-old girl is forgiven for everything, or almost everything, especially one who is dressed in pink from head to toe like a Barbie doll.

The tension of the trip home is eased a bit by the story of my brother's twelve months in Italy. There is a pause for the presentation of the golden bracelets, passed from mother-in-law to her future daughter-in-law. Unfortunately for my mother, western women have much larger bone structure than eastern women. This had never crossed her mind. Obviously, the bracelets didn't even make it halfway over Maria Cristina's left hand.

My mother takes this as a bad omen, and uses three different English accents to apologize—one indigenous, one British, and the third somewhere between American and the undulation of a boat.

"Nahi, nahi, maaji, aap mat parishan kigie," responds the girl. "Don't worry about it at all."

Her words are an electroshock for my folks.

"But you speak Hindi?" I ask, since I am the only one not short-circuited.

"Yes, or at least I try," responds Maria Cristina.

"Don't believe a word she says," reveals Ravi. "She just finished translating the *Dhyna Bindu Upanishad* into Italian."

My father's eyebrow asks what the devil he's talking about, and Ravi explains that it is a sacred treatise on the sound "Om" and its mystical revelations.

"Of course it is," responds my father's right eyebrow, the one adept at the manifestations of skepticism.

"Mom, Dad, did you know that Maria Cristina teaches yoga?" says Ravi, his voice full of pride.

Mom and Dad look at the girl in the same way they looked at our dog Ricky when I told them that I taught him to shake hands. These foreigners learn to do two somersaults and cross their legs and they call themselves yoga masters. They put two sticks of incense in their houses and they call themselves Hindu. Then they give up meat on Fridays and they call themselves enlightened: the modern world is full of so many little buddhas.

"Good, good, we'll do a couple of exercises together in the morning," Dad says benevolently.

"With pleasure, what type of yoga do you practice, sir?" the girl asks with interest.

Dad shrugs his shoulders. "I do whatever comes to mind. Whatever I remember seeing my father do. In fact, I was the one who taught Ravi those exercises for his back pain. Do you still do those exercises I taught you, Ravi?"

Ravi starts to laugh. "You know, you're playing with fire here, Dad. Maria Cristina is a follower of Swami Paramahansa Yogananda and a master of Kriya Yoga. She hardly practices Hatha Yoga."

"There's nothing wrong with Hatha Yoga," murmurs my father.

"Yes, but these smalltime exercises won't bring you the cosmic reawakening of the consciousness that Maria Cristina is seeking."

Maria Cristina is visibly embarrassed. "Come on, Ravi, it would be a pleasure to meditate with your father." She turns toward my dad and says they can meet tomorrow at the *Brahma Muhurta*.

Dad has no idea what the *Brahma Muhurta* is and mumbles an excuse about having a very important condominium meeting in the morning.

"From three to six in the morning?" asks Maria Cristina, her eyes bulging open in surprise.

My mother manages to change the subject. "Ravi, my son, I bet you have really missed my home cooking, right?"

Ravi admits that he hasn't missed Indian foods in the slightest because Maria Cristina is an excellent cook.

"Yes, but I bet she cooks you English crème and Russian salad and roasted chicken," says Mom smiling.

"Actually I'm vegan and *sattvik*, ma'am," admits Maria Cristina. "That's why I'm always so happy to come to India. And find good spiced potatoes with onion and chapatti instead of the brioches filled with fat and cholesterol that you find in our country."

"But do you drink coffee for breakfast?" Mom asks.

"No, ma'm, it's forbidden by the Laws of Manu."

I see my mother fall prey to panic. Aunt Preeti had filled her head with Arabic and robust blends and who knows what else, but hadn't mentioned the Laws of Manu.

Fortunately my father intervenes, happy to demonstrate his extensive knowledge of Indian philosophy. "It's an ethical code written by the sage Manu. It describes all the foods permitted and forbidden for a Hindu."

"Actually," Maria Cristina clarifies, "Manu is not a person. It's a term that means 'Caretaker of the Earth.' There have been many Manus in the course of history. Also, I love spiced tea and can't stand coffee. But you all don't observe the five *Maha Yagna*? Ravi told me he came from a family of orthodox Brahmans."

Mom hides her hands underneath the fold of her sari where she can squeeze and turn them as much as she likes without being seen. *"Rama Rama, Rama Rama,"* she murmurs. I even see her cross her fingers and curse Aunt Preeti who was so insistent about buying that infernal coffee maker with its grinders and filters of three different sizes.

When we finally arrive home, Mom exits the car and walks up to the house while the others deal with the bags. Aunt Preeti opens the door in her splendid peach suit.

"Well, how is she? How is she?" she asks, excited, patting her stylish hair and rubbing her lips together to redistribute her lipstick.

Mom looks at her and lowers her eyelashes slowly. She makes a face and answers, "He had to go halfway around the world to find someone like this? Go in the kitchen and see if there are vegetables to make the *bhaji* and enough potatoes for breakfast tomorrow."

"The Egyptian Lover"

Yousef Wakkas

Translated by Robert Morse

Cleopatra, whose real name was Semiha Husein, was born in upper Egypt to parents descended directly from a well-known scribe of King Necao. She had gotten off the boat at the port of Genoa near the beginning of the nineties. In her arms was a secondhand Vuitton suitcase that held everything she owned, including her burdensome past. She had just a few dreams, but they were remarkable. She wanted to meet a movie director at Cinecittà and make a neorealist film with him. She really liked the role of Sophia Loren in *La Ciociara,* but had her sights set on *La Dolce Vita.* She could have done the Trevi Fountain scene better than Anita Ekberg. Not that the scene was poorly acted, but it lacked the couple of tears that would have made even the cold-hearted policemen understand the kind of suffering that hung over people like her.

"Madame, don't cry," the policeman consoled her, taking note of the dream she had written under her entry visa.

"Unfortunately," he added, "for the moment, it is difficult to work with Nanni Moretti. They say he is turning Rome inside out in search of his *Caro Diario.*"

At this point, Cleopatra didn't wait. "I'll think about it," she said. She appealed to her practical side, put away her dreams, and made her way through the crowd. After passing through customs, she pulled a note out of her bra with the address of the pensione where she was going to stay. She showed it to the taxi driver who, pretending to be nearsighted, brought it close to his nose, read it, and sniffed it several times. The womanly scent made him dizzy. After several endless minutes of emotional agony, he spoke to her in an English learned with great pains thanks to the *De Agostini* language courses.

"Make war, no love." Then he explained in Italian, "No . . . no, excuse me, that wasn't it, and I just read it last night. Anyway, Madame, it's better to make love than war."

Cleopatra still had in mind her most recent experience with Marc Anthony, and she was determined not to trust men. "First work, then talk," she thought seriously.

"I not whore!" she replied, resorting to the few phrases she had learned as a little girl in the Italian quarter in Alexandria.

When the taxi pulled up to the sidewalk in front of the pensione, Carmelo, an up-and-coming "boss," was just exiting the main door and was swearing. Their eyes met, and someone, perhaps his guardian angel, whispered to him that this girl had been made just for him.

"But that day, I was really mad," began Carmelo. He had just arrived from another institution to serve a twenty-five year sentence with us. "My last lover knew six positions by heart, and during her orgasms, she said phrases in Portuguese, German, and Spanish. I didn't pay any attention to it, because I thought, 'When in Rome.' When she began to use phrases in the Neapolitan and Genoese dialects, however, I lost my patience and hit her a few times. Do I look like a Neanderthal to you? Nobody had ever called me that before. Neanderthal! What an ugly word."

Then, before taking Cleopatra away from the taxi driver, a strange thing happened to me. One day, while I was unloading two cases of homegrown tomatoes for a friend, who later became mayor, I read on the outside wall of my house an unusual phrase: "What life do we lead, and above all, what life do we learn?" I felt as if that phrase were slowly sneaking in under my skin, deeply disturbing my conscience. I began to meditate by drinking eight cappuccinos and smoking three packs of Marlboros a day, but I still didn't understand the meaning of those mysterious words. Was it a message from my rivals to intimidate me? Or was this some hidden prophesy of Ezekiel that was unknown to us? I thought about it for a long time—two, three, or four months —I couldn't tell you how long. But one evening, opening my eyes, I found myself in the hospital. There I thought calmly in my bed: five years as a brick worker, twelve years that I can't tell you about because I am sworn to silence, and seven years in a fruit and vegetable shop that had annual revenues of six hundred million lira. Now, imagine how hard it was to convince the tax authorities that the former owner sold it to me willingly and knowingly without being threatened or intimidated. I remember the day he came to visit me at my house. "My old friend," he said to me, "I am tired, my old friend. They have burned my car, and they are threatening me with worse things. Do something, for the love of God!" The call was as clear as the voices of the saints in their eternal prayers: help your fellow man. I immediately made out a check to him for two hundred million lira and advised him to move to Barbados. There he would have been able to live peacefully and live longer than in Italy. In reality, a shop like that in the fruit and vegetable market would have cost three times as much, but nobody would have bought it. People, out of respect, hesitated to compete with me. Perhaps there was a hidden threat, as the judge maintains. I didn't need the money, I simply wanted to find a job to pass the time. In fact, with my first earnings, I bought a coupe and two cashmere sweaters for Cleopatra, and we left for Egypt to see the pyramids. It was a fun trip. But, what can I say about when she confessed her love for Richard Burton? Me, who hadn't even finished my compulsory education, how could I understand these breathtaking colossal pyramids? At one point, I lost my head and roamed around the Hilton, reading all the books about the secret lives of the pharaohs, from the first dynasty to the discovery of the Tutankhamen's treasures. At my side, she wept for Nasser and said she was sorry because the streets of Cairo were dirty. I asked her to stop it. It was only then that I understood the meaning of the phrase that was tormenting my life.

While in Cairo, I didn't lose contact with my wife. I called her every night, but she had decided to leave me, without realizing that such a move would make me lose face with my friends. In fact, when disaster struck, and I ended up in prison with the defamatory charges of homicide and association with organized crime, I wrote her immediately saying I had broken off all ties with Cleopatra. Naturally it wasn't true, but that fact didn't come out until I made a little written request to buy a panettone for Christmas. The next day, I found three guards and the *educatore* himself in front of my cell.

"Pandoro or panettone?" they asked me with their usual arrogance. I was in the middle of writing. The letter to Cleopatra was on the right, the one to my wife on the left.

"It's in my request," I replied.

"Pandoro or panettone?" they repeated again. I realized they wanted to stir me up, so I read it out loud to them: "The undersigned

C.M., requests permission to buy one panettone pandoro. I thank you in advance." You're not Italian, you don't understand our language well, but if I asked any Italian what that meant, he would reply without hesitation that it meant a panettone. By arguing with them, I lost my clearheadedness, and caught up in the confusion, I put the letters into the wrong envelopes. A week later, the postman came to my cell and delivered two parchment letters sealed with the mark of the duke of Parma. I thought they were some promotional items for the election, like those they give away during the Sunday referendums, but when the red wax seal was broken, Cleopatra jumped out shouting, "Me, a whore? You bugger!" while my wife showed the *brigadiere* the letter in which I described her as an old witch.

I don't know where you come from, but where we come from a wife is untouchable. I care very much about my family, flesh of my flesh. Starting from this principle, that same night I wrote a short note to my friends: Cleopatra and her daughter are going away because I am not sure whether she got pregnant by me or the taxi driver. My wife is entitled to the sports car and the cashmere sweaters. I will never forget that day. That evening, while I was watching the news on TV, to my surprise, I saw Cleopatra with her daughter in tow, throwing stones at the generals of an Allied patrol! So, what can I tell you? I spent that Christmas with no panettone. Those idiots, I think they did it to me on purpose.

Contributors

Fatima Ahmed is of Somalian and Cambodian descent. Her short story "Shanti" is included in the volume *Pace in Parole Migranti* (Peace in Migrant Words) published in 2002. In 2000, she won an award for short fiction from the Literary Prize for Immigrant Writers "Eks&Tra."

Adrian Nazareno Bravi is originally from Buenos Aires, Argentina and moved to Italy in 1990. In 1999, his first novel *Rio Sauce* was published in Buenos Aires.

Viola Chandra is the pseudonym of Gabriella Kuruvilla. She was born in Milan, where she currently resides. Her father migrated to Italy from India. She holds a degree in architecture, and works as a journalist for an interior design magazine. She is a poet, novelist, and also a painter. *Media chiara e noccioline* (Light Beer and Peanuts, 2003) is her first novel.

Christiana de Caldas Brito originally came to Italy from Brazil. She lives in Rome where she works as a psychologist. She has published numerous short stories, a novel, *500 temporali* (500 Storms, 2006), two collections of short fiction: *Qui e là* (Here and There, 2004), and *Amanda Olinda Azzurra e le altre* (Amanda Olinda Azzurra and the Other Women, 1998), which was awarded first prize in the Literary Award "Il Paese delle donne" in 2003. She has also published a children's book, and adapted her short story "Ana de Jesus" into a play, which has been performed widely throughout Italy.

Amor Dekhis was born in Algeria and currently resides in Florence. He has published numerous short stories and a novel, *La notte dei lupi* (The Night of the Wolves, 2005), which was a finalist for the Italo Calvino prize.

JADELIN MABIALA GANGBO was born in the Congo in 1976 and came to Italy at the age of four, where he was raised in a religious institution. He has appeared as an actor in a short film *Il contratto* (The Contract, 2002), has published numerous short stories, and two novels, *Verso la notte Bakonga* (Toward the Bakonga Night, 1999) and *Rometta e Giulieo* (2001), the latter of which has been adapted for the theater and performed throughout Italy. He has completed another manuscript with the working title, *Una congrega di falliti* (A Bunch of Losers), for which he is in search of a publisher.

GABRIELLA GHERMANDI was born in Ethiopia in 1965 and moved to Italy in 1979. She currently lives in Bologna, where her father is from originally. She has published several short stories and has won two awards for short fiction from the Literary Award for Immigrant Writers "Eks&Tra" (first place in 1999, and third place in 2001).

KOSSI KOMLA-EBRI came to Italy from Togo in 1974 at the age of twenty. He completed medical studies in Bologna in 1982 and moved to Como with his wife and two children, where he practices medicine. In May, 2001, Komla-Ebri became the first African-Italian to run for Parliament. He is co-director of *El Ghibli,* an online journal for literature by migrant authors in Italy. He has published a collection of short stories, *All'incrocio dei sentieri* (At the Crossroads, 2003), and a novel, *Neyla* (2002). The novel was translated into English by Peter N. Pedroni and published by FDUP in 2004. Komla-Ebri is also the author of two collections of anecdotes, *Imbarazzismi: quotitidiani imbarazzi in bianco e nero* (Embaracism: Daily Embarrassments in Black and White, 2002) and *Nuovi Imbarazzismi: quotidiani imbarazzi in bianco e nero . . . e a colori* (New Embaracism: Daily Embarrassments in Black and White . . . and Color, 2004).

RON KUBATI has published two novels, *Va e non torna* (Leaving with No Return, 2000) and *M* (2002), both of which concentrate mainly on the inability to communicate between cultures. He grew up in Albania, and before migrating to Italy in 1991 for political reasons, Kubati published a collection of poetry.

TAHAR LAMRI was born in Algeria in 1958. He moved to Libya in 1979, where he completed his studies in law and worked as a translator for the French Consulate. He moved to Italy in 1986 after having resided in France and other European countries. He currently resides in Ravenna, where he works as a translator and linguistic consultant. He has published numerous short stories and authored several plays that have been performed by Ravenna Teatro. Lamri has adapted for the theater his short story, "The Pilgramage of the Voice," which he performs. His collection of short stories, *I sessanta nomi dell'amore* (The Sixty Names of Love), was published in 2006.

IMED MEHADHEB was born in Tunis in 1961 and has lived in Italy since 1982. He has published several short stories, three of which have received awards in the Literary Awards for Immigrant Writers, sponsored by the Association Eks&Tra. His short story "La colpa" ("The Blame") was awarded first place in the Literary Award "Emanuele Casalini" in 2002.

MARTHA ELVIRA PATIÑO was born in Mexico where she completed degrees in Communication and Journalism. In 1985 she moved to Italy, where she worked as a radio and magazine correspondent for Italy and the Vatican. She has recently completed making a short film about migrant women in Italy for the Association No. Di (I Nostri Diritti) in Rome.

CARMELO QUIJADA was born in Venezuela and currently resides in Genova. He won a prize at the fourth Literary Award organized by the Association Eks&Tra in 1999.

IGIABA SCEGO was born in Rome in 1974 after her parents had migrated to Italy from Somalia. She graduated with a degree in languages and currently writes for several magazines that are dedicated to issues of migration: *Migra, Carta,* and *Latinoamerica.* Her first novel, *La nomade che amava Alfred Hitchcock* (The Nomad Who Loved Alfred Hitchcock) was published by Sinnos in 2003. Together with Gabriella Kuruvilla and Mubiayi Ingy, Igiaba Scego wrote and edited a collection of short stories entitled *Pecore nere,* published by Laterza in 2006. She is currently pursuing a PhD at the Università La Sapienza in Rome.

BARBARA SERDAKOWSKI has lived in Italy since 1999. She was born in Poland, grew up in Morocco, and later migrated to Canada. She has published numerous works of short fiction, which she writes in

French and Italian, and poetry, which she composes in all the languages that comprise her linguistic background. In collaboration with Cesare Oliva, she cofounded the Centro d'Arte e Ricerca Magma in Florence, where she currently lives and works.

LILY-AMBER LAILA WADIA was born in Bombay and currently resides in Trieste, where she works as a linguistic expert and translator with the University of Trieste. In 2004, she was awarded first place for short fiction in the Literary Award for Immigrant Writers "Eks&Tra." Her collection of short stories *Il burattinaio e altre storie extra-italiane* (The Puppetmaster and Other Outer-Italian Stories, 2004) was published in a series edited by Armando Gnisci.

YOUSEF WAKKAS, a medical doctor, migrated from Syria to Italy in 1982, where he had problems with the law. He was incarcerated in 1992, and began writing in prison in 1995. He is currently on day-release. He has published two volumes of short stories: *Fogli sbarrati: Viaggio surreale e reale tra carcerati migranti* (Loose Leaf Paper with Bars: Surreal and Real Voyages among Migrant Prisoners, 2002), and *Terra Mobile* (Moving Earth, 2004), and has received multiple awards for his short fiction. His story has been made the subject of a made-for-TV movie produced by the Italian national channel, RaiTre, as well as a documentary for Swiss-Italian television.